Alien Challenge

Derkat screams echoed in the night. Finally a torch was lighted, and Poco saw the derkat leader approach.

Ho-law sat on a length of yellow cloth. Her belt of authority lay across her knees. She coughed in greeting.

Poco returned the cough and sat quietly waiting.

For long moments, Poco and Ho-law just stared at each other, blue and yellow eyes locked in combat.

Ho-law's fingers began to move. "As the one challenged, I will state my demands first," she signed. "Agreed?"

"No," Poco signed.

SHADOW SINGER

Marcia J. Bennett

A Del Rey Book

BALLANTINE BOOKS • NEW YORK

A Dey Rey Book
Published by Ballantine Books

Copyright © 1984 by Marcia J. Bennett

Library of Congress Catalog Card Number: 84-91033

ISBN 0-345-31776-9

Manufactured in the United States of America

First Edition: September 1984

Cover art by Barclay Shaw

Map by Shelly Shapiro

This story is dedicated to my parents,
Richard and Reatha

With special thanks to Kristin,
who introduced me to Screech.

Chapter 1 🦋

Singer, Singer,
set the pattern.
Those who follow,
will be friend.

THE SONG CAME EASILY TO HER LIPS. ONE OF THE OLD songs, it told the story of the Ni-lach Seeker Toreth and his journey to the lake valley of Mar-lion, where the first Ni were said to have walked on land, leaving the security of their water homes in exchange for unknown dangers on a green world where draak and gensvolf had reigned supreme for thousands of years.

As Pocalina-fel-Jamba sang about the valley's tree-shaded hills and open fens, she drew pictures on the stone walk before her. Words, song, and chalk flowed together, and a dream that was born in the mind was given reality by voice and hand.

Her gift of song came from her Ni father; her talent for drawing was a skill she had developed in order to survive.

Poco finished her song and looked down at her work. Of all those for whom she had sung, only Dhalvad had seen her pictures come to life, as they did for her. She

1

looked up, wondering what was keeping him. He had promised to meet her in front of the Varda Inn well over an hour ago.

Poco cleaned her hands on the rag lying across her knees as the crowd milled around her. The clink-clink of coins being dropped into her chalk bag was music she liked to hear. That night they would eat the best!

Poco looked at the men and women who had been drawn to watch her work. The crowds in Port Sulta were larger than those she had known in Port Bhalvar, but perhaps that was because chalk artists were rare in that part of the Enzaar Sea.

Poco and her companions had been in Port Sulta three weeks, camping on the outskirts of the city. But Poco knew that soon they would have to move on. The Sarissa were in the process of enlarging their empire, and, according to rumor, Port Sulta stood next in line. If the Sarissa overran Letsia, Dhalvad would be in danger again. The question was, where were they to go? Was any civilized place safe from the Sarissa?

Someone asked her to sing again. She flipped her long, black hair back off her shoulders and nodded.

Suddenly the crowd parted and a tall, gray-furred derkat stepped into view. He moved with the easy grace natural to his kind.

Poco swallowed a smile as the humans moved out of his way. Ssaal-lr was well aware of the reaction to his presence. His growl of annoyance only made everyone move back a little faster.

"No more songs today, folks," Poco announced. "Thank you for your time. Come back tomorrow if you will."

As the crowd began to disperse, the derkat crouched in front of Poco and coughed a greeting, his tufted ears forward, his large yellow eyes alert. His breath carried the tangy smell of jinsa bean.

Poco leaned forward and imitated the coughing sound, then signed with her hands. *"You are late, Screech. Where is Dhal?"*

"*Docks*," he signed.

"Trouble?" she said aloud.

"*No.*"

"He hasn't been healing again has he?"

"*No. He has found another Green One.*"

"Where?"

"*Lower market. Dhal says to come.*"

Poco nodded and started to gather her chalks.

Ssaal-lr stood and looked up and down the tree-shaded street. While he waited, he scratched at his blunt nose, which was all but lost behind the two overlapping layers of light and dark gray fur surrounding his eyes.

Finally, Poco handed Ssaal-lr her pouch of chalks. "I'm ready. Let's go."

Ssaal-lr took the pouch with his long, prehensile tail and hung it over his left shoulder. With both hands free, he led the way down the street.

"Screech, did you see the Green One yourself?" she asked.

Ssaal-lr clenched his left hand into a fist, furred fingers down and in, signing yes.

"Any chance he may be half-blood?"

"*No.*"

They had located thus far seven half-bloods, most of them trying to hide their Ni bloodlines. Half-blood herself, Poco was not ashamed of her Ni blood; she was, in fact, rather proud of it. But with her dark hair and light blue eyes, she could easily pass for full-blood Sarissa, so she had never had to hide herself in order to survive. Years ago, when the Sarissa had made war on the Ni-lach, it had been death to be labeled a Green One. The disappearance of the Ni-lach from the Enzaar Sea territories was total. But for a handful of half-bloods like Poco, the only Ni left to trouble the Sarissa was Dhalvad sar Haradan, her lover.

Dhalvad had lived twenty-six years knowing nothing of his heritage; but the discovery of his healing powers by the authorities in Annaroth had forced him to flee with his foster father, Haradan sar Nath. He had learned then what it meant to be Ni-lach, and had dreamed ever since of finding his own people.

Poco brought her attention back to Screech, who was signing to her. *"Is something wrong?"*

"No," she answered. "Just thinking. Tell me about the Ni that Dhal has found."

"He is full-blood; green hair, ice eyes. He belongs to a fisherman. Dhal offers to buy him but needs money."

"The Ni is a slave?"

"Yes. Fisherman wants a high price for him."

"How much?"

Ssaal-lr opened and closed his four-fingered hand five times.

Poco thought about the meal she had planned for them that night and shrugged. She decided that she wanted a look at this Ni before they did any buying; twenty marks was a lot of money. They did, of course, have a few pieces of Ni jewelry left to trade, but they were all loathe to part with them.

Unconsciously, Poco touched the carved, wooden pendant hanging from her neck. She knew she would go hungry before giving it up. She believed that Screech felt much the same about the two gold armbands he had brought from the treasure cave in the ruins of the Ni-lach city, Val-hrodhur.

Ssaal-lr cut his stride to match Poco's; still she was feeling the pace by the time they neared the fishmarket. As she hurried after him, the smells of salt water, seaweed, and fish wafted around her, reminding her of her home in Port Bhalvar. Then Screech, taller than Poco by a head, spotted Dhalvad seated on the railing of a ramp leading down from one of the port inns.

Poco smiled when she saw the small ball of fur leaning over Dhal's lap, pointing to something down in the market. Gi-arobi was covered head to toe with short, rust-color fur, and all that could be seen of his face was a pair of golden eyes. The bond between Dhal and the olvaar was very similar to the one Poco and Screech shared.

Dhal saw them and jumped down from his perch. Though small in stature, as were most Ni when compared to men, he was strong and quick, his movements betraying an inner energy that set him apart.

Dhal kissed her as they met. "Sorry about our meeting, Poco."

Poco nodded. "You are forgiven. Screech tells me that you have found another Ni."

Dhal pointed to the docks. "He is over there. Come look."

Dhal's green, shoulder-length hair and crystal eyes were shadowed by his cowled tunic, so no one took notice as he led Poco over to one of the fish stalls.

"How much money do you have?" he asked her.

"Thirteen marks and some smaller coins. You?"

"Three. The man wants twenty."

As they approached the selling stall, the fisherman greeted Dhal with a grin. "Back again?"

"Yes. I would like to see the Ni again, if you are agreeable."

The man turned and glanced behind him. Poco followed the direction of his gaze and saw a bundle of cloth on the ground. Sticking out of the bundle she could see a head and a pair of thin arms; the arms were wrapped around a pair of legs which were tucked up against the body.

"He is sleeping right now," the man said. "We were fishing until late morning. It takes a lot out of him."

"Can we see him?" Dhal asked again. "It won't take long."

"Still interested in buying him?"

"Perhaps, but first I want my friend to see him."

The man looked at Poco and nodded, then he glanced at Screech and Gi-arobi. A puzzled expression touched his face. "What are you planning to do with the Ni? Start a zoo?"

"Zoo?" Dhal echoed.

The man indicated Screech and Gi. "Looks like you already have a good start."

"They are our friends, fisherman," Poco said firmly.

The man shrugged. "If you say so. Well, you can look at him, but don't scare him. I told you before, he is simple and he frightens easily."

"I remember," Dhal said, as he stepped past the fisherman.

Poco squatted beside Dhal as he touched the Ni on the shoulder. For a moment the Ni did not respond, then slowly his head lifted. His green hair was long and tangled and looked as if it had not been combed in months.

"Avto," Poco said softly, greeting him in the Ni tongue. "What is your name?"

"He won't answer, Poco." Dhal pulled a tangled lock of hair away from the Ni's forehead. A visible scar ran from the right temple well back into the hair.

Poco took only a moment to see past the beauty of the Ni's eyes and become aware of the emptiness there. "How long has he been like this?" she asked the fisherman.

"I have had him five years now," the man answered. "Before that he belonged to a man in Janchee."

"Do you know what happened to him?" she asked.

"No, but from the scar on his head, I would say he was wounded back when the Sarissa were hunting the Green Ones, fifteen, twenty years ago."

"Does he have a name?"

"No, miss, not really. The man I bought him from called him Taav. He answers to it after a fashion."

"You told me he helped you catch fish," Dhal said. "How do you get him to work for you if he doesn't even know his own name?"

"Fishing comes natural to his kind; so does eating. When he gets hungry, he fishes real well . . . so I keep him hungry most of the time. If you are going to use him to fish, you will have to make sure he doesn't gorge when you aren't looking. You will also have to keep his neck

collar and line on when he is in the water or you will lose
him. He—"

"Thank you," Dhal said, standing. "But we have other
plans for him." He glanced down at the Ni. "How much
do you want for him?"

"I told you before," the man replied. "Twenty marks."

"Too much for damaged goods," Dhal said. "We can
offer you ten."

The fisherman shook his head. "He earns me that much
in three weeks."

Poco stood and took Dhal's arm, pulling him away from
the stall. "Let's talk a few minutes, Dhal."

When they were alone, Poco turned and looked at Dhal.
His face was still and unreadable. Since leaving Val-hrodhur in the Mountains of the Lost, he had become very
adept at hiding his emotions. Poco wasn't sure she liked
the changes taking place in him. The shy and innocent
wilder with whom she had fallen in love was quickly becoming a stranger to her, driven by his need to find others
of his kind.

"Dhal, what are you thinking?"

"I want him," he answered.

"Why? What are you going to do with him?"

"Help him."

"You mean heal him?"

Dhal nodded.

"From what the man said, he was injured a long time
ago. Do you think your healing powers can make any
difference now?"

"I healed Efan's spine and his injury was well over
two years old."

"Paralyzed limbs are one thing, Dhal, but a brain—
that may be a little more than even you can handle."

"I know, but I want to try."

"Because he may know something about a Ni-lach
sanctuary?"

"That is part of it," he answered. "But I also want to
help him because he is Ni. I cannot just pass him by

without trying to do something for him. Look at him, Poco! He is being starved to death!"

"I can see, Dhal, and I know what you are feeling," Poco said, trying to calm him. "But what if you do buy him free and we take him with us? What if you try to heal him and it doesn't work? Have you considered what will happen to him then? You know the kind of life we have been living these past few months, and you know how good the chances are of the Sarissa moving in on the Letsians any time now. If that happens, we will have to get out of here and get out fast! There won't be time to care for someone who is unable to think for himself. He might just be better off here with the fisherman."

"Better off?" Dhal shook his head. "No, I think not!"

"He would be alive."

"Then he is better dead!"

Poco realized that Dhal was deadly serious about the Ni; either he would heal him, or he would see him dead. She also knew that things were never that simple; that between the saying and the doing stood many other choices. But Dhal was not in any mood for arguments.

"All right, Dhal," she said. "Your way. But first we will have to get the fisherman to trade. We have only sixteen marks between us."

"If he won't come down on his price, I'll trade him one of the Ni brooches I still have."

"Wait, Dhal. Give me a chance to talk to the man first. I think we can deal with him."

Chapter 2

*P*OCO SAT QUIETLY WATCHING SCREECH FEED THE NI.
Keeping a steadying hand on one thin shoulder, the derkat placed bits of food to Taav's lips. Within seconds the food was chewed and swallowed. Taav had the appearance of an abandoned child, skeletal from starvation, his face devoid of emotion. Completely oblivious to his surroundings, he showed no interest in anything but the food being offered him.

Poco silently cursed the merchant who had owned Taav. She could not understand how anyone could so misuse another person. In the morning she would have to return to Port Sulta to see about trading another piece of Ni jewelry. For twelve marks down and twelve payable within three days, the fisherman had consented finally to sell the Ni. Looking at Taav, Poco still wasn't sure who had made the better bargain.

Dhal touched Ssaal-lr's shoulder. "No more food for him now, Screech. We don't want to make him sick."

Screech signed agreement and moved out of the way, allowing Dhal to take his place beside the Ni.

Poco looked down as Gi-arobi stirred in her lap. "Dhal heal now?" Gi asked.

"I don't know, Gi," she said, keeping her voice low so as not to disturb Dhal. "Do you think he can?"

Gi patted her arm. "Dhal knowing what he does."

I hope, she thought. She settled back against the trunk of a young aban tree and pulled her blanket closer around her shoulders. The air was cool with the feel of rain. The cold season was near its end and soon the warm spring rains would arrive, making travel and outdoor living something to avoid.

Sheltered in a dense copse of trees, their camp was reasonably secure from any night-wandering draak, the large reptiles abundant in that land. But draak were not the only threat to someone living outside the manmade stockades that surrounded all villages and cities; one had to be alert for gensvolf and venom-shooting feeders, night creatures which mesmerized their victims with dancing lights. To be on the safe side, Screech had tied climbing vines to the branches above, giving them all easy escape routes.

Poco turned her attention back to Dhal, who sat quietly stroking Taav's shoulders, arms, and legs. She realized that he was looking for some kind of a response from the Ni; but it did not look as if Taav was about to cooperate.

Dhal lifted Taav's face so he could look into the Ni's eyes. For long moments those twin pairs of crystal gazed at each other, then suddenly Taav pulled from Dhal's hold and ducked away, scrambling on hands and knees toward a nearby clump of bushes.

Dhal went after Taav, but Screech was faster. The long-bodied derkat lunged from a reclining position and threw himself in front of Taav, catching the Ni around the shoulders and rolling over with him.

"Be careful, Screech," Dhal cried. "Don't hurt him!"

Dhal went to aid the derkat and between the two of

them they got Taav back near the fire. "Sit down, Screech," Dhal said. "And hold onto him."

Screech wrapped his strong arms around Taav's chest and arms, then kicked Taav's feet out from under him and sat down. While Screech held the Ni as still as possible, Dhal crouched in front of them, his hands going to Taav's forehead.

"What are you going to do, Dhal?" Poco asked, alert and ready to help.

"Make him sleep," Dhal answered.

Poco could not see Taav's face, but only a moment or two passed before he stopped struggling. When Dhal leaned back, she could see the Ni resting quietly in Screech's arms.

Poco came to stand behind Dhal. Her hand dropped gently to the top of his head. "What happened?"

Dhal looked up. "I don't know, Poco. I must have done something that frightened him."

"You had not started to heal him?"

"No."

"Are you going to try to do anything now?"

Dhal took Poco's hand and pulled her down beside him. Poco felt a tingle of happiness as their glances locked. How much she loved him. Did he know? she wondered. With his head filled with stories of the Ni-lach and his dreams of finding them, did he realize how important he had become to her?

"There is no reason to put it off," Dhal said, answering her question. "Either I can help him or I cannot. I think I'll know once I'm inside."

Poco shook her head. "It still sounds strange to me when you speak of going inside another person's body. Were you never afraid of becoming trapped, of losing your own identity?"

"It isn't like that, Poco. I told you before, it is more like slipping inside another set of clothes, where you can feel every wrinkle of material, every tight seam. When I am *inside* I can feel if there is anything wrong with the body, a hurt or an illness; and when I find it, I picture things as they should be, rather than as they are. Somehow my thoughts become a healing energy that kills disease and stimulates new cell growth in bone, blood, and muscle. Then, when everything is as it should be, I leave."

"You make it sound simple," Poco said.

"It is—for me."

"Perhaps, but I know for a fact that your healing is not accomplished without cost. You were weak for a day after healing Screech that one time, and when Saan Drambe stabbed you with his knife, you took four days to recover."

"So?"

"So what happens if we have to move fast? There are rumors that the Sarissa plan to invade Port Sulta soon."

"We have been hearing those rumors ever since we arrived here."

"That is no reason to dismiss them, Dhal. If you try to heal Taav and end up flat on your back for days, you might well be putting us all in danger."

Dhal looked down at Taav. "Yes, I know," he said.

But Poco knew that if Dhal had set his mind on something, he would go through with it. "When do you start?" she asked.

Dhal turned and smiled at her. "Thanks, Poco."

"For?"

"Understanding."

Don't I always, she thought. She looked down at Taav and for the first time noticed the bruises on his arms. Suddenly she saw something she had missed before.

"Scales!" she cried softly. "Dhal, he is atich-ar, one of the scaled ones! They are said to be direct throwbacks to the first Ni, those who are supposed to have lived in water."

"Yes, I know," Dhal said. "It means that he is full-blood Ni."

Atich-ar were rare among the Ni-lach, so rare that they were almost legendary. The scales were small, almost invisible from any distance. Poco reached out and gently laid her fingertips on Taav's arm. His skin was not rough, as she had supposed it would be, nor was it as soft as her own; it was just different. His nose was straight, with very narrow nostrils; his lips were thin; his cheekbones were high. Winged eyebrows accented crystal-gray eyes that were so like Dhal's.

"He looks so vulnerable, Dhal. What will it be like for him? Will it hurt?"

"I can dull the pain centers for most of the body, but for the mind itself I am not sure. Sometimes in order to feel the *wrongness* in a body, I must be able to feel its pain. I don't want to hurt him, Poco, believe me."

"Is there anything we can do to help?" she asked.

Dhal looked at Screech and Gi-arobi. "Screech, I want you to stay close, in case Taav wakes and becomes violent again; and Gi, you be our watch. If anyone comes this way, whistle."

"And me?" Poco asked.

"Just stay close. If anything threatens us, you will have to try to wake me. It won't be easy and you may not succeed. It will depend upon how far I am inside."

"What happens if I can't reach you?"

"Leave me or—"

"No!"

"—try to hide me. Screech can carry me and I am sure you can carry Taav. He is not very heavy."

"I don't like this, Dhal," Poco said. "I wish we could do this in a more protected place, perhaps somewhere inside the city gates. We could rent a room for a few days. We have to trade another piece of jewelry to pay for Taav anyway. We will have plenty left over."

"Poco, we are as safe here as we would be in any of the port inns. Here no one will ask questions or become curious about the company we keep. We have come far together, the four of us, and I don't want us splitting up. I have seen enough of the Letsians to know that none of them would sell us a room if they knew we intended to share it with Screech and Gi."

Screech coughed softly, seeking Dhal's attention. *"If it is safer to heal the atich-ar in a protected room, go. Little Fur and I will stay here."*

Dhal watched Screech's hands carefully, for he was still in the process of learning the derkat sign language. He shook his head. "No, Screech. I want us to stay together. It is safer."

"Healer fears something?" Screech signed.

"No."

Though Screech sat perfectly still, Poco saw the end of his tail rise and fall in a gesture she had come to recognize as impatience.

"Is Healer afraid I will not look after Little Fur?" Screech signed.

Gi-arobi stood at Dhal's right shoulder, his glance darting from one speaker to the next. He answered before Dhal could. "Dhal trusting Screech. Knowing Big Fur is friend to Gi, but Dhal right. Staying together, us, is safer."

"I know you and Gi would be safe together, Screech," Dhal added. "I trust you with his life and my own, but if Poco and I took Taav into the city and tried to heal him there, Poco would be alone to watch over us until I regained my strength."

Dhal glanced at Poco and smiled. "Not that I have any doubts that she could do that, but it would be a lonely vigil, and with Taav the way he is, I would like her to have your strength to call on."

Screech looked at Poco and saw her nod; then he turned back to Dhal and signed agreement. *"Poco will not be alone."*

After Screech boosted Gi up into the lower branches of a nearby aban tree, he returned to take a position opposite Dhal, the slumbering Taav between them.

Poco sat to Dhal's right and slightly behind, where she could feed the fire and keep an eye on Dhal at the same time.

Dhal reached out and placed his left hand on Taav's forehead over the scar; his right hand hovered over Taav's abdomen. A moment later Dhal's head dropped forward, his eyes closed.

As the minutes passed, Poco traced each line of Dhal's body, her gaze finally coming to rest on his hands. She had felt both the strength and the gentleness of those hands, but had yet to experience his healing touch, unless he had used it one of the times he had soothed away her fears.

The Sarissa were fools to have made Dhal an enemy, she thought. The Ni-lach jewelry hidden at Val-hrodhur was nothing compared to Dhal's gifts as Healer and Seeker, yet in their greed the Sarissa would have murdered Dhal as they had Haradan.

Poco looked up to check on Gi-arobi, who sat perched on a branch overhead. The olvaar saw her and waved a furred hand. All was well with him. Poco then checked on Screech, but the derkat was watching Dhal work his healing magic and did not look up.

Poco placed several small branches on the fire, then turned back to watch Dhal. She barely managed to suppress a grasp of wonder when she saw the aura of green, translucent light which surrounded Dhal's hands and Taav's head.

Poco decided that when Dhal was finished, she would ask him more about his *gift*. Dhal spoke of the green aura as a manifestation of healing energy. In the back of her mind she wondered if such power was hereditary or a learned skill, one that others might be taught to use.

The air cooled as night closed around them. All was still but for the sound of small insects flitting in and out of the campfire light. Poco studied Dhal's back. She was growing worried; the green aura from Dhal's hands had faded well over an hour before and still Dhal had not moved.

Poco looked up and found Screech watching her.

"Does the Healer sleep?" he signed.

Poco leaned forward and touched Dhal's shoulder. "Dhal, are you awake?" When he failed to respond, she shook him gently. "Dhal, are you all right?"

Still there was no response.

Poco moved to Dhal's left and took his wrists. She heard him sigh deeply and mumble something as she pulled his hands away, then suddenly, he slumped to the side. She caught him before his shoulder hit the ground.

Screech jumped over Taav and crouched next to Poco, ready to help.

"Straighten his legs," Poco said. "Let's get him comfortable."

Quickly Poco checked Dhal's breathing and heartbeat. Once satisfied that he was in no danger, she told Screech to get Gi-arobi.

The anxious olvaar peered at Dhal's relaxed features, then looked up and nodded. "Not worry. Dhal sleeping."

"How long will he sleep, Little Fur?" Screech signed.

"Gi not knowing. Much energy lost in healing. We watch and keep Dhal safe now, yes."

"Gi, what about Taav?" Poco asked. "Should we try to wake him?"

The olvaar looked down at the atich-ar. "Can try."

Poco sat back a few minutes later. She had tried everything she could think of, short of pricking Taav with a knife. "No luck," she said. "All we can hope for is that one or both will wake sometime tonight or tomorrow. We will just have to stay close to them until they do. Screech, let's lay them together over there near the tree. We can use the windbreak you and Dhal made the other day and form a shelter over them. The air feels like rain tonight."

Screech nodded and bent to pick up Dhal. A little while later they had both Taav and Dhal under shelter.

Toward morning, Gi woke Poco, his soft whistle-click close to her right ear. They had been sharing two-hour watches and she had just fallen asleep.

"What is it, Gi?" she asked, sitting up. Quickly she glanced around camp. A light mist had put their campfire

out, but to the east the sky was beginning to show a haze
of light.

Poco felt Gi's round, furred stomach press against her
arm as he leaned close.

"Taav moving," he said. "Makes waking noises."

Poco kicked free of her blanket and crawled deeper
under the shelter, where she could just make out the two
blanketed forms. Gi was right. Taav was moving; his hands
were clenching and unclenching and his head was rolling
from side to side. The noises which escaped his lips were
without meaning, unless they echoed pain or troubled
thoughts.

She listened to Taav for a few minutes, but there was
no change. Gently she laid a hand on his forehead,
smoothing back his tangled hair, then she began to sing
a lullaby. Taav soon quieted.

Poco continued to sing and watched as Taav's hands
relaxed. He may not understand what we say to him, she
thought, but he does hear. It's a step.

She returned to her blanket and found Gi waiting for
her. The olvaar tipped his head up as she sat. "Poco sing
for Gi?" he asked.

Fully awake and no longer sleepy, Poco pulled the
blanket around her shoulders and silently offered Gi a
place beside her. As the olvaar settled down, Poco dropped
the blanket around him. She liked the feel of his soft fur
and did not mind as he snuggled close. "What song would
you like to hear?" she asked him.

"Gi liking all songs," he responded.

"You are easy to please. All right, one song, just for
you."

Poco sang "The Seven Words of Wisdom," a song she
had learned from the dockworker Trass, the half-blood
Ni who had answered her questions and taught her the
language of the Ni-lach.

Orphaned at an early age Poco had lived a lonely,
furtive life until meeting Trass. In those early days after
the war, it had been dangerous to speak Ni or to be con-

sidered a Ni sympathizer. But Trass had provided her sanctuary on the lower tier of streets near the docks; had offered her his protection against the local authorities; and had taught her to use her voice to earn honest wages.

Each time Poco sang "The Seven Words of Wisdom" she thought about Trass—and his death.

When she finished the song, she lay back down. Gi's whistled thank you helped to drive away sad thoughts of friends long dead. She had new friends who needed her; there was no sense in dwelling on the past.

Chapter 3

*P*OCO WAS RESTLESS. *TWO DAYS OF INACTIVITY WERE AL-*most more than she could stand, and her growing worry over Dhal's sleeping state made her all the more irritable.

Poco crawled into the shelter and knelt beside Dhal. She spoke his name softly, but there was no response. She watched the rise and fall of his chest, then felt for the pulse at his throat. He seemed to be all right; still, she was worried. By holding him up, she and Screech had managed to get him to drink several times each day, but as yet he had not eaten anything, and if he did not eat soon, he would be weak for days.

She looked at Dhal and Taav, lying side by side under one blanket. Their green hair, pale skin, and beardless faces left no doubt about their common ancestry.

Poco leaned over and felt Taav's hair. It was dry now. That morning she had clipped and washed it as best she could. She hoped that when he woke up he would not be

angry; among the Ni-lach, long hair and the style in which
it was worn usually symbolized age and rank.

Taav moaned in his sleep and rolled onto his side,
taking the blanket with him. Poco reached across Dhal
and pulled back the blanket to cover them both once
more.

A little while later, Poco went to check on Gi-arobi,
who had been on watch since early morning. She found
him sitting on a branch in a nearby aban tree.

"Poco wants?" he whistled, as she approached.

"Nothing, Gi. I was just checking to see if all is well
with you. Here," she said, tossing him a half section of
golden kansa fruit. "I thought you might be hungry."

"Gi always hungry," he said as he caught the offering.

Poco grinned. "Gi, that is an understatement."

Gi cocked his head to the side. "What meaning, under-
stay-mint?"

Poco laughed. "In this case it means a large truth that
is spoken in the mildest of terms."

"Not understanding, Poco."

"Never mind, Gi. I am only teasing."

Gi popped the last piece of fruit into his mouth. "Dhal
waking soon," he said.

"Is that a question, Gi, or a statement?"

Gi made a thrumming noise in his throat, the olvaar's
form of laughter. "Is under-stay-mint, Poco. A truth, yes?"

Poco shook her head, not exactly sure she understood
this time. "Are you telling me that Dhal *will* wake soon?"

"Yes," Gi said.

"How do you know?"

"Gi knowing here," he answered, patting his head.

Poco smiled. "If you say so, Gi." She had been too
long around the olvaar not to trust what he said. If he
said that Dhal would wake soon, he would; until then she
would just have to be patient.

Ver-draak was a green and sparsely populated world.
Its twin suns, Ra-shun and Ra-gar, lighted the mint-green

sky twenty-two out of thirty hours a day, creating lush jungle forests and green oceans of bush and grass.

Late in the afternoon, Ra-gar was low in the western sky; her sister, Ra-shun was already lighting another part of the world. The patch of sunlight Poco had been watching had finally succumbed to shadows.

After she checked on Dhal and Taav, Poco built a fire and fixed a cup of tea using some rayil leaves Dhal had gathered days before. She sat quietly by the fire, breathing in the tea's spicy aroma and thinking about all that had happened during the months she had spent with Dhalvad. She thought about their run into the Mountains of the Lost; their finding the Ni city of Val-hrodhur; she remembered Haradan's death, and Efan's; and the treasure chests they had left behind.

She set her tea aside and caught at the chain and pendant hanging from her neck. Of all the things she had brought out of Val-hrodhur, that one piece she liked the best. She could not have explained why. A seven-pointed star formed the outline of the pendant. On one side an intricate pattern of curving lines was carved around a pair of interlocking suns; on the other side of the pendant there were symbols which Poco was unable to decipher.

As she turned the pendant over seeking a maker's sign, she remembered that some pieces of Ni jewelry were functional rather than decorative. By accidentally activating the green fire stone within his ring, Dhal had discovered a doorway into the past. The fire stone, he had learned, was a shard of the Tamorlee, the great crystalline life form that was the Keeper of Ni-lach history. The energy of the Tamorlee enabled Dhal and other Seekers like him to teleport to other destinations with nothing but thought and their own inner vision to guide them.

Poco traced the curving lines and noticed that they doubled back upon themselves in a pattern that drew the eyes to follow. She began to hum a favorite melody she had learned from Trass.

Unconsciously her humming rose in tempo as she traced

the pattern over and over. Suddenly she felt light-headed; then, between one breath and the next, she lost the pattern of the design and found herself surrounded by a gray mist, where dark blue shadows fought to push their way into her line of vision.

At first the shadows had no meaning, then slowly they began to form into recognizable shapes. It took her a moment to realize that she was still singing, and that her voice seemed to influence the shadows.

Like a child finding a new toy, she experimented with her voice. She watched the shadows grow tall and slender and weave and dance to her song. There were bird-shadows that circled and dipped, and spirals of darkness that grew smaller and smaller until they melted into nothing. The shadows changed again and again, flowing together to create scenes of draak and ships, of towering buildings and oddly shaped trees.

Suddenly Poco realized that she was singing a song she had never heard before. The voice was hers, but the words and music came to her as if from someone else's memory.

She stopped singing, shocked by the impossible. The shadows solidified as the words of the mystery singer faded from her mind, and then she was looking upon a scene that was not of her making.

Down to her left there was a narrow body of water, black in its depth. Green, tree-shaded hills rose steeply to either side of the water, and out toward the horizon she could see different shades of green which spoke of distant hills or a large body of water. And above, the sky was—blue?

Poco blinked to clear her vision, but the color of the sky stayed the same.

Feeling suddenly uneasy, Poco looked to her right, and through an opening in the trees she saw a cream-colored, stone temple standing at the edge of the river. The seven, round towers on the tall, thick, outer walls made her think

of the great Trade Hall in Upper Port Bhalvar, a building
said to have been designed by the Ni-lach.

A strange tree stood in the center of the large courtyard
at one end of the temple. The leafless branches grew in
a maze of interlocking circles. Poco turned to study the
other types of flora in the valley. Where were the giant
aban trees? she wondered. And the most common among
trees, the rilror pine? Where were the sturdy genna bushes
and stalk grass?

The clanging of a bell drew Poco's attention back to
the courtyard. There, a line of people emerged from a
door in the far wall to a circle around the strange tree.
Seized by a desire to get closer, to see what they were
about, Poco tried to move—and suddenly became aware
of her own body, sitting, not standing. Then she remembered where she was, and realized that what she was
seeing was not real—or if real, then only to her.

Like ripples on water stirred by the dropping of a leaf,
the scene before her wavered, then disappeared.

"Poco?"

She opened her eyes and found Dhal kneeling before
her. Happy to see him awake she was more than willing
to put her dreaming aside for a while.

"Welcome back," she said. "How long have you been
up?"

"Not long," he answered.

She thought Dhal looked tired still, but his smile was
encouraging. "Did my singing wake you?" she asked.

"Both of us," he answered.

"What?" She turned and looked back to see Taav was
sitting up, watching them. "I did not think I was singing
that loud."

Dhal looked deep into her eyes. "Some songs are different than others, Poco. Had you whispered that last
one, we still would have heard you."

"What one?" she asked, a cold chill skittering down
her spine.

"I heard only one. It must have been the last." He

frowned. "Poco, where did you take us? What was that place?"

"You saw the temple?"

Dhal nodded.

Impossible! she thought. How could Dhal see without a chalk picture to guide him? Poco rubbed her hand across her forehead, shielding her eyes. What had happened to her—to them? What was the song she had sung?

"Poco, are you all right?"

Poco looked up. "Yes, Dhal. I am just a little confused. That song you heard, it was not one of mine! It might have been my voice you heard, but it was someone else singing." Poco lifted the pendant. "I was looking at this, trying to read the inscription on the back. I started to sing a song Trass taught me, then suddenly I noticed these shadows; they moved to the sound of my voice. I couldn't take my eyes away from them. Then there was this other song, one I have never heard before. It was my voice, but it wasn't me doing the singing!"

Poco drew a deep breath and released it, realizing that she was not explaining things very clearly. "This all sounds crazy."

"Never mind how it sounds," Dhal said. "Go on, tell me what happened."

Poco shrugged. "I stopped singing, then I was looking at this place. There was a valley with a river running through it and there was a temple, or at least what looked like a temple." She hesitated, then continued. "I saw some people in one of the courtyards and thought about going down to take a closer look, then I remembered where I was and the vision faded."

"Vision or reality, Poco?" he asked softly.

"I don't know, Dhal. I also don't know how you were able to see what I saw. I didn't use my chalks this time."

"Perhaps you don't need to draw pictures, Poco. Your talent for creating living scenes might just originate in your mind and voice, rather than in your skill with chalks. That building, that place, are you sure you have never seen it before, or heard about it in a song you picked up some-where?"

"No! And I told you, it was not my song we were seeing!"

"Whose song then?"

"I don't know!" she snapped.

For a moment or two their glances locked. Poco was the first to look away. "Sorry," she murmured.

"May I see your pendant, Poco?" Dhal asked, holding out his hand.

She lifted the pendant from around her neck. "Do you think it might have something to do with what happened?"

"It was made by the Ni-lach, Poco. My ring enables me to teleport to other places. Perhaps your pendant has a similar function."

"But we didn't *go* anywhere—did we?"

"No," he answered, bending over the disc, "but we certainly did *see* a somewhere."

Dhal studied the pendant, turning it over and over in his hands. Finally he looked up. "Several of the symbols on the back are similar to ones I saw in the sun chamber of Val-hrodhur, but the writing is beyond me."

Poco felt a chill as she recalled the vision they had just shared. "Dhal, did you notice the color of the sky?"

His crystal eyes seemed to darken as he handed the pendant back. "Yes. It was blue, a blue I have never seen before."

"And not a color that I would ever chalk a sky, Dhal! That frightens me." She shook her head. "There is some-thing strange going on here, something I don't understand. Did you notice that odd-looking tree in the center of the courtyard, the one with the tangled branches?"

"Yes. It must have taken someone a long time to re-shape it."

"Unless the shaping is natural," she said softly. She glanced down at the pendant. When she looked up, she found Dhal watching her intently.

"Where did you take us, Poco? Was it an alternate world?"

There! Poco thought. He has said it! He is thinking just what I am.

Dhal believed that the Ni-lach and the Tamorlee had escaped the Sarissa through something he called a world gate, a kind of door into parallel worlds. Poco did not even pretend to understand the different realities Dhal described when he talked about world gates. All she knew was that she did not like him poking his nose into things about which he knew nothing. He was too new to his power as a Seeker to have learned caution. A practical person herself, Poco liked to know the depth of the water before jumping in.

"Dhal, listen," she said. "Isn't it possible that what we saw was just an imaginary place, something I dreamed up?"

Dhal reached out and took her hand. "Poco, when I first started to use the Seeker ring, I knew nothing about the energy forces I stirred. Every time I entered the world I saw in the fire stone, I thought I was just dreaming. Now I know differently. Do not ask me how it works, but somehow I tapped into the energy reserves of the Tamorlee as it existed in the past, and I used it to travel backward in time. I formed a link with the Tamorlee and became a Seeker. If it—"

"But I don't carry a fire stone!" Poco protested. "My songs have no link with the Tamorlee!"

"No direct link perhaps, but all life is energy of one form or another. That I learned from the Ancients."

"So?"

"So your songs are the product of a very special form of energy. When you sing, you create more than music, you create an energy pattern that produces a reality, your own special version perhaps, but how do we know whether that reality is not one of the alternate worlds we seek?"

"You are reaching, Dhal."

"Am I? Perhaps, but it is something to think about. If

the Tamorlee was taken into an alternate world for safety's sake, the only way we are going to find it and the Ni-lach of our own time, is to delve into those alternate worlds."

"Have you ever thought that we might be getting ourselves into something that is over our heads?"

"Yes, but I cannot stop myself. Finding the Ni-lach is something I have to do, and I will go wherever my search takes me."

Dhal's voice softened. "Haradan died trying to help me find my people. If his death is to mean anything at all, I must continue my search."

A lump came to Poco's throat for she knew how much Dhal mourned Haradan. She reached out and laid her hand on top of his. "Haradan was a good man. He was strong and wise—and a good friend. I miss him too."

Eyes moist with feelings he could not hide, Dhal leaned forward and kissed her.

Poco returned his kiss and held him a moment, wishing she could take some of the pain from his grieving.

He drew back. "I think I will go and see if Taav is all right."

Curious to see if there was any change in the atich-ar, Poco rose and followed Dhal as he walked a little unsteadily on his feet toward the shelter. She noticed that Taav's eyes remained fixed on her as she knelt before him. She was excited by the possibility that Dhal had accomplished another successful healing.

"Avto, Taav," she said softly in Ni. "We are friends. How are you feeling?"

There was no response.

Dhal's command of the Ni language was not the equal of Poco's but he was learning fast. "Taav, we are your friends. Do not be afraid."

Taav looked from Poco to Dhal, then back.

Suddenly Poco felt something brush her hand. She looked down and saw Taav's fingers move from her hand to her leg. He was touching her almost as if he feared she would break or melt away like ginsa smoke if he moved too quickly.

Poco caught his hands. "Taav, do you understand what we are saying?"

Taav's face lifted at the sound of her voice. Tears rolled down his cheeks.

Disconcerted, Poco looked at Dhal, silently appealing for help.

Dhal shrugged. He too was surprised by Taav's tears. "Try to get him to lie down," he said.

"I'll sing to him. It calmed him before."

As Poco started to sing, Dhal moved away. Within a few minutes Taav was lying down again. His tears had stopped and his eyelids had fluttered closed. Poco sang a little while longer, then covered him with a blanket and left the shelter.

Dhal had a fire going by that time, and he swung the water pot over the flames as she sat down. "Tea?" he asked.

"Sounds good."

Poco waited patiently while Dhal rummaged in one of the packs. When he found the small pouch of tea leaves, she passed him two cups.

"Dhal, what do you suppose caused Taav to cry?" she asked.

"I don't know. He is aware and he can hear, but beyond that I would only be guessing.

"What was wrong with him?"

"That scar he wears was caused by a blow from something sharp, probably a sword." He shook his head. "When I first joined him, it felt like I was wearing a rock in my head. There was pressure here, and here." He touched his forehead and the right side of his head over the ear.

"What did you do?"

Dhal looked down at his hands. "There was damaged brain tissue. I envisioned it as whole and surrounded it with a green healing light. The stronger the light, the faster the healing."

Poco tried to make sense out of the impossible. "This light, what is it really?"

"I believe it is a form of energy, something that is there all the time, something I can tap into and use to heal. Some of the energy comes from within, but I believe a greater portion comes from outside my body, from the very core of existence."

"Are you talking about a god, Dhal?"

He shook his head. "I don't know. Am I?"

"It sounds like it."

"Haradan took me to Drimdor once, to hear a Religious speak," he said.

"What did you think about it?"

"*It* meaning the man or what he taught?"

"Both," she replied.

"I liked the man. He had an easy voice to listen to. I can still remember the story he told; it was about the first men to come to Lach. He told how his god had saved them in order that they might build a new and better world where all men could live together in peace. Then he started to talk about the Sarissa needing money to build a great temple. That is when Haradan brought me away."

"Haradan didn't agree with the speaker?"

"Something like that. He said that the Sarissa would only use the temple to get more money away from the poor people. He said that if the Sarissa had any god at all, it was a god of greed."

"He was right there."

"Poco, do you know if the Ni have a religion?"

"If you mean the worship of a god, no; but if by religion you mean a belief around which they center their lives, then the answer is yes."

"And that belief is?" he asked.

"In the sanctity of life. The Ni-lach believe we are all a part of a whole. It is their belief that the inner being is continually being recycled, living one life after another until there is a time of complete understanding of the whole."

"And then?" he pressed.

"With complete understanding comes peace and a full acceptance of life in all its forms." She paused. "It is a simple religion, if one can call it a religion. To the Ni-lach it was just a way of life."

"Do you believe as the Ni-lach did?" he asked.

"It is a good religion, one I could live with."

Dhal nodded, then suddenly changed the subject. "I haven't seen Screech around. Where is he?"

"He went to Port Sulta this morning to sell one of my Ni bracelets. He'll pay off the fisherman who owned Taav, get a few things we need, and bring back the change. That should keep us in supplies for a while."

"You think he'll be all right alone?"

Poco smiled. "Who would bother him? Don't worry, he should be back soon. You still look tired. Why don't you eat something and lie down again. I'll keep watch and wake you when he returns."

Dhal accepted her suggestion, knowing that his strength would return only with rest.

Chapter 4

*P*OCO ROSE EARLY THE NEXT MORNING. SHE SLIPPED QUI-
etly out from between the blankets she shared with
Dhal and went down to the small rivulet that provided
them with drinking water.

After she satisfied her thirst, she washed and returned
to camp. The morning stillness was eerie, but the sight
of Dhal sleeping peacefully where she had left him instantly chased away all feelings of loneliness.

She got out her pack and quickly sorted through the
clothing she had accumulated since their arrival in Port
Sulta. After changing her underclothes, she slipped into
a long-sleeved, blue tunic that laced from chest to neck.
She brushed off the pants she had been wearing, deciding
they would do for another day or so. She was in the
process of lacing up her ankle-length, draak-hide boots
when she felt something behind he. She turned, her hand
going to the knife in her wrist sheath, but relaxed when
she saw Gi-arobi.

"Morning, Gi," she said, keeping her voice down.

Gi bobbed his head in greeting, then came to stand at her shoulder. "Poco going?" he asked.

"Yes," she answered.

"Where?"

"To find Screech. When Dhal gets up, tell him I have gone to Port Sulta. I'll be back as soon as I can."

"Big Fur lost?"

"I don't know, Gi: I'm going to find out."

"Gi come?"

"No, not this time." Poco patted Gi's round stomach. "Take care of Dhal until I come back, all right?"

She picked up her bag of chalks and threaded her way through the dense undergrowth that hid their camp from the main trail. The great aban trees lining the manmade roadway formed a dark green canopy overhead. She watched for movement in the nearby bushes as she started downhill. The chances of meeting draak or gensvolf so close to the port were slim, but one had to be cautious just the same.

Poco knew that Dhal would be angry at her for leaving camp alone, but she also knew that if she had waited for him to wake up he would have insisted that she stay in camp with Taav while he went to look for Screech.

Dhal could be very protective at times. It was nice, she thought, but hardly necessary. She had survived alone for twenty-seven years among the dockworkers of Port Bhalvar. Working as a Chalk Master, she had earned their respect; but she had learned also how to protect herself.

She laughed. If she needed any protection at all, it was from one green-haired, crystal-eyed Ni, whose dream of finding his people was taking her far from her homeland.

The sky was growing light by the time Poco approached the port gates leading to the docks. Once she had passed the gate guards, she made straight for the fisherman's stall and there learned that Screech had been there the day before and had paid off their debt.

"When he left, did you see which way he went?" Poco asked.

The fisherman nodded. "That way," he said, pointing toward the center of the market.

The open-air market boasted of over one hundred vendors. Poco had to talk only to five before she found one who remembered seeing the derkat the day before.

"Sure I remember him," the merchant said. "His kind usually travel in numbers. I thought it odd to see one wandering around alone. He bought a packet of salt and a pouch of dried fruit."

From there Ssaal-lr's trail was easy to follow at first. He had purchased fish-hooks and a knife at a metalworker's stall; then he had looked over several leather pouches at a hide shop, but had not chosen one. From there his trail led to a food stall, where he had purchased and devoured a large portion of draak meat.

Poco began to wonder how much money Screech had received for the Ni bracelet she had given him. She trusted him to make a good deal but hoped the sale had been a private one, for it was not wise to advertise the possession of such trade items in a district where there were more thieves than honest folk.

She moved deeper into the marketplace, her own hunger stirred by the various odors wafting out of the inns and open-air cooking stalls. Out of habit, she had brought her chalks along, but she was not ready to stop and ply her trade; nor was she willing to part with one of the two rings she had taken from the Ni-lach treasure chests.

She looked down at her right hand. The bird images carved into the shell on top of the rings caught at colors, folding them one inside the other until the birds seemed to move in the light. No, she thought. You I keep. If I have not found Screech in a little while, I will do some chalking, just enough to earn a meal, then I'll go looking again.

Three hours later, Poco finally gave in to hunger. She had lost Ssaal-lr's trail and was beginning to work her way out of the tangle of streets surrounding the market-place. She stopped, turned, and went back the way she had come. She chose a section of the slate-walk that was large enough to work yet out of the middle of traffic.

She quickly slid her chalks from her pouch and began to draw. She chose a sea draak for her subject, and as she drew, she sang one of the songs of the Draak Watch, a loose organization of Ni who used their voices to control draak and keep them away from the homes of Ni and the croplands of men.

At one time no village or holding had been without at least one or two members of the Draak Watch; but now they were gone and lands that once had been tilled and planted had gone back to wilderness.

Poco knew seven different songs used by the Draak Watch. The words were in Ni, but she had mastered them easily. Her song quickly drew a crowd.

She was aware of the people standing around her, but she did not look up. As the last words of the song floated into the air, Poco concentrated on the picture before her. The draak moved its head as if searching for the singer who had called it from the depths. It was alive...one moment...two...then the silence was broken by hands clapping, and the draak stilled.

Poco looked up, wondering if she alone had seen the draak move. She searched the faces above, looking for that one small flicker of surprise. But no—no one had seen the draak live.

She looked down at the picture. Dhal would have seen, she thought. Why not others? Is it our Ni blood?

"Another song," someone in the crowd called out.

"Yes, another, please."

Poco glanced at the few coins which had been dropped onto her cloth bag; not enough for a good meal. She nodded and moved over to a smaller piece of slate nearby.

She sang again, chalking a picture of a ship. The crowd responded with more coins. Poco decided she had enough money for a meal and started to gather her chalks.

Suddenly a hand dropped onto her shoulder. "Singer?"

Poco looked up. The man standing behind her was tall and muscular. His brown hair was trimmed neatly; his beard was shaped to a point a finger's length below his chin. He wore the dress of a sailor; sandals, knee-length pants, a loose-fitting, white shirt, and a weapons belt. But Poco knew the man had another trade, for no sailor ever had hands so well-tended. Thief or cardman, she thought.

The man knelt beside her. "Someone told me that you are looking for a derkat."

Poco did not like the way the man's dark eyes searched her face. She hesitated before answering. "You have seen one?"

"Better than that," he responded. "I know where you can find him. I saw him go into Eyson's Tavern yesterday. He never came out."

"Was he alone?"

"No. He was with a man."

"How do you know he never came out?" Poco asked.

"I followed him," the man answered. "I was curious. You do not see a derkat in Port Sulta every day."

"Do you know what happened to him?" Poco asked, wondering when the man would demand money for the rest of the information he had.

"The derkat got into a fight with three men who did not approve of serving animals in the tavern. He killed one of them before the other two knocked him senseless. I understand that sar Eyson is holding him in the cellar."

Poco stiffened at the word "*animal*" being used to refer to derkat. She tried to hide her anger as she looked at the man. "There was a death and the authorities were not called?"

The man shrugged, his grin supporting Poco's guess that he was not just the curious spectator he had claimed to be. "Sometimes it is wiser to leave the authorities out of things," he said in a lower voice. "The man who was killed was a loner. His friends were easily bought off. Verg sar Eyson plans to make a profit by selling the derkat to someone in Annaroth, an exotic-animal importer named Arre. Ever heard of him?"

Poco nodded. "Do you know how much sar Eyson hopes to get for the derkat?"

"I heard that the price was one hundred marks."

"You seem to know a lot about all of this. What is your percentage?"

The man hesitated, then shrugged. "Twenty percent of any bid over seventy-five marks. Eyson can sell him to Arre, but it would mean time and waiting. If he can get a buyer here in Port Sulta, so much the better. Does your pet mean that much to you?"

"He does," Poco admitted. "But I haven't much money."

The man glanced down at the rings on Poco's right hand. "But you do have something to trade," he said.

"Perhaps." Poco stood. "I suppose you can tell me where Eyson's Tavern is?"

The man's smile showed strong, white teeth, and his quick look of appraisal left nothing in doubt: He liked what he saw and was not shy about making it evident. "I can tell you, Singer, but I would rather show you."

Poco deftly sidestepped his hand and shouldered her chalk pouch. "Good," she said. "Then you can lead the way."

The man's smile faded. The cool, steady look he gave her made Poco feel uneasy. A man-snake if ever I met one, she thought.

The man turned without a word and headed back through the marketplace. Poco kept pace with him, walking to his left and slightly behind, where she could keep her eye on him.

"Do you have a name?" she asked.

The man slowed and glanced back at her. "Jesh."

"Do you work for sar Eyson very often?"

"Off and on."

"You dress like a sailor, but you have the hands of a cardman. Do you have a profession?"

Jesh turned and continued walking, not once pausing to see if she followed him.

The man-snake does not like questions, she thought. Screech, what have you gotten us into? Poco checked the knife hidden in her tunic sleeve; she had a feeling she was going to need it before long.

They left the marketplace and turned south toward the docks. The Street of Taverns was narrow and crowded with day traffic. The majority of small shops that snuggled in between the taverns and inns catered to a man's appetite, offering exotic foods, wines, gaming, and bodily pleasures. Poco tried to disregard the leers of the men lounging in the doorways of the shops and taverns, but their lewd comments were not so easily ignored, and soon her face warmed with color. She had known of streets like this in Port Bhalvar, but she sensibly had avoided them.

Suddenly someone bumped into her from behind. Poco turned, but before she could draw her knife Jesh was standing at her shoulder, glaring at the bearded man who had appeared out of nowhere.

"Something you want?" Jesh growled at the man.

The stranger's eyes widened as he shook his head. "No, Jesh. No, nothing. I just thought I knew her. I was—"

Jesh looked at the man, then with a tip of his head, ordered the man to leave.

The man scuttled away, heading for the nearest doorway.

Poco turned and found Jesh watching her. His glance fell to where her hand still hovered by her knife hilt.

"Stay closer to me and you won't need that," he said.

"How much farther?" she asked.

"We are almost there," he replied.

As they continued on, Poco looked from one side of the street to the other, suddenly wishing she had not been so independent and had brought Dhal along.

Jesh stopped before a large, log building. Weathered

to a light gray color, it reminded Poco of a water draak carcass she had seen on the banks of the Gadrocci river near Janchee, its bleached bones sticking skyward. Wooden steps led up to a porch where a small group of dockside loungers sat enjoying an early drink. Several of the men spoke to Jesh as he climbed the steps, but he merely nodded and kept walking. At the main doors he stepped aside, indicating that Poco should precede him.

Poco hesitated, then went in. Jesh followed close behind. She felt his hand drop onto her shoulder, steering her to the right.

"Over there," he said. "Verg is probably in his office."

Poco shrugged away from his hand and walked across the room. Her eyes quickly adjusted to the semidarkness of the interior. At that moment, the dingy eating hall was empty, but after supper hour the room would fill with drinkers and gamblers and those looking for excitement.

When they reached the other side of the room, Jesh stopped at a door and knocked. A voice from inside told him to enter.

Poco stepped aside as Jesh reached for the doorknob. "You first," she said.

"You don't trust me," he said, smiling.

"I trust my instincts, and they tell me to let you go in first."

"All right, I'll go first, and when you are satisfied that it is safe, follow."

Jesh opened the door, then pushed it all the way back to the wall so Poco could see inside. Then she followed him through the doorway and quickly glanced around. The room was empty but for Jesh and a man who sat behind a large desk on the other side of the room.

Vẽrg sar Eyson stood and came around the end of the desk. He was dressed in a white shirt, a blue overvest, and a pair of dark pants. He was heavyset and balding, and he had the blotchy face of a man who liked to drink. He stopped in front of Poco, his heavy-lidded eyes sparkling with interest. "What have you brought me this time, Jesh?"

"Someone who is interested in finding a certain derkat," Jesh replied. "Singer, this is Verg sar Eyson, the owner of this establishment."

"Do you have a name, Singer?" Verg asked.

"My name is Pocalina."

Verg looked Poco up and down with the expression of a man checking over merchandise for sale. Poco was accustomed to such rude appraisals, and stifled her disgust by reminding herself that Ssaal-lr's life might depend upon her convincing this man to trade with her.

Sar Eyson leaned back against his desk. "So, you have an interest in the derkat I am holding."

"Yes," Poco answered.

Sar Eyson nodded and returned to his chair, sitting down heavily. "What kind of an interest?"

"He is a friend. I want him freed."

Verg glanced at Jesh, who was leaning against the wall to Poco's right. When Verg looked at Poco again, his glance went from her head to her toes and back to her face, assessing.

"Has Jesh told you what the derkat did?" Verg asked.

"He said that he killed a man."

"You say that as if you do not believe it, Singer."

"Oh, I believe it," Poco said. "But I would bet that if he killed someone, he had just cause."

Verg frowned. "Well, he did kill a man, and he caused a lot of damage while he was about it! Damage that someone has to pay for. Are *you* willing to pay?"

Careful, Poco thought, careful. "How much?" she asked.

"One hundred marks should cover it."

"I don't have one hundred marks, but I have something that is worth that much." Poco held up her right hand, showing him the ring on her middle finger. She had carefully removed the second ring during her walk from the marketplace.

"It is made by the Ni-lach and is worth three times what you are asking," she said.

Verg held out his hand. "Let me see it."

"First I want to see Screech."

"Screech?"

"The derkat," Poco answered.

"Damn good name for him," Jesh observed. "Those noises he makes are enough to stir a herd of draak. We had to knock him out just to get some sleep last night."

Poco felt her heart clench. She turned to Jesh. "I want to see him, then we can talk about a trade!"

Verg stood and moved around the desk. "All right, come on. He is in the cellar. Jesh, you had better come along too, just in case he decides to give us trouble."

Poco followed Verg down an unlighted corridor that ended in the tavern kitchens, where a door led to the cellar. Verg and Jesh each lighted a candle to take down into the darkness. Poco walked between them, uneasy and all too aware of the danger of a trap.

Verg stopped before a large door at the bottom of the steps and slid back the heavy bolt. Poco followed him into a dark room; she was acutely aware of Jesh close behind her.

Several stools and a small table stood in the center of the room. On the table sat an oil lamp, which Verg lighted with his candle. Poco looked around the room, but saw nothing but a jumble of empty wooden-slat crates and a pile of loose sacks. Then something moved in the far corner, and yellow eyes shone out of the shadows.

"Screech?" Poco said, starting toward the corner.

A hand caught her arm, holding her back. "Better be careful, Singer," Jesh said. "If he is as mad right now as he was last night, he might not recognize you as a friend."

"Let me go!" Poco's command was reinforced by the point of her knife, pressed against Jesh's stomach.

Jesh released her and raised his hands in a gesture of peace as he backed away. "Easy, Singer. I was just trying to warn you."

Poco backed toward the corner. The sound of chains clanking against the floor made her turn, and she saw that Screech was trying to move. The short chains linking his wrists and ankles prevented him from rising.

Screech coughed a greeting.

Poco answered in kind. "Stay quiet, friend," she said, as she touched his shoulder. "I am going to try to buy your freedom."

Suddenly Poco felt the sharp prick of claws in her left leg. She looked down and saw Screech's fingers moving in sign language. She tried to read his signing, but the shadows made it difficult.

"————me. Wants Healer. Watching us—— ——. Used me to—— —— ——. Don't trust them. ——Ni-Lach——"

"All right, Singer!" Verg snapped. "You have seen him. Now let us do some trading."

Poco turned. "He is hurt. I want some light to see if—"

"No! You've seen him! He is alive, and if you want him to stay that way, you will let me see your ring. Right now! Jesh, bring her over here!"

Poco returned to the table before Jesh could act on Verg's orders. She slipped her knife back into her wrist sheath and pulled the ring from her finger.

Verg looked the ring over carefully, holding it to the lantern light. Then he looked up. "Is this the only piece of Ni jewelry you own?"

"It is worth more than you are asking," Poco replied.

"Yes," Verg said, "it probably is. But seeing this and the armband your pet was wearing makes me wonder what other valuables you and your boyfriend possess—you know, the one who goes around with his head covered. You make quite a trio: a derkat, a chalk artist, and—who is your other friend, Singer? We are most curious, Jesh and I. We have even made bets on his parentage. According to one of the merchants we talked to, your hooded friend has the eyes of a Ni."

Poco cursed silently to herself, realizing that she and

Dhal had been watched since their arrival in Port Sulta. And she knew why: Because of the few pieces of Ni jewelry they had used in trade that first week.

She pulled her knife and threw herself at Verg. Catching his arm, she jerked him forward a step. As he tried to regain his balance, she ducked around behind him and stuck her knife into his side.

"Stand still!" she yelled at Jesh, who had started toward her. "Stand still or I kill him!"

Jesh came to a lurching stop, his leg bumping the table. The lantern started to tip over. Verg lunged forward to catch it.

Poco felt her knife drag across something soft. Verg cried out; as he fell over a stool, one of his legs slammed into Poco's side. Before she could recover her balance, Jesh grabbed her knife hand and slammed her up against the nearest wall.

Poco heard Ssaal-lr's scream of rage just before her head struck the stone wall.

Chapter 5

POCO'S FIRST AWARENESS WAS OF COLD, THEN OF PAIN in the back of her head. For a moment she could not remember where she was. She started to roll over and accuse Dhal of taking all the blankets, when she heard voices. She opened her eyes and saw Jesh standing with his back to her. She swallowed convulsively as everything came back to her.

She took a few seconds to get herself under control. When she opened her eyes again, she saw that Jesh was looking over a piece of clothing, carefully searching pockets and hems with long, nimble fingers. Poco knew that the clothes he was searching were hers, for she was stripped to the skin and could feel the cold stone beneath her back, buttocks, and legs. Her lack of clothing made her feel vulnerable so she searched for a quick way out.

She rolled her head to the side, careful not to alert either of the men to her return to consciousness. She

43

looked under the table, past the chair upon which Verg sat, and found a pair of yellow eyes watching her.

Seeing that she was awake, Screech made a small movement with his head, indicating that he wanted her to remain still.

"Find anything?" Verg asked.

Jesh dropped Poco's pants onto the table. "Nothing. Have you checked the pouch she carried?"

"Yes. Just chalks and a few coins. Let me see that necklace she was wearing."

"It is made of wood," Jesh said, handing it to Verg. "But it is Ni. I can tell that stuff anywhere. Personally, I think the rings are the best of the lot, including the armband the derkat was wearing."

"I agree." There was a moment or two of silence, then Verg spoke again. "I wish we could find their new camp. I would bet my soul that there is more where this came from."

"We located their first camp. We will find their new one eventually."

"If they don't move again."

Jesh shook his head. "I don't think the Ni will go very far without the woman. In fact, she should make a good lever when we catch up with him."

"I just hope all of this is worth the effort," Verg complained. "I do not like getting cut up for just a few pieces of Ni artwork."

"You were lucky she did not prick you a little deeper." Jesh laughed. "I warned you that she might be just as dangerous as the derkat. You never know with women. They can be all sweetness one minute, and the death of you the next." Jesh picked up the golden armband belonging to Screech. "As for what we get out of this job, a lot will depend upon whether or not her lover is the Ni who escaped the Sarissa authorities in Annaroth months ago."

"Do you think the Sarissa are still offering a reward for him?" Verg asked.

"I am not thinking as much about a reward right now, as I am about the reason for their posting the reward, *and* the stipulation that he be captured alive. Why alive and why the high price? Who is he and what does he have or know that makes him so important to them? If we can learn that, I think we might have something a lot better than the money the Sarissa are offering."

Jesh held the armband up, turning it around so he could inspect the inside. Poco cringed inwardly when she realized that it was probably Jesh who had removed her clothes.

"Jesh, has it occurred to you, that if the man is Ni, we might be borrowing more trouble than we can handle?"

"Relax, Verg. That rumor about Ni massing in the north is a pile of draak shit. They are gone for good, at least in this part of the Enzaar Sea. Those who escaped the Sarissa purge are probably hiding so far back in the northern forests that we will never hear of them again."

"I was not thinking about them. I was referring to the Ni outside the gates. If he is the one who escaped the Sarissa, who knows what kind of powers he might have. It could be dangerous to corner him."

"We have enough men, and remember, we also have something that belongs to him, something that should buy us his good behavior."

Poco closed her eyes as Jesh turned from the table. A moment later she felt the toe of his sandal nudge her hip. "Pretty bitch," he said.

Poco knew exactly what could happen to her if she failed to escape; the slave markets and brothels were always ready to buy healthy young men and women who had no friends or connections.

"Is she still out?" Verg asked.

Poco was aware of Jesh as he squatted down over her, his nearness like an enveloping fog. She forced herself to relax as she felt his fingers at her throat.

Satisfied that she was still alive, Jesh moved his hand

down to gently touch Poco's left breast. "Very nice," he murmured.

"Enough of that!" Verg growled. "Come here and look at this. The two rings are—Damn it! Jesh, come here! There will be time for that later. If you would keep your mind on—"

Jesh pinched the tip of Poco's breast. Her cry of pain brought a wicked grin to his face.

Pain and rage brought Poco up fighting.

Jesh ducked her first swing, then lunged for her wrists, leaving himself wide open. Poco's knee came up with a speed Jesh could not outmaneuver. He grunted in pain and rolled away, clutching himself and swearing. She brought her legs up and rolled onto her back. Before he could get away, she kicked out and caught him in the neck and head with the heels of her feet.

Everything happened so fast that Verg was just rising as Jesh's shoulders hit the table. Verg was thrown backward, and the lantern on top of the table fell over, sending oil and flame across the table top and onto the floor. Some of the oil splattered onto Jesh.

Poco heard Ssaal-lr's yowl of triumph, followed by a man's scream. She rolled over and quickly came to her feet. Through the flickering firelight, she saw Screech atop Verg's twitching body; the derkat had his teeth fastened in the man's throat.

Poco turned away, swallowing quickly to quell the sudden queasiness in her stomach. No man should die like that, she thought.

All thoughts of Verg were driven from her mind as Jesh let loose with a roar of pain. He was rolling over and over on the floor, batting at the flames which licked at his shoulders, chest, and head.

Poco looked around for something with which to beat at the flames, but before she could move, Jesh was up and running for the door.

She ran around the burning table as Jesh disappeared up the cellar steps. She and Screech had to get out of there before Jesh sent someone to stop them. She crouched beside Screech. The derkat had given up his hold on Verg's throat and was fumbling at the man's pockets.

"*Find keys*," he signed.

Poco quickly checked Verg's belt. She heard the clink of metal against the stone floor and turned the man over. A moment later she held a ring of keys. She fought the trembling of her hands as she tried each key in the locks holding Screech prisoner. While she was busy with the keys, Screech untied Verg's money pouch.

Seven keys and still she could not find the right one! Poco looked at Screech and saw that his attention was now on the cellar door. She listened and was sure she heard people moving overhead. Hurry! she told herself. Hurry, but don't fumble.

Finally one of the keys slid into the lock. There was a click and Screech shook off one leg chain; he was impatient to be free.

The moment Poco released the last manacle, Screech stood and glided toward the cellar door. The table was still burning; the smoke was growing thick.

Poco grabbed up her pants, tunic, and boots. Then she saw Screech's armband and her pendant and rings, which had been knocked off the table during the scuffle. She picked them up and joined Screech at the cellar door.

She started to say something, but Screech signaled her to stand quietly. All was silent above.

Poco slipped her tunic over her head; then suddenly Screech was moving. She followed him up the cellar steps and prayed that they would not meet any resistance above.

Screech paused at the top step and poked his head out around the doorway. Voices could be heard coming from the main dining room.

"Come on," Poco whispered urgently. "Let's get out of here!"

Screech bobbed his head, then he took her wrist and led her across the kitchen toward a side door.

He made sure the back alley was clear, then together

they raced down the narrow dirt lane leading east away from the tavern. They stopped before they reached the main street, and Poco finished dressing.

She pulled her boots on and stood up. Screech was watching her; the blood around his mouth and over his neck and chest reminded her of Verg's death. She had never seen Screech kill, not like that—and never a man.

He placed furred hands to her shoulders. Bending down so his face was even with hers, he coughed softly, his warm breath scented with blood.

Poco ignored the odor as she returned the cough, the derkat sign of acceptance.

"*You saved my life*," he signed.

"And you mine," she replied. She hesitated. "I have never seen you kill anyone before."

"*The men hurt you. Might have killed you. You are of my radg. It is my duty to protect you.*" He paused then finished. "*Angry?*"

Poco shook her head.

"*Does the Healer know you came to look for me?*"

"I left before he was awake. I told Gi where I was going. I was worried when you did not return last night."

"*Men want to find the Healer.*"

"Yes, I know. It means we will have to leave here."

"*Where do we go?*"

"Jesh spoke about the Ni gathering in the north, and Dhal believes Jjaan-bi lies somewhere beyond the Chengarry Mountains. Since we cannot go back to Port Bhalvar or to any of the other port towns on the Enzaar Sea, it leaves us little choice."

"*We must cross the High Plains to reach the Chengarry Mountains.*"

Poco nodded. "Derkat territory, Screech. Home for you."

"*My radg is my home*," he answered.

Poco smiled in understanding: The derkat's home was wherever his family was, and that meant her. "Come on, Screech, let's find Dhal and tell him what has happened.

Oh, here, I picked this up before we left." She handed him the single armband she had brought away with her. Her neck pendant already hung down inside her tunic.

Screech slipped the armband onto his lower right arm, then surprised Poco by pulling her close in a hug. Poco returned the embrace, carefully trying to avoid the drying blood on his chest fur.

Upon returning to camp, Poco convinced a very angry Dhal that Port Sulta had ceased to be a refuge for them. Dhal's anger cooled as she explained the reason for Ssaal-lr's abduction. She neglected to tell him the details of her own capture and humiliation, and finished by warning him that Jesh was not the kind of man to give up easily. "If we do not leave soon," she said, "we may never leave at all."

Chapter 6 🖎

TWO DAYS LATER, DHAL LED THE WAY INTO THE SMALL
town of Anatat. Using the last of the money from
Verg's pouch, they purchased some supplies; but they did
not linger, fearing that Jesh or his men might not be far
behind them.

The narrow trail north from Anatat was overgrown
with vine and grass. The giant aban trees to either side
of the road formed a continuous canopy of dark green
leaves. At the first touch of the spring rains due in a few
weeks, the old leaves would fall off and for a short time
sunlight would filter through to warm and revive the smaller
plant life below. Poco shared Dhal's love for the warm
season and eagerly awaited the flowers and new growth
that would soon abound in the woodlands.

Late in the afternoon they passed an abandoned holding. The buildings were weathered, the stockade broken.
Without a Draak Watch to patrol the area, the land had
been left to return to wilderness.

Poco shook her head as they passed the holding. The more she became involved with Dhal and his search for the Ni-lach, the more she realized how foolish the Sarissa had been to drive the Green Ones away. Without a Draak Watch, no one could plant or harvest the vast acreage needed to fill the stomachs of the hungry; and without the Watch, there could be no outward growth into new territories.

Poco was appalled by the very scope of the disaster facing mankind on Lach: She felt insignificant and a little guilty. True, she was half-blood Ni, but the blood of men also flowed in her veins. Was she betraying her mother's people by searching out the Ni-lach? And if she and Dhal did, by some remote chance, find the Ni-lach, could she live among them and forget that elsewhere men were fighting draak to hold onto the little land they still possessed?

She stopped and looked back the way they had come. They had been climbing steadily since leaving Anatat, and in the distance she could see the green water of the Enzaar Sea. During her lifetime she had never been more than a few hours away from the sea. She could not help but wonder if she would ever return that way again.

Her thoughts were interrupted by a deep-throated growl.

Screech and Taav had stopped in the middle of the pathway ahead. When Poco caught up with them, Taav turned.

She looked into his eyes, searching for that flicker of presence that spoke of a thinking entity; but his eyes remained the same, open and watching, but somehow empty, as if conscious thought had been suspended.

He was dressed in one of her tunics and a pair of pants that belonged to Dhal. Gone was the pitiful bundle of bones and rags; after Dhal's healing touch, and a few days of solid meals and exercise, Taav had become a new person.

Now, Poco thought, if we can only get Taav to talk to us.

She looked over the top of his head. She was about to

ask Screech why they had stopped, when she saw Dhal running back down the trail toward them. Gi-arobi was down on all fours, running right behind him.

"Draak!" Dhal yelled. "Off the trail! Climb!"

Screech grabbed Taav around the waist and lifted him up and over his shoulder, then followed Poco into the dense underbrush at the side of the road.

Poco pushed her way around bushes and vine and headed for the nearest aban trees, looking for a tree strong enough to withstand the assault of an adult draak. She heard Screech growl and turned to see him point to a huge tree with branches reaching down far enough to make for easy climbing. She nodded.

When she reached the tree, she swung onto one of the lower branches and pulled herself up. Screech was right behind her with Taav.

"Keep climbing, Poco!" Dhal shouted as he ran past. "I'll try to lead them away!"

Them? Poco's heart dropped as she continued to climb. Damn fool, she thought. Probably get himself killed!

Poco heard the hiss of an aroused draak and turned to look back toward the road. She saw the head of a draak appear over the tops of the genna bushes lining the road, and right behind the one, came two more. The three draak were immature blues, perhaps four or five years old. Land draak were lighter in build then their water cousins, but it was not unusual for an adult land draak to stand as tall as a rilror pine.

The draak followed Dhal downtrail, their long, scaled necks outstretched, their tails whipping back and forth as they ran. Though draak looked ungainly, their lower bodies almost dragging on the ground, they moved quickly. Poco watched as they continued on out of sight, hissing and roaring at their escaping quarry.

She adjusted her hold on a branch above; then Screech climbed up beside her and pushed Taav into her lap. "*Stay here*," he signed. "*I will go help the Healer.*"

Poco nodded and grabbed Taav around the waist. "Be

careful," she cautioned as Screech dropped quickly down from branch to branch. "And keep an eye out for Gi. I doubt he was able to keep up with Dhal!"

Poco interpreted the derkat's growl as an affirmative, and turned her attention to her charge, who at that moment was sitting balanced on her right leg, his hands clutching her arm. She wondered if he was aware of what was going on.

She carefully inched her way along the branch until her back was against the trunk of the tree; she then clamped her legs around the limb and relesed her hold on the branch above. She finally maneuvered Taav's left leg up and over so that he joined her in straddling the limb.

Sure that their positions were as secure as she could make them, she turned to listen to the sounds of the draak chase, trying to judge the direction of the hunt. "Just don't let them get too close, Dhal," she whispered softly.

Poco patted Taav's shoulder and readjusted her arm about his waist. "We will just have to trust him to know what he is doing, won't we, Taav? Are you comfortable?" She did not expect him to answer.

Time dragged on. The sounds of the chase had long since died away. The stillness of the forest was broken by the call of a neeva bird, a trilling sound that ended with a high note repeated four times. Poco noticed that Taav turned to listen when the call was answered by another neeva bird.

"Do you like that, Taav?" she asked softly, her lips close to his ear. "That is a neeva bird. Have you ever seen a neeva, Taav?"

Poco shrugged when Taav failed to respond to her voice. Dhal thinks you can talk, friend, she thought, but how long do we wait? If you do not show some signs of improvement soon, what will we do with you?

Time stretched on and still there was no sign of Dhal or Screech. Poco was worried, and Taav was growing increasingly restless. She did think about leaving her perch to look for her friends, but she feared that she lacked both

the strength and coordination to help Taav climb down;
a fall from such a height would kill.

Poco readjusted her hold on Taav and tried to ease
cramped muscles in arms, back, and legs. Suddenly, Taav
leaned forward over her arm, reaching for a branch.

"No, Taav! Sit still!" Poco cried. "I cannot hold you
if you are going to—I said, stop it!"

Taav twisted around and began to emit strange mouth
noises. Before Poco could stop him, he brought his left
leg up and over the branch and was slipping out of her
grasp.

Poco clamped her legs tight around the limb and readjusted her hold on Taav, using both arms to quell his
struggles. She was not sure what had set him off and could
think of only one way to quiet him.

She chose a song about the flying griff which hunted
the high plateaus of Sala, far east of the Reaches. Poco
had never seen one of the winged cat-creatures, but she
had heard them described, and in her mind she likened
them to sleek fishing vessels, their billowing sails lending
themselves to imagery of great wings dipping to currents
of air blowing across open water.

Taav stilled his struggles as the first few notes of song
trembled in the air.

Poco continued to sing and carefully pulled Taav up
until he again sat on the main limb, his legs dangling to
one side.

Suddenly Taav turned to look at her. Poco was startled
by the directness of his gaze and stopped singing; but the
pause was only momentary, for as soon as the music
ended, Taav tried to push away from her.

All right, so I sing, she thought. She started a familiar
dock song and Taav went still once more, his gaze never
leaving her face.

She sang the chorus of the song, which described old
wooden docks lying in the sun and wharfmen moving
about their work, nodding to one another as they laid
their catches out to dry. Suddenly she became aware of

movement reflected in Taav's eyes, of shadows which began to take the form of ships and docks.

She drew back, startled. The song died on her lips.

Taav sat perfectly still in a trancelike state.

Poco shivered as she stared into his eyes, for the scene reflected there was achingly familiar: Port Bhalvar! There was no mistaking the place where she had lived so long.

She shook her head, unable to believe what she was seeing. The picture she had drawn was etched with words this time, not chalk, and in Taav's eyes rather than on a stone walk.

She leaned closer, searching the scene before her, waiting for it to shimmer and vanish. Her song pictures always disappeared a few moments after she stopped singing. Taav's eyes were tiny compared to the wide stone slates to which she was accustomed, still she could easily see everything in the song: boats, docks, men.

Minutes passed and still the scene remained. Poco drew a shaky breath.

She was mesmerized by the living world within Taav's eyes. The scene, once so familiar, reinforced her belief that what she was seeing was real, both to her and in some way to Taav. But why didn't the scene fade as it always did? Was Taav responsible? Was he doing something to hold the door to elsewhere open?

She felt her flesh crawl as the word door echoed and reechoed through her mind. Dhal had called the world gates doors through time and space—was it possible that Taav could be of some help in finding such a door?

Fool! Poco swore silently. You are letting your thoughts run wild! Taav is in no mental state to do anything but absorb your stupid songs and blank out whatever little mind he has left! Snap him out of it before he is hurt!

"Taav!" Poco tapped the side of his face lightly, then harder when he failed to respond. "Taav, do you hear me? Come on, wake up! Come back to me!"

Poco's third slap stung her fingers. Taav blinked rapidly, his eyes watering from the blow. For a moment there was a spark of awareness shining back at her, then his eyes closed and he slumped in her arms.

Not long after that, Dhal, Gi, and Screech returned, giving Poco the all-clear signal. Screech climbed up the tree and carried Taav back down. Poco stretched cramped muscles and followed, her mind still busy with thoughts of Taav and his reaction to her singing.

Poco gave Dhal a quick hug when she reached the ground, glad to see that he had come to no harm. "It looks like you went through some heavy underbrush," she said.

Dhal nodded and continued to pull small stickburrs from his pants. "It was quite a run, something I would not want to do every day. Screech and Gi helped distract one while I lost the other two farther downtrail. It took us a little while to find each other."

Dhal looked down at Taav, who lay at Ssaal-lr's feet. "What is wrong with him?" he asked Poco.

"Do we have time to sit and talk?" Poco asked.

Dhal frowned. "Something *is* wrong."

"Yes," she answered.

Dhal turned to Screech and saw him nod; they would be safe there for a little while. Dhal took Poco's hand. "Sit down and tell me what happened."

Poco sat next to Taav, unsure of where she should begin. She rubbed at the frown lines on her forehead and tried to gather her thoughts. "You are not going to believe what I have to tell you," she warned.

A small, furred hand touched her arm. Gi stood at her right shoulder, his head cocked to one side. "Tell us," he lisped. "We believe."

Poco smiled and drew the olvaar close. "You, I love," she said, rubbing her cheek on the top of his head.

Gi thrummed laughter and contentment. "Gi making Poco happy, Dhal," he said.

Dhal smiled at the olvaar, knowing full well how Gi affected everyone. Then he reached out and drew Gi from Poco's embrace. "Enough with happiness for a little while, Gi. Let's hear what Poco has to tell us, all right?"

Ssaal-lr knelt behind Poco as she started to tell them about Taav's reaction to her singing. The derkat's strong fingers moved over her back and shoulders, massaging and easing her tired muscles.

Words came more easily as Poco relaxed to a familiar touch.

Poco looked down at the red bruise on Taav's cheek. "I had to slap him to wake him up," she finished ruefully. "After he passed out, I just held him until you came."

Screech was the first to offer an opinion. *"Your songs live for you and for the Healer. Not for me or Little Fur. Now they live for the atich-ar. Your songs are a form of Ni bonding, yes?"*

"Yes," Dhal agreed. "I begin to think so. Whatever Poco's special talent is, it only seems to affect those of Ni blood."

"That I can accept," Poco said. "But why was it different this time? Why did the scene hold so long? It has never lasted more than a few seconds before."

"It has to have something to do with Taav, or his state of mind, I think," Dhal responded.

"Or lack of it," Poco added, looking down at the unconscious atich-ar. "Dhal, do you think he will ever be any better than he is now?"

Dhal smoothed the hair from Taav's forehead. "I don't know. I could try to go back inside again, to see if there is something I missed."

"That would be dangerous right now if Jesh is behind us."

"I agree."

A few minutes passed as each of the four was caught up in his or her own thoughts. Finally Poco spoke.

"Dhal have you decided which way we are going?"

They had talked about their options every night since leaving Port Sulta, but had not yet made a firm decision. Their goal was the Owri River deep in the Chen-garry Mountains. According to all Dhal had learned from talking to traders in Port Sulta, the Owri had once been used as a route in reaching Jjaan-bi. They had two choices. In order to reach the Chen-garry Mountains they could go straight north across the High Plains where radgs of derkat roamed freely, or they could go east to the Reaches, a natural flood plain where vast food crops were grown for trade in Annaroth; but the men of the Reaches were closely tied to the Sarissa Empire and therefore might look upon Dhal as an enemy. If they did chance the western route, it would take them a month longer to reach the Owri.

Dhal was set on a route straight north, which meant that their last stop for supplies would be the small trade town of Bannoc, deep in the Semco Hills. The only problem with Bannoc was that Ssaal-lr would be in danger there, for it was a trade center built and governed by men who dealt in the procurement of animal pelts. Some of the pelts brought more than a man's weight in spices, a rare commodity in Letsia and derkat pelts were among the most precious.

The derkat were native to Lach and considered by most men to be little more than gensvolf, animals to be hunted and put in cages. The only time men would lower themselves to trade with the derkat was when the furred ones had something men wanted, such as draak hides or amber nodules.

Poco knew that if they went into the Semco Hills it would be extremely unwise for Screech to enter Bannoc without a full radg to protect him. Those derkat who were taken by trappers were usually loners or the very young, caught straying from their radgs during the yearly trek across the plains. The bronze-skinned Utura trappers were responsible for Ssaal-lr's abduction to Port Bhalvar years before.

Poco looked at Ssaal-lr. Knowing the depth of thought that could go on behind his still, yellow eyes, she could not help but wonder if men would ever waken to the realization that they were not the sole possessors of intelligence on Lach, that mind could not always be judged by form or lifestyle.

Poco watched Dhal stand and move away, his eyes turned to the trail north. "Bannoc?" she asked.

Screech growled; his eyes narrowed with distaste. He was not afraid of returning to his home territory, but he wanted nothing to do with the men of Bannoc.

Poco realized that if Dhal said yes, they likely would lose Screech; if not to Utura trappers, then to his own people. Returning to his clan if the opportunity presented itself would only be natural. The thought of separation brought a lump to her throat.

Dhal turned and nodded. "Bannoc. Who knows, maybe the Utura will know something more about Jjaan-bi."

"I hate the thought of crossing the plains. I wish we could just turn around and go south again, maybe down-coast toward Port Cestar."

Dhal looked at Poco. "Port Cestar belongs to the Sar-issa in all but name, Poco. We would be right back where we started."

"What about Amla-Bagor or even beyond. It's a big world. The Sarissa don't own it all!"

"No, but they do own enough of it to keep us jumping." Dhal squatted next to her. "You are afraid," he said. "Of what? Of getting lost on the plains?"

"No. I am not afraid of getting lost."

"What then?" he pressed.

Poco hesitated, then answered. "I am afraid of finding what we search for."

"Jjaan-bi?" he asked, disbelief plain in his look.

"Yes."

He shook his head. "I don't understand. If we find Jjaan-bi, we find the Ni-lach, and maybe the Tamorlee."

"What if Jjaan-bi is deserted, like Val-hrodhur? What then? Where do we go from there?" she asked.

Dhal hesitated. "I don't know, Poco. I guess that I have just been hoping that it won't be deserted."

Poco realized that Dhal had had his mind made up for some time. Was there any chance at all to dissuade him? she wondered.

"Dhal, when we found Val-hrodhur, we lost Haradan. Who will it be this time? Screech? You? Me?"

"Poco you are not making any sense. No one need die this time. If Jjaan-bi is deserted, there is no danger, and if it is not, the Ni we find there will see us as friends."

"How can you be so sure, Dhal?"

He pulled her close. "I am not. There is no way of knowing what we will find in Jjaan-bi, but not knowing should not keep us from looking. I think—I know Haradan would want us to go on."

He released her and pushed her to arm's length. "You do still want to find the Ni-lach and the Tamorlee don't you?"

Poco finally gave a reluctant nod. "Yes, I guess so, but I want your promise that you will go slowly if and when we do find your people."

"Look who is cautioning who, will you? Who was it who slipped off on her own to rescue Screech and got herself caught?" Dhal laughed and pulled her close again, kissing her soundly.

Poco struggled for a moment, then returned his kiss.

Dhal stood and gave her a hand up. "Will that bolster your courage for a little while?" he asked, smiling.

An answering smile tugged at the corners of her mouth. "I did not know Healers were capable of granting courage."

"Only to very special patients," he replied.

Chapter 7

THEY TOOK EIGHT DAYS TO REACH BANNOC, WHERE THEY intended to purchase supplies and mounts for the trek across the High Plains. Taav's inability to keep to a steady march slowed them down considerably. Although he seemed to have recovered from the trance touched off by Poco's singing, he tired easily and there were times when he seemed to walk in a daze; he would come to a standstill and move only if someone pulled him along. And still he did not try to communicate.

Leaving Screech, Gi, and Taav hidden in a narrow, tree-shaded valley a half-day's march from Bannoc, Poco and Dhal continued on alone.

"Have you ever ridden a bomal, Dhal?" Poco asked as they walked up the roadway.

The Utura trappers had domesticated one of the larger variety of bomal, a fleet-footed, four-legged animal that stood shoulder high to a man, its slender neck raising its head an arm's length taller. The trappers used the bomal's strength to travel over great distances and to outmaneuver draak, gensvolf, and derkat.

"No," Dhal answered. "The bomal in the marshlands are small and shy and seldom seen, even by wilders. I have heard about the greater bomal, but have never seen one."

"I have seen two, and they were beautiful. They have big, sad eyes and long curled horns. I admit, though, that I am a little nervous about riding one."

"Before you worry about that, let's worry about getting the money to buy them. Verg's money is almost gone."

The road widened as it neared Bannoc. To either side lay small, freshly turned fields, surrounded by thick, briar-twined fences. The town was situated on a ridge of a hill. The stockade that encircled the town was built to with-stand the attack of even the largest of land draak.

When they reached the main south gate, Poco and Dhal were stopped and asked what business had brought them to Bannoc. Dhal was careful to keep his eyes shadowed by his hood as he explained their need to purchase several bomal to use as pack animals.

"I am a wilder by profession," he told the two gate guards. "My mate and I tire of carrying everything on our backs. Herbs and spices can get heavy when one has to travel long distances."

"Do you have a trade route?" one of the men asked.

"No," Dhal answered. "Not yet."

"We could use a good wilder here," the man said. "All of our medicines have to come from Port Sulta. You might do well to set up a route between here and the Reaches. You would not have much competition."

"No competition," the other man said, smiling. "But lots of draak." A burly fellow, he seemed more interested in looking at Poco than in hearing what Dhal had to say. "But you both look like you would be fast on your feet," he added. "You especially, blue eyes."

Poco smiled and nodded. "I have outrun a few draak, but I find climbing a tree much easier."

"I'm sure you are good at it," the first man said.

"She looks like she would be good at everything," the second man added.

Before things could go any further, Dhal politely reminded the men he was there. "If you have no more questions for us, may we pass?"

"Sure," the first man said. "Welcome aboard. Good luck to you in your buying."

Dhal turned to look at Poco as they started toward the center of the town. "They liked you."

"So I noticed," she responded, smiling.

"Sometimes I wish you were not so beautiful."

Poco looked down at herself. Her shirt was torn in several places; her pants were dusty and grass-stained; and her boots were definitely the worse for wear.

"You *are* beautiful, Poco," Dhal said. "No matter what you wear. I know it and those men back there know it. I just hope it doesn't get us into trouble here."

Poco nodded. "I'll be careful. I promise. No flirting back." She smiled. "No matter how tall and handsome he may be."

Bannoc was not large. The collection of buildings situated at the very top of the hill boasted of only four main streets and was bare of trees except for those that sheltered the large bomal enclosure at the north end of town.

"Shall we go and look at the bomal first?" Poco asked.

Dhal was watching five men who sat on a porch on the right-hand side of the street. "Yes, it might be a good idea."

Poco was also aware of the men watching them. "We are strangers, Dhal. They are only curious. They probably don't get many visitors here."

"I hope that is all it is," he murmured.

Suddenly Poco was chilled by an unpleasant thought. "Dhal, do you think Jesh's men are still after us?"

"I don't know, Poco. Still, it would be wise to assume the worst and keep our eyes open."

"Yes," Poco agreed, "and start thinking about ways to earn some money."

"We still have a few pieces of Ni jewelry left, but I would rather not do any more trading unless we have to. One band of thieves following us is enough."

Poco nodded, her thoughts already turning from Jesh's men to the money they needed for supplies. "I lost my pouch of chalks at Verg's place, so chalking is out. Even if I had them, there is no place to do any sketching, unless I used one of the porches we passed."

"Would anyone pay just to hear you sing?"

Poco knew better than to take Dhal's question as an insult. "Back in Port Sulta I would say yes; but here I am not so sure. I could try."

They walked on in silence, passing the last of the wooden buildings on the street and approaching the bomal enclosure.

Dhal adjusted his backpack, easing tired muscles. "I have an idea."

Poco looked at him. "What?"

He met her glance, then hesitated and looked away, shaking his head. "No, I guess not."

"What? What were you thinking about?"

"Never mind."

"Come on, Dhal. If you have thought of something, tell me."

"I could heal," he said, not looking at her.

Poco slowed her pace, then stopped. Dhal walked a step or two beyond her. When he turned to face her, Poco just stared at him, shocked and surprised by the inner conflict she felt. Was it wrong for him to profit by such a gift? Was it really any different for him than it was for her? She had used her gift for song to provide a living for many years; but his gift for healing was so very special that to put a price on it would be like putting a price on a miracle. And though the Letsians had never treated the Ni-lach as had the Sarissa, neither had they offered them sanctuary—there was no telling how they might treat Dhal should they learn of his bloodlines.

Poco closed the distance between them. "Dhal," she said, carefully judging her words. "I think I would rather trade every piece of Ni jewelry we own than to have you sell your power to heal. I know what healing means to you, how you become linked with everyone you touch. You cannot sell something like that. Not you! And I think it best to keep your secret to ourselves, even here."

Dhal took a deep breath and nodded, relief plain in his voice. "It was just a thought."

Poco slipped her arms about his waist and pulled him close. "Come on, let's go look at the bomal."

Down at the bomal enclosure, Dhal pointed out several bomal that he thought might make good mounts. Suddenly Poco became aware of a man standing behind them. She had not heard him approach.

"Like what you see?" he asked as she turned to face him.

"They are beautiful," she answered. "Are they as fast as they look?"

"Faster." The man smiled and stepped closer, then Dhal turned and the man's eyes widened.

Too late, Dhal pulled his hood forward, shielding his eyes.

The man hesitated, then spoke. "Are you two interested in buying?"

"Perhaps," Poco answered. "It depends upon the price."

"You are strangers in Bannoc." When neither replied, the man continued. "We don't get many strangers here. Those who come usually have a pretty good reason." The man looked at Dhal. "You are Ni, aren't you?"

Dhal hesitated, then nodded.

"Running?"

"Let us just say that we have some place we want to go," Poco said. "And we need bomal to get there. How much for three?"

The man rubbed the back of his jaw with his hand, his

glance taking in their clothing and their tattered packs. "Why three?" he asked.

"One extra to carry our supplies," Poco answered quickly. "How much?"

"Two hundred marks each," the man answered.

"It's too high, Dhal! We would never be able to—"

The man cut Poco off. "How many bomal have you ever bought, miss? That price is not high. It's standard."

"Would you trade?" Dhal asked.

"No, Dhal!" Poco protested.

"I know what I said, Poco, but we haven't much of a choice. It would take us a week to earn money to pay for the bomal." He turned to the man. "Would you accept something in trade?"

"Like what?" the man asked.

Dhal unlaced the flap of his belt pouch and brought out one of the two pieces of Ni artistry he had left. The large brooch of wood overlaid with carved shell depicted a gensvolf attacking a berryl cat half its own size. The workmanship was exquisite.

Dhal hated to part with the brooch, but knew from the man's expression of desire that he had chosen correctly.

"For that you can have two bomal," the man said, reaching for the brooch.

Dhal drew back his hand. "Three bomal and whatever gear is needed to ride them."

The man hesitated only a moment. "All right, three— and gear." The man quickly took the brooch. "Do you want them now?"

"No. Tomorrow," Dhal answered.

"Do you have a name?" Poco asked the man.

"Rahn sar Evvan," he answered.

She nodded. "We will be back later to talk with you, Rahn. We are inexperienced riders and will have to trust you to choose our mounts for us, and give us instructions in caring for them, if you will."

"My pleasure."

"That was easier than I expected," Dhal said, as they made their way back up the dirt road to the main street.

"Too easy maybe," Poco said.

"What do you mean?"

Poco looked at Dhal, wondering how so intelligent a person could be so innocent. True, his upbringing in the Deep had sheltered him from some of the grimmer aspects of life, still she found herself continually amazed at his trusting nature. Would he ever change? Did she want him to?

"Poco?"

"I just don't trust him, Dhal. I can't tell you why."

"Should we go back, get the bomal and leave?"

"No. Let's go and see what I can earn by singing a few songs. We still need some supplies if we're to make this trek across the plains. You know what wild roots we can eat, and Screech told me he can supply us with water, but we ought to have several more water flagons to carry and another sword or two; one for me, one for Screech."

"Can you handle a sword?" he asked seriously.

"Not with any finesse, but I can learn. You will have to be my teacher."

"I only know what Haradan taught me."

Poco smiled. "He was good with a sword. If you can make me even a third as good, we should have no problem."

"What about Screech? Can he use a sword?"

"Yes, but I think he prefers claws and teeth when he fights."

"I've been thinking about Screech," Dhal said, his face suddenly grim, "and what could happen to us if we run across some of his kin."

"As long as he is with us, we should be all right. And if we are mounted, we can always outrun them." I hope, she added silently.

Chapter 8

LONG AFTER THE SUPPER HOUR, POCO NOTICED FIVE newcomers enter the dining hall. She continued to sing the last verse of "Guard the Gates," and watched as the men moved around the crowded dining tables, making their way toward a bench situated along the south wall of the inn.

Something about the men made Poco feel uneasy. A moment later she realized what that something was: the men were not dressed as Bannoc traders; their tunics were cut differently, and not one of them wore the baggy pants common to the plainsmen.

The five late arrivals took seats where they could find them, two down on the far end of the hall, two at a table in the back of the room. The last man stopped near an open window to her right. Poco did not like the satisfied grin on his face as he leaned back against the window ledge and folded his arms across his chest.

She glanced over at the proprietor of the inn, a heavy-shouldered man with whom she had contracted to perform that night. When Benjor caught her eye, he nodded, his grin telling her that he was pleased with the number of patrons she had drawn into his establishment.

She returned his nod and glanced at the side door just behind him. She was looking for Dhal to return. He had left over an hour ago; certainly he had had time enough to pay for the supplies they had ordered and return to the inn. So, where was he?

She glanced at the five men who had entered last and quickly decided that it might be best if Dhal did not return to Benjor's at that moment.

Poco had been singing off and on for about three hours, and had more than met her agreement with Benjor, so she felt no qualms about calling it a night. She cut the chorus of the song she was singing and signaled Benjor that she intended to take a break.

The men and women who had drifted in and out of Benjor's inn during and after the supper hour had been attentive and generous. The coins thrown to her during the first hour were worth twice what they needed to pay for the things she and Dhal had chosen from the well-stocked shelves at the trade shop down the street.

Poco deftly caught several coins tossed her way as her audience showed its appreciation by stamping their feet and clapping. Someone called for another song. But Poco slid off the table upon which she had been sitting and raised her hands.

"You have been kind to a stranger, ladies and gentlemen," she said, giving them her best smile. "If you will permit me some time to catch my breath, I will be happy to rejoin you in a little while."

A spatter of hand-clapping followed Poco as she made her way to Benjor. One man caught her wrist as she passed his table. He pressed a large coin into her hand.

"I have not heard singing like that since I left Port Bhalvar years ago. Do you know Port Bhalvar, Singer?"

"It was my home until recently," Poco answered, smil-

ing. "But I have restless feet and am prone to wander."
She held up the coin and nodded. "Thank you for this. It
is a gift much needed right now."

Poco quickly reached Benjor, who was waiting for her
near the side entrance. "Has my friend returned?" she
asked.

"No. I haven't seen him. Pocalina, you *will* sing again
won't you?" Benjor asked.

"I need some air," she answered, avoiding a direct
reply. "Does this door lead outside?"

"Yes. Go down the hall to the left and it takes you
out."

Poco started to turn away, but Benjor held her arm.
"You're doing a good job here, daughter of Jamba. Would
you consider a more permanent arrangement?"

"I might," she lied, anxious to leave and look for Dhal.
She definitely did not want him returning to Benjor's inn.
Either he was still at the trade shop or he had taken
everything down to the bomal pens. He had to be one
place or the other—or somewhere in between.

Damn, she thought, we should have stayed together!

Benjor released her arm. "Back in a few minutes, then?"

Poco nodded. "As soon as I get my breath back."

She stepped into the hall and closed the door behind
her. She was sorry to have to lie to Benjor, but her instincts told her it was time to leave as quickly as possible.

She was halfway down the hall when the door to the
dining hall opened and a man wearing a hooded tunic
appeared. By his size Poco knew it was not Dhal. As he
hurried after her, she ran toward the door at the end of
the hallway.

Hands grabbed her from behind and jerked her backward. She started to scream for help, but a hand slapped
over her mouth, cutting off her cry.

She brought her right knee up as her attacker slammed
her up against the wall. The man turned sideways, as if
anticipating that move.

"Not again, you she-cat!"

The voice was familiar! Suddenly the man's hood fell back to reveal the ugly mask that was Jesh's face: Where there was no bandaging, his burned skin was swollen and oozing, and a great patch of hair was missing from the right side of his head. Poco's eyes widened.

Jesh pushed his face down close to hers. "It took some doing, but I finally caught up with you, Singer! You are responsible for this! And I swear, you will pay for it if I have to chain you in a cellar and sell you to every man in Port Sulta!"

Poco tried to slip out from under the arm pressing against her throat, but Jesh was strong and she was no match for him. Remembering her knife, she changed tactics.

Jesh swore and loosened his hold as she kicked him in the legs. At that moment she reached for her knife.

She was not fast enough. Jesh blocked her thrust and captured her hand, bringing it back and banging it against the wall. The knife slipped from Poco's fingers as her hand went numb with pain.

Jesh laughed. "You are not going to come quietly, are you? No matter. I don't need your cooperation. It will be more fun this way."

The horror of Jesh's scarred face leering down at her made Poco feel sick inside.

Suddenly the door to the street slammed shut. Jesh turned to see who had interrupted him.

In three running steps, Dhal was on top of Jesh, his knife drawn. Jesh managed to evade Dhal's first thrust by turning sideways. But the moment Jesh released Poco, she kicked out. Her foot connected with his leg, knocking him off balance.

Jesh grabbed for his own knife but with snakelike speed, Dhal struck a second time, his knife plunging into Jesh's stomach and ripping up.

The big man screamed and staggered, then slowly crumpled to the floor.

"Are you all right?" Dhal snapped as he turned to glance at her.

Unable to find her voice, Poco nodded. Everything had happened so fast. She looked down at Jesh and saw him shudder once, then still.

Dhal leaned down and withdrew his knife.

"Is he dead?" Poco asked softly.

Dhal pulled Jesh over onto his back. One glance at Jesh's staring eyes gave Poco her answer. Slowly, she bent to retrieve her knife.

"I was afraid you would come back and walk into a trap," Poco said. "It looks like I was the one to—"

She stopped short at the sound of the hallway door banging open. Two men appeared; she could hear others behind them. "You!" one of the men yelled. "What's going on? What are you doing—"

Dhal leaped up, grabbed Poco's arm, and started for the door. "Move!" he shouted.

Out on the street, they hesitated as two men ran around the corner of Benjor's inn, cutting off a direct run to the bomal pens.

"This way!" Poco cried, running toward the trade shop a few doors down.

Dhal followed. They cleared the porch steps in several bounds and went in through the trade shop door. Dhal slammed the door behind them and quickly located the bolt.

"What are you doing?"

Poco whirled to face the tall, thin proprietor of the shop, the same man she had seen earlier that day.

"Someone is after us," she explained. "Have you another way out of here?"

"Who are you? What is going on?" the man demanded.

"We came in earlier, remember? My friend came back after supper to pay for the things we ordered."

The man looked at Dhal. "Oh, yes, now I—"

Heavy pounding erupted at the front door. "Open up!" someone outside yelled.

The man looked at the door, then at Poco and Dhal. "What have you done?"

"Nothing!" Poco answered. "The men out there are thieves! They followed us all the way from Port Sulta!"

The men outside began throwing their weight against the door.

"Quick! Another way out!" Poco cried, moving away from the door.

The man growled a curse at strangers and their problems, then waved toward the back of the shop. "Through that doorway and take a right. There is a door to the outside in the room at the end of the hall. Go on, I will see if I can hold things up here."

Poco did not wait to thank the man. She and Dhal were around the end of counter and into the back of the shop before the owner could order the men outside to stop pounding on his door.

Dhal and Poco followed the directions given and stepped out a back door into an alley. Avoiding the main street, they made their way down a narrow, dirt lane between some one-story buildings. They came out into the open by the main stockade gates facing south, the same gates through which they had entered the town earlier that day.

They paused and studied their surroundings. The sky was still light though evening shadows were growing longer. They had two choices: hide and wait for dark, which would give Jesh's men time to regroup and start searching, or try to circle around to the west and return to the bomal pens where they had left their packs.

After talking it over, they decided to move on. Staying to the low side of the hill on which they stood they crossed the road and circled the last building at the end of the street. From there they threaded their way through small gardens and around an odd mixture of cages and holding pens. Some were empty, others held birds and small animals. At one point they passed a stone ledge enclosing a pit where a pair of gensvolf paced restlessly.

When they reached the trees near the bomal pens, Dhal carefully led the way to the stockade wall.

"After I had the packs ready and the bomal saddled," he explained, "I led them down here out of the way, then I went back to speak to Rahn a minute. I wanted to ask him if we would have any trouble leaving Bannoc after dark. I was thinking about the gate guards.

"When I reached the barn, I saw Rahn talking to two men so I hesitated. Something about the men made me nervous, so I made my way down alongside the barn until I was close enough to hear what was being said.

"You were right about Rahn, Poco. He told the two men about us and charged damned high for the information."

"They were probably more of Jesh's men," Poco said.

"They had to be. Who else would be asking about us? Anyway, I thought of you up at Benjor's. Not knowing how many more men Jesh had sent, I got back to the inn as fast as I could."

"You could not have timed it better had you planned it," Poco said, as she moved into Dhal's arms. "He must have wanted us badly to have come after us hurting like he did."

Poco shivered. "Gods, but his face was a mess!"

Dhal held her close a moment. "Hate can do strange things to people."

"What do you think Jesh's men will do now that he is dead?"

"Nothing, once we are out of Bannoc. Men like that need a leader. Without Jesh to drive them, they will go back where they came from."

I hope so, Poco thought, as Dhal helped her mount one of the bomal. I sincerely hope so.

Chapter 9

*P*OCO LOOKED UP THROUGH A BREAK IN THE LEAVES overhead. The stars above made her thoughts turn to the legends of the first men, the Ral-jennob, who were said to have come to Lach from a far distant star.

Poco knew that the written history of man on Lach went back over two thousand years, and began with the founding of the rock city of Annaroth. Whether or not the Ral-jennob and man were one and the same only the winds knew. If the legends were true, Poco thought, man had come far from his home world but had lost much in the coming.

She looked at Dhal, riding just ahead of her. Man lost his own world and now claims yours, Dhal, and you can do nothing about it but run and hide and hope that somewhere there will be safety.

Man and Ni, we are so much alike, she thought. Why can't we live together in peace?

Dahl turned in the saddle. "Everything all right, Poco?"

"Yes."

"Getting tired?"

"A little," she replied. Poco's first experience at riding bomal had proven to be pleasant, for the large, horned animals were gentle and easily guided; but after hours in the saddle, her body ached and her legs kept going to sleep.

Dhal pulled his mount's head around. "Do you want to stop and rest a few hours?" he asked.

Poco nodded thankfully. Dhal loosened the draak-hide saddles, then showed her how to adjust the foot rests to ease the numbing of her of legs.

"I wish I had known that before," she said.

"Sorry," Dhal apologized. "I should have told you. Why not lie down and rest a while, Poco. I will call you when it is time to leave."

"You need rest too," she said.

"I'm fine. I'll get some sleep when we meet with Screech and Gi. I think it will be best if we do most of our traveling by night until we reach the plains. There will be less of a chance of anyone seeing us."

Poco agreed. She unrolled one of the blankets they had purchased at the trade shop, and lay down. The last thing she remembered was feeling Dhal's hands rubbing her back and legs.

After Dhal's ministrations and a good sleep, Poco found the second half of the ride more comfortable than the first.

"We had better go slow," Dhal said, as they approached the sheltered camp where they had left their friends. "Rahn told me that bomal become extremely unmanageable if they scent derkat. It seems that bomal make up a large portion of the derkat diet."

Poco swore softly under her breath. "That means that Screech will not be able to ride with us."

Dhal nodded. "He will have to go ahead of us, or follow behind; but don't worry, it will work out all right."

He stepped down from the saddle and whistled. A trilling whistle sounded from the tree ahead; Poco recognized the olvaar's all-clear signal.

She left her mount with Dhal and walked toward the sheltered hollow just ahead. Her eyes quickly adjusted to the blue-green shadows and a moment later she saw Screech and Taav sitting together near a dead fire.

Taav looked up as she approached; then suddenly he was on his feet moving toward her. Screech followed— his left wrist was attached to Taav's right by a stout piece of vine.

When Poco stopped, Taav knelt before her; he wrapped his arms around her legs and began to hum softly.

She looked from Taav to Screech, wondering what was going on. Screech signed a welcome, to which Poco nodded.

"What is this all about?" she asked Screech. "Taav acts as if he has been frightened."

"*Not frightened,*" Screech said, as he untied the vine cording from Taav's wrist.

Poco frowned. "Why the rope?"

"*He tried to leave. Made humming noises, like now, and started walking. Happened twice. I tied him to keep him here. Little Fur thinks he was trying to follow you.*"

Poco took Taav's arms and pulled them apart, freeing herself. Taav stopped humming and lifted his head.

She stared down into his eyes and for a moment she thought she saw a flicker of awareness.

"Taav?" Poco reached out and brushed the hair from his forehead. "Taav, do you understand what I am saying?" She spoke in Ni, the language she suspected he knew and would use, if he chose to speak.

Taav opened his mouth, but no words were forthcoming.

"Try again, Taav," Poco said softly. "You can do it."

Taav did try, but the movement of his lips produced no matching sounds. His eyes filled with tears.

Poco pulled him close, comforting him as she would a child. When she looked up, Dhal was standing beside her.

"He understands, Dhal," she said.

"So I see."

"What are we going to do with him?"

Dhal touched the back of Taav's head and stroked the straight, green hair. "We will have to take him with us, Poco. There is no other choice. We cannot leave him here and just hope he will be able to take care of himself."

"I didn't mean that."

"What did you mean?" he asked.

"What Taav needs right now is a place to stay, somewhere quiet, where he can relearn the things he seems to have forgotten. What if we postpone our trip across the plains for a few weeks, and find a place around here where we would be safe? We could spend some time with Taav and you might even try healing him again."

"We haven't supplies enough to stop anywhere very long and I don't like the thought of returning to Bannoc right away. Leaving bodies for others to bury does not make for welcome returns. I think it best we continue our journey while we can."

"Do we leave now?" Poco asked.

"No. We will eat something, and rest a while. We can leave after supper."

Later Poco woke to find Taav lying beside her; his eyes were open and he was watching her. She wondered if he had slept at all.

She sat up and glanced around the small glade. Nearby, Dhal was tending strips of meat that hung from a branch over the fire, and Screech was busy drawing a picture of something on the ground.

Screech dropped his stick and signed to Dhal. When Poco realized that the derkat was talking about their proposed trek across the plains, she got to her feet. Better find out what is going on, she thought.

She turned and extended her hand to Taav. "Come with me, Taav?" she asked in Ni.

Taav pushed to a sitting position and looked from her face to her hand. Poco waited, hoping that patience might accomplish what strength of will could not.

Taav timidly placed his hand in hers. She allowed herself a smile, which she quickly swallowed as Taav's head lifted. She did not want him to think she was laughing at him.

Dhal looked up from Ssaal-lr's dirt drawing as Poco and Taav approached. "Sleep well?" he asked.

Poco nodded and pulled gently on Taav's hand as she sat down. "Sit, Taav. Dhal is fixing something to eat."

Dhal and Screech watched as the atich-ar looked from face to face. Both of them sensed a change in Taav, but neither could tell what that change meant to their present situation. Was Taav going to be easier to control, or more difficult?

With her free hand, Poco signed to Screech and Dhal to go on about what they were doing. She waited a moment, then pulled on Taav's hand a second time, silently inviting him to join her on the ground.

Free from the scrutiny of the other two, Taav sank to his knees; he did not let go of Poco's hand as he settled back on his heels.

Ignoring Taav for the moment, Poco looked at the crude, dirt map. "Is that where we are going?" she asked.

Screech nodded and began pointing things out as he explained what obstacles they would face on the High Plains, such as, a scarcity of water until the spring rains came and a lack of cover in case of attack by gensvolf or draak. Also, there was the possibility that they would not be able to cross the plains without meeting one or two radgs of derkat.

Not long after Screech had finished describing their route, Dhal announced that supper was ready. He said, "Wake Gi, will you, Poco?"

She nodded and turned to look at the small ball of fur lying curled up beside one of their packs. She freed her

hand from Taav's grasp and reached for Gi, then noticed
that Taav was watching her.

"Taav, would you like to wake Gi?" she asked in Ni.

Taav looked down at the sleeping olvaar.

"There is nothing to be afraid of, Taav," Poco reassured him. "Gi won't hurt you. He is a good friend. Go
ahead, wake him so he can eat with us."

Slowly Taav reached for the olvaar, his fingers extended.

"Gently now," Poco said softly.

Taav's hand trembled, but he did not draw it back.
Dhal and Screech watched Taav closely, ready to move
quickly should the atich-ar do something that might hurt
their small comrade.

Taav's fingers brushed Gi's back; at that soft touch
the olvaar uncurled and sat up, golden eyes blinking away
sleep. Taav withdrew his hand.

Gi stood suddenly, his glance darting from face to face.
"What wrong?" he asked.

Dhal smiled at the olvaar's confusion. "There is nothing wrong, Gi. It is time to eat again. Taav did not want
you to miss a meal."

Gi looked at the atich-ar, head cocked to one side.
"Thanking Taav," he said. "Gi always hungry."

After Poco repeated Gi's words in Ni, Taav reached
out and gently touched the top of Gi's head.

"I think you have made another friend, Gi," Poco said,
pleased that Taav was beginning to react to those around
him.

Their meal consisted of dried fruit, a handful of hiat
nuts, several cups of hot rayil tea, and thin strips of roasted
aybar, a heavy-breasted wild bird common to the area.
Screech had caught the aybar earlier that day and had
saved it for their evening meal.

They finished eating and while Poco and Screech packed
their few belongings, Dhal went for the bomal. Screech
slipped out of camp when Dhal whistled that he was ready
with the mounts.

They decided that for the meantime Taav would ride with Dhal, and Gi-arobi with Poco. The multilayered saddles were built in a crescent shape, allowing plenty of room for two riders. They secured their packs across the saddle on the third bomal.

Dhal mounted first, and with Poco's help he pulled Taav into the saddle in front of him. Taav leaned back against him and gripped Dhal's arms as if he feared to fall off.

Dhal brought his right arm around Taav's waist and pulled him close, giving the atich-ar a sense of security, and at the same time giving himself a good hold should Taav try to leave the saddle without warning.

Poco reached up and touched Taav's arm. "You are going to be all right, Taav. Dhal will not let you fall."

"Never mind, Poco. Let's go. He will get used to it after a while," Dhal said.

Poco put Gi up in the saddle first, then mounted behind him. Gi was fairly bouncing with excitement. One small furred hand latched onto Poco's tunic sash, the other touched the reins which Poco held down in front of him.

"All set, Gi?" she asked.

Gi whistled an affirmative.

Poco smiled. "All right, sit down and hang on. If you get tired, let me know. Dhal has rigged a sling that will hold you safe."

"Gi not needing sling," the olvaar replied indignantly.

"Perhaps not," she said, as she rubbed her thumb against Gi's stomach. "But if you change your mind, just give a whistle."

Gi bobbed his head, then turned to look out past the bomal's horns. "Going now," he said.

"Yes, now."

The bomal were rested and set out at a good lope. They left the valley and turned north, following the trail of broken branches left by Ssaal-lr.

Several hours later their pace had slowed. Night shadows grew long as they left the rolling hills and tree-shaded valleys behind to enter a land of grassy swells. The scarcity of trees bothered Poco at first, but after a while, when her fear of a draak looming out of the tall grass failed to become a reality, she began to relax and listen to the sounds around her, the swish-swish of grass as the bomal cleared a path, the trill and chirping of small insects she could not name. The air was different too, warmer and drier, lulling the senses.

Poco turned and looked at Dhal. They had been riding side by side for some time and had not spoken five words to each other. She thought Dhal's eyes looked heavy and wondered if he had slept at all that afternoon. Taav seemed easier in the saddle, but Poco was not sure if that was due to acceptance or simple exhaustion.

"Is everything all right?" she asked, catching Dhal's eyes.

Dhal nodded. "My arms are getting tired but he is quiet."

"How much longer do we ride?" Poco asked.

"Screech will find us a place to camp. We will stop when we catch up with him," Dhal answered.

"What about the bomal?"

"They should be all right as long as Screech keeps his distance. They may smell his scent in the air, but I do not think they will panic unless he comes close."

"I don't like us to get too far apart. There is safety in numbers."

"Don't worry," Dhal assured her. "Screech will stay as close as he dares." He paused. "He loves you very much, you know."

Poco smiled. "Jealous?"

Dhal looked at her, his face sober. "Yes, sometimes."

Poco was surprised that Dhal had taken her teasing seriously. She reached over and put a hand on his arm.

"I love you, Dhal, more than anyone I have ever loved before. I love Screech too, but it is a different kind of love. Should I be jealous of the love you feel for Gi?"

Dhal glanced at the olvaar, who was fast asleep in the saddle. "No," he said. "I guess I am just being foolish."

Poco smiled again. "Foolish I can deal with. Jealous, I can't."

Chapter 10 ✎

*P*OCO LOOKED UP AT THE HEAD-HIGH GRASS THAT SUR-
rounded their camp; it was brown and brittle and had
a tangy, grain smell. As soon as the spring storms came,
the old grass would succumb to high winds and torrential
rains, and that which was brown and dead would spring
to life again, green upon green until land and sky merged
together in a haze of new color.

Taav retrieved his blanket from the pile of saddles and
packs, and crossed the trampled grass of their campsite.
He unrolled his blanket next to Poco's and sat down,
ready to begin his evening lesson.

Poco looked past Taav and saw Dhal sitting astride one
of the bomal. He was checking the surrounding territory;
from the ground, it was often impossible to see out over
the top of the grass.

They were three weeks out of Bannoc and as far as
they could tell, they had not been followed. They had also
been lucky not to run afoul of any of Ssaal-lr's kin, though

they had seen signs of their passing. Ssaal-lr, who still ranged ahead of them each day, had cautioned them to remain alert at all times, for the occasional great swaths of trampled grass were signs that the derkat radgs were on the move in that territory.

Their trek thus far had been a lonely one, but Poco did not complain, for they finally had a respite from the tensions of being hunted. As minds and bodies began to relax, both she and Dhal had turned their attention to Taav, whose progress so far had been gratifying. As his mental reactions grew sharper by the day, Poco could not help but feel that they had made the right choice in bringing him along.

She looked at Taav and smiled. "*Avto, friend, Taav*," she signed. Though Dhal believed that Taav would be able to speak eventually, he thought it wise to have Poco teach Taav the rudiments of signing so he could begin to communicate.

As Poco began the night's lesson, she noticed that Taav's face, arms, and legs were dirty. His clothes were little better, with food and grass stains vying for attention over several large holes in his pants at thigh and knee. He also had lost the lacing at the neck of his tunic.

Poco shook her head, realizing that she was not much cleaner. They all needed a bath, and time enough to spend a day washing and drying their clothes. There were times when she wondered if her life would ever again take on a semblance of order.

Poco returned to the job at hand and went over some of the easier hand signs, watching as Taav imitated the movements. She repeated the signs she had taught him the last few nights, then put several words together to form a sentence. She spoke as she signed, reenforcing the signing by sound; the language was always Ni.

"*Where is Dhal?*" she signed.

Taav turned and looked behind him. "*Dhal horned ones*," Taav responded, meaning Dhal was with the bomal.

Poco nodded. "*That is right. Where is Gi?*"

"*Gi go derkat.*"

"*Why?*" she asked.

"*Take food derkat.*"

Poco smiled, pleased with Taav's answers, for they proved that he was thinking, and that he did understand the signs he was learning.

Dhal finished hobbling the bomal and joined them. Poco moved over on her blanket, offering him a seat beside her.

Dhal signed to Taav as he sat down. "*May I join you?*" Taav frowned, not understanding.

"You signed too fast, Dhal," Poco explained.

"Sorry," Dhal said.

"Never mind. Do you want to practice with us?" she asked.

"Yes. I still do not understand half of what Screech says when he signs," Dhal answered.

Poco started with action verbs, signing and explaining at the same time. She then suggested they play a game where Dhal and Taav took turns pointing at something; she would name it using sign language.

The derkat used body language and sounds, such as coughs and growls, to reenforce their signing; so acquiring a good command of the derkat language was something that required a lot of practice. Sometimes the signing grew quite complicated and both Dhal and Taav became confused.

Poco touched Taav's arm, drawing his attention from Dhal, who was practicing the sign for danger and adding symbols for draak, gensvolf, and storm.

"*Taav happy speaking with his hands?*" she signed.

Taav hesitated, as if thinking it over; then slowly his fingers moved in answer to the question. "*I happy speaking hands.*" No smile attended his words.

She looked at him, wondering if the atich-ar even understood what happiness was. What thoughts lay behind the waiting expectancy she saw in his eyes?

Suddenly Taav lifted his hands and signed to her. *"Shadow talker...talk me?"*

Poco repeated the words in her mind, trying to make sense out of the message.

Dhal's voice broke into her thoughts. "What did he call you? I missed the first symbol."

Poco frowned. "The first symbol was *shadow*; the second was talker or singer. Shadow singer, sing me. Is that what you wanted to say, Taav?"

The atich-ar nodded and pointed at her. He then opened his mouth, and moved his fingers in the symbol for sound.

"I think he is asking you to sing, Poco," Dhal said.

She nodded. "I know, but where does he get Shadow Singer from?"

Dhal shrugged. "Maybe that is the way he thinks of you."

Another thought occurred to Poco, one she was reluctant to voice. The last two times she had sung to Taav, he had become so caught up in her singing that he had slipped into a trance.

"Poco, what is wrong?" Dhal asked.

"I think that I will have to be careful about the songs I sing when Taav is listening."

"What do you mean? He likes to hear you sing. So do I. It has been a week since you last sang."

"And do you remember what happened that night?" she asked.

Dhal glanced at Taav. "You put him to sleep if I remember right."

"Taav was not asleep, Dhal. He was in a trance of some kind, a trance caused by my singing. When I went to say good night to him, he was lying there with his eyes open. The moving shadows I saw in his eyes mirrored the words of the last song I had sung. I had to slap him to bring him out of it."

"Why didn't you say something?"

Poco shook her head. "I don't know. I should have. It has happened twice now. Once, before we reached

Bannoc, that day Taav and I spent several hours up in that tree; then again last week. I told you about the first time."

"Yes. I remember now."

"He is like an empty slate, Dhal. I can draw my songs on his mind and see the results in his eyes. No one else has ever been affected that way."

"I have seen your chalk pictures live, Poco," Dhal said.

"Yes, but I have never put you into a trance!"

"Perhaps we are both reacting to your singing, but in different ways. I told you once before that I thought your songs were a form of Ni energy."

Taav was becoming impatient with all the talk. He reached out and touched Poco's arm. *"Sing me?"*

"Go ahead," Dhal said. "Sing him a song. He would not ask if it bothered him."

"What if I put him into a trance again?" she asked.

"What if you do? He came out of it all right each time." Dhal smiled. "Come on, sing us a song."

Poco shook her head in defeat. "All right, something light then."

She searched her memory for a song that she hoped would entertain without bringing her special gift into play. She chose a rousing dock song with a repeating chorus which Dhal joined her in singing. Taav clapped his hands in time to the beat, enjoying the song even if he could not sing.

There followed two more songs; one called "Bran's Lament," a sad love song with a tragic ending; the other, a song Poco particularly liked called "Green Draak Dreaming."

"The Green Draak is dreaming;
    he wakes to find the day.
        He cries for the singer
            who walks the patterned way.
Singer, singer, set the pattern.
        Those who follow will be friend.

> Shadows lengthen, turn, and spin.
>   Worlds are born when dreams begin."

Taav clapped his hands when Poco finished singing, but Dhal sat quietly lost in his own thoughts.

"You didn't like the song, Dhal?" Poco asked.

His crystal eyes focused on her and for a moment or two he was silent; then he spoke. "Yes, I liked it—very much. There was something about it that made me feel as if I should—understand something, something important."

"About green draaks?" She laughed.

"No," he responded, his expression serious. "Something about singers and patterns. Poco, would you do me a favor?"

The tone of Dhal's voice wiped away her smile. "What?" she asked.

"Sing me another song, a very special song."

"What song?"

"The song about the white temple," he answered.

Poco frowned as she searched her memory. "I'm sorry, Dhal, I don't think I know that one."

Dhal looked at her, his crystal eyes intent. "You know it, Poco."

She shook her head, not understanding.

"Ever since we left Port Sulta I have been haunted by a song," Dhal said. "The one you sang that night in our camp; the one that let us see the white temple in that other place."

Unconsciously Poco's fingers brushed the Ni pendant hidden inside her tunic. A tingle of fear skittered down her back and came to rest in the pit of her stomach.

"I know how much that song bothered you," he said. "That is why I have kept my peace this long. But I have been thinking about that place we saw and I need to see it again!"

Poco shook her head. "I cannot sing that song, Dhal. I know the one you mean, but—"

"We will never know more about that place unless you sing it up again, Poco." He took her hand. "If I could see it clearly just one more time, I might be able to focus my Seeker energy on it and go there."

"I cannot sing it! I don't know the words or the song!" she snapped. "I told you before, it was not *me* singing!"

"Perhaps not," he conceded calmly. "But what you did once, perhaps you can do again, if you do exactly as you did before."

"To what purpose, Dhal?"

"Poco, suppose that other place was not in our world! Remember the sky and the trees? What if, by chance, you have located a world gate? I know that all of this frightens you, but I think we have to find out one way or another. If what we saw is real, then there must be a way to get there—and just maybe *there* is where the Ni-lach have gone. It is a possibility, one I have to check out."

Poco's mind whirled with arguments against further probes into the unknown, but deep in her heart she knew that those arguments would have little effect upon Dhal. She could, of course, simply refuse to sing the song; but if she did refuse, he would only grow more sure of his need to see the place again and eventually she would cede to his wishes if only to please him.

"What about Taav?" she asked.

"He will be all right," Dhal assured her. "I will keep my eye on him."

Dhal took Taav's hand. "If he gets restless," he said, lifting their linked hands, "I will know."

Poco still hesitated.

"Please, Poco," Dhal pressed. "Please just try."

She drew a deep breath, trying to calm the flutter in her stomach as she reached into the neckline of her tunic.

She looked at Dhal, wishing she could say something that would make him change his mind.

"Ready?" he asked her.

"Yes, I guess so," she responded unhappily.

"Do you remember what you were singing that day, before the other song came to you?" he asked.

"Yes, it is called the 'Penthor Draak Watch'."

Poco lifted the pendant and began to sing. With her eyes she traced the curving lines on the back of the pendant, following the pattern over and over.

She was aware of Dhal sitting close beside her. She squeezed his hand and he squeezed back. His silent encouragement was all she needed to continue.

Her thoughts centered on the song she was singing. As she sang, she felt a deep sadness, for the Draak Watch was gone now, lost to mankind by its own greed.

She became less and less aware of Dhal and her surroundings as the song took hold on her thoughts. In her mind she envisioned the Penthor Draak Watch circling a large, green land draak. The song that the Ni sang brought the huge reptile to a halt. The Ni signaled to each other and their song changed. The draak turned and followed the Ni, enticed by a sound it could not resist.

Suddenly Poco became aware of another song entering her mind, and the scenes she had created began to melt away. Blue shadows danced to her voice as the mystery singer took over and slowly another scene began to emerge within her mind.

She remembered Dhal and Taav, and she wondered if they were seeing what she was seeing. She shivered as the last few lines of song left her lips.

> "*Light and dark, their minds repel.*
> *All friends be warned to guard the gate,*
> *For evil spawned seek entrance.*"

The song was finished, yet it held Poco with invisible bonds. She tried to break free but could not escape the command to carry the warning to— To who? she cried silently. Who am I to warn?

"Poco! You did it!"

Dhal's excited cry tore at her mind, releasing her from

the song. She opened her eyes and found Dhal standing beside her. A warm puff of air hit her face; it held the scent of grain.

"Look, Poco! It's there, just as before," Dhal said, as he pointed to the valley below them.

Poco recognized the scene. The cream-colored temple stood stately and serene beside the river; the seven towers cast long shadows across the valley as the sun slipped toward the horizon, shading the blue sky to the color of slate.

"It seems so real," she whispered softly, afraid to break the spell.

"Because it is, Poco," Dhal replied. "Look around you! We are not just seeing it this time, we are living it. Poco, do you realize what you have done?"

"I am not sure I want to know."

"That song must have been some kind of a pattern to a world gate!"

Poco moved a step closer to Dhal and took his arm, trying to calm the sudden flutter in her stomach. "Dhal, are you telling me that it is not just our minds that have gone traveling this time?"

"Feel the air, Poco! Smell it! Believe it or not, you have projected us into one of your visionary worlds!"

"But I am no Seeker, Dhal! I am not capable of anything like that!"

"Perhaps not, but I am. The scene you created was so clear that my Seeker powers must have—" Dhal was turning as he spoke. Suddenly his hand tightened on her arm. "Poco, look! It's Taav!"

Poco turned and saw a green mist behind them. Through the mist she saw someone sitting cross-legged on the ground. As tendrils of fog shifted, Taav's face became clear. Noting his trancelike state, Poco swore softly.

"Dhal, I don't like this." Her voice was unsteady. "What has happened to us?"

Dhal frowned. "I am not sure, but I think we have

projected ourselves into another world and have left Taav behind."

"You mean he is back on the plains?"

"Yes," he answered. He looked at the haze of fog that separated them from Taav and shook his head in wonder. "Poco, look at the size of the doorway you have created. I think you could ride a bomal through it."

"Never mind its size," Poco snapped. "Let's go back through before the damn opening closes!"

"Wait!" he cried, grabbing her around the waist as she started forward.

"For what?" she demanded, pushing away from him.

"Whenever I used my Seeker power to travel, I always traveled alone. If that doorway has anything to do with my powers, I want to be sure I am able to take you back through with me."

Poco's heart sank to her stomach. "You brought me here, didn't you? I mean, we came together. Shouldn't the same thing work going back?"

"I don't know *what* brought us here, Poco. My power? Your song? Maybe a combination."

"Damn!" Poco turned to look at the gate. I knew I should not have sung that song! Now we don't know where we are, she thought, and there is a damn good chance that we—or I—might be stuck here. Damn! Damn! Damn!

"Poco," Dhal said softly.

"What?" she snapped, without turning.

"It is going to be all right. I just don't want us to make any quick moves without thinking things out."

"I wish you had said that earlier!"

When Dhal failed to reply to her rebuke, Poco turned and looked at him. "Sorry, I did not mean to snap."

Dhal reached for her and drew her close. "It is going to be all right, Poco. We got here. We will get back."

"What about Taav?" she asked. "Without us there he might wake up and wander off."

"Gi will come back soon. He will watch over him until we return."

"Gi is awfully small to do much looking after."

"Don't judge him by his size, Poco. He has been watching over me for years now and I am still in one piece."

"What will he do when he finds us gone?"

Dhal shook his head. "I never predict what Gi will do, but I do trust him. He won't leave camp without having a good idea of where we have gone. Personally, I am more worried about Screech and what he will do if and when Gi confides in him."

"You don't think they would try to come through there?" she asked, indicating the strange doorway between the two worlds.

"They might not even be able to see it, Poco. If they can, there is no telling what they might do."

Chapter 11

POCO LOOKED AT THE OPEN WOODLAND BEYOND THE GATE she had created. "I think it will be dark soon, Dhal," she said.

"I know, but I want to look around a little before we try going back."

If we can go back, Poco thought, as she followed Dhal to the crest of the hill overlooking the temple.

"If we could talk to some of the people we saw down in the temple, we could find out where we are, and when," Dhal said.

"What do you mean by *when*? Do you think we have gone backward in time, as you did in Val-hrodhur?"

"It is possible." Dhal turned and looked at her, his crystal eyes intent. "Anything is possible when dealing with forces such as those used by the Ni-lach and the Tamorlee."

"I wish I knew more about this Tamorlee. The things you have told me seem hardly credible. How can a rock—"

"A crystalline life form," he corrected her.

"All right, a crystalline life form, how can it control or direct anything when it cannot move or speak? I know you said it communicates mind to mind, but still, how does it work? Where does the energy it uses come from?"

"From all around us, Poco," Dhal answered. "Everything that is, is energy. As to how the Tamorlee absorbs and uses energy, how do we work? If I knew the answer to that question, I think I would be the god we were talking about once before."

Dhal looked at his ring. "I do not know how the Tamorlee works, but I have felt its presence, and I know it is an entity with an enormous appetite for knowledge, which it gathers through fire stones like the one I carry. Each of the stones is a shard of the Tamorlee, broken off during its growth periods. According to what the Ancients told me, these shards are somehow locked into the parent crystal; through these stones and the Ni who carry them, the Tamorlee learns. It is also believed that the fire stones enhance the Ni's natural talents, whether that Ni be a Healer, a Seeker—or a Singer."

Poco continued to scan the woodland around them. "I do not see how the Tamorlee could have any effect on my talents as a singer. I do not wear one of the fire stones."

"No, but you do stand close to one who does."

"Could that alone cause . . ." Poco's words trailed off as she saw movement down through the trees. "Something is moving over there, Dhal."

Dhal looked, then led out, cutting down behind the crest of the hill and working his way through a wooded area which stretched from the top of the hill down to the edge of an open field. Poco noticed the absence of vell vine and clingor grass, two types of foliage common to wooded areas. She started to point out her observation, but Dhal cautioned her to be silent. They stopped just within the shelter of the trees and looked out onto the open fields, where naked people were working. Most of the workers were male.

Suddenly Dhal squeezed Poco's arm. "Poco, look at their hair! It's green! The Ni-lach—we have found them!"

Poco's heartbeat quickened as she stared at the Ni-lach workers strung across the field. After all the time they had spent searching for the Ni-lach, it seemed impossible to her that they could have stumbled across them by accident.

Dhal watched the Ni who was working the edge of the field not more than two hundred paces away. "I knew our luck was going to change," he whispered softly. "I just knew it! It was the temple, the first time I saw it I knew— I knew it was Ni!"

Poco looked at Dhal, caution fighting for control of her emotions. "Dhal, what are we going to do?"

"I don't know," he said, his glance sweeping across the field of workers. "Talk to them, I guess. Maybe we can find out where we are."

Poco watched one of the workers approach their position; the rhythmic swing of his sickle made a soft shushing sound as it cut the grass ahead of him.

Dhal took Poco's arm and pulled her back behind the trunk of a large tree.

"What is wrong?"

"Nothing," he answered softly. "But I think we should stay hidden until one of them gets closer. I want some answers, and I do not want to frighten them away."

Poco and Dhal stood quietly until the Ni worker was within twenty-five paces of them, then stepped out of hiding. They held their hands down at their sides, palms forward, showing that they were unarmed and approaching in peace.

Poco made herself study the Ni worker closely, though she was embarrassed by his lack of clothing. He was older than she had first guessed; his legs, abdomen, upper arms, and neck all showed the loose flesh and wrinkles associated with old age; his light green hair also showed patches of white.

The Ni laid his sickle down and bent to scoop up an

armful of grass. When he straightened he saw Dhal and
Poco. Startled, his crystal eyes opened wide and the grass
fell from his arms.

Dhal looked ready to lunge forward should the Ni decide to bolt. Poco hoped to forestall such action and quickly
placed her hands together before her and bowed to the
Ni.

"Avto, friend," she said in Ni. "Do not be afraid. We
are strangers who are lost and in need of guidance."

The Ni's eyes widened further. "You are Ni," he said,
looking at Dhal. He looked at Poco. "But you are not.
Where do you come from?"

"Do you speak trader?" Dhal asked.

The Ni hesitated, then nodded.

"Good," Dhal said. "Though I am Ni, I am not very
familiar with our language yet and it would be easier
if—"

Suddenly the old Ni caught at Dhal's arms and pushed
him back into the shelter of the trees. "Where do you
come from?" he demanded. "Tell me quickly!"

"I was raised near Annaroth," Dhal answered in trader.
"My friend comes from Port Bhalvar."

"May the twin suns never fall, it has happened! You
are from Lach!" he cried. The old one continued to speak
in the Ni tongue. "After all these years, someone has
finally gotten through!"

"What do you mean, *through*?" Dhal asked.

The old one, fairly dancing with excitement, ignored
Dhal's question. "Who sent you? How many hold the
gate? Quickly, tell me! We have waited so long!"

Dhal held the old Ni by the arms, steadying him.
"Waited for what, Old One?" he asked, switching to the
Ni tongue. "What are you talking about?"

The old Ni glanced up through the trees that covered
the hillside.

"How many are with you? Are they on the other side
of the gate? If they are, you had better have them move

quickly, because soon it will be dark and the atich-ar will start clearing the fields!"

"Old One, listen to me," Dhal said firmly. "There are no more of us. We came alone and we are lost. We don't know where we are."

The old Ni shook his head in confusion. "You say you are alone?"

Dhal nodded. "I am sorry, but we do not know what you are talking about. Could you please tell us—"

"But you are Ni-lach!" the old one cried. He reached out and lifted Dhal's hand. "And you wear a Seeker ring!"

"That is true," Dhal admitted.

"Then who sent you?"

Dhal withdrew his hand gently. "No one sent me, Old One. I have only my own curiosity to blame for being here—wherever here is."

The old Ni shook his head, disbelief plain in his eyes. "You did not come looking for us?"

"Who is us?" Poco asked.

The Ni turned to her. "We are the Ni-lach of Val-hrodhur, those who went with the Tamorlee. Have you never even heard of us?"

Poco shook her head. "We found Val-hrodhur, Old One, but it was empty. Dhal and I are—"

Dhal interrupted. "The Tamorlee—is it here with you now?"

"It is here," the old Ni answered, "but it is no longer in our possession. Did you say that Val-hrodhur was abandoned?"

"It was when we found it three months ago," Dhal answered. "But tell us about the Tamorlee? Is it—"

"They have all gone to Jjaan-bi," the old Ni said. "With all of us gone, it would be the only thing left to them."

Poco shook her head, confused by the old Ni's muttering. "Old One, what is your name?" she asked, hoping to calm him.

The old Ni looked at her. "My name is Retath. I was once the—"

A loud clanging of bells came from the temple down in the valley. The old Ni jumped at the sound and looked back into the field. "They are coming for us," he cried. "You will have to go! If they see you, you are lost!"

"Who is 'they'?" Dhal demanded, growing uneasy under the frightened eyes of the old Ni.

"They! The atich-ar! We thought they were our friends! We thought we could trust them, but they betrayed us to gain the Tamorlee! They killed most of our Singers and Sensitives, those who could make and hold the gate between our worlds; then they tried to force the Seekers to work with them. But we wouldn't! Even though they tortured some of us. When we brought the Tamorlee through the world gate we numbered one hundred and thirty. Now we are but thirty-seven."

"Where is the Tamorlee?" Dhal interrupted. "Down in the temple?"

"Yes! And there it will remain until the atich-ar learn how it functions; then they plan to invade Lach in order to seize more of our gifted ones. This we know!"

"Invade Lach?" Dhal repeated, incredulous. "Are they strong enough to do that?"

"Yes," the old Ni snapped. "They have many fighters to call upon and they have our Seeker rings and the Tamorlee knows the pattern for the I-naal gate!"

"The Tamorlee would not betray the Ni-lach!" Dhal said fiercely.

"It has not, so far," the old one said. "But how long before someone among the atich-ar learns how to tap the core of knowledge buried within the crystal? They experiment all the time. They try to use those of us who are left, but—"

"Someone is coming this way, Dhal!" Poco said quickly.

The old Ni turned to look, then he was pushing them back further into the woods. "Go quickly! They have not seen you! Go to Jjaan-bi and warn our people about the atich-ar! Tell them to guard the I-naal gate! Tell them to—"

Dhal grabbed the old Ni by the arm. "Come with us! We will need your help to find Jjaan-bi! We do not know where it is!"

Retath hesitated a moment, then he was running beside Dhal, the fear in his eyes replaced by hope. "The gate," he panted, as the grade grew steeper. "Who holds the gate for you?"

"A friend," Dhal answered.

Dhal looked behind him and saw two long-haired Ni hit the bottom of the slope behind them. They were clothed in open vests and short pants; their feet were shod in sandals. But what captured Dhal's attention were the long, curved blades they carried; a single blow could easily decapitate an opponent.

"Move, Poco!" Dhal yelled. "They are right behind us!"

"Where are we going?" she yelled back.

"The gate! Hurry!" he answered.

Poco ran up the incline, dodging small trees or using them for handholds. She turned once to see Dhal and Retath close on her heels. The enemy atich-ar who scrambled upslope behind Dhal were silent in their pursuit as they concentrated all of their energies on catching up with the fugitives.

Poco reached the place where she and Dhal had stood overlooking the temple, and ahead of her saw the circle of mist which marked the gate to their own world; there was a greenish cast to the mist, something she had not noticed before.

Poco stopped before the world gate and turned. A few running steps brought Dhal to her side. He thrust Retath into her arms. "Hold onto him," Dhal cried. "Do not let go! We will try to take him back through with us!"

One of the atich-ar raced toward them, his sword upraised. Suddenly Retath pulled free and lunged forward, straight into the path of the atich-ar. "Go!" Retath yelled. "Forget about me!"

The oncoming speed and weight of the enemy atich-ar

carried Retath back into Poco. The old Ni grunted in pain as he fell against her.

Poco knew a moment of disorientation as she was pushed backward through the world gate. In one instant the wooded hillside was gone. She looked at the forest of tall grass which surrounded her and knew she had returned to their camp on the High Plains.

Retath was suddenly heavy in Poco's arms; his body slipped to the ground. Before she could change her grasp on his arms, she was bumped from behind. She fell over Retath and landed on her right elbow, jarring her shoulder and head.

Poco rolled free of the old Ni and turned to see Dhal grappling with the atich-ar who had attacked them. Somehow Dhal got his leg hooked around and behind his opponent's leg, pushing the atich-ar off balance. They fell together, the atich-ar on the bottom.

Poco started to go to Dhal's aid, but suddenly Retath pushed himself up onto one elbow and caught at her ankle. "The gate!" he cried.

Poco kicked free.

"The gate!" Retath cried again. "Close the gate before others come through!"

Poco glanced at the mist-shrouded gate, then looked at Taav. In that instant she understood what the old Ni wanted. She ran to Taav and knelt before him. She looked into his eyes and saw a reflection of the wooded hillside overlooking the temple.

Suddenly there was something else there—a tall dark shadow. No, Poco thought, not a shadow—another of the atich-ar!

"Behind you!" Retath yelled suddenly.

Poco turned. A second atich-ar had joined the first one!

Unaware of the danger behind him, Dhal fought on, his head down to protect his face and throat from the fist of his opponent.

Gi-arobi's shrill, whistled warning sounded as Poco launched herself at the second atich-ar. Her knife sank into his back just as he raised his sword to slash down at Dhal's unprotected neck.

The atich-ar cried out and stumbled backward several steps, shaking Poco free. Before she could recover her balance, he turned and the flat of his sword struck Poco's shoulder, knocking her down.

As he raised his sword for a second blow, he faltered and fell to one knee. Poco saw her chance. Fear giving her an agility she did not know she possessed, she leaped from the ground and locked her hands around the atich-ar's wrist.

The atich-ar twisted to one side and Poco lost her balance. At that moment the atich-ar brought his knee up, catching her full in the stomach. Her feet left the ground, then she was falling. A blur of grass was followed by a moment or two of darkness as the breath was driven from her lungs.

The darkness cleared and Poco found herself curled into a tight ball. She opened her eyes and saw the atich-ar pushing to his hands and knees; his crystal eyes were filled with pain and anger.

Suddenly, a small, red-brown ball of fur darted between Poco and the enemy atich-ar. The atich-ar cried out as Gi's teeth caught in his lower arm just above the wrist. He dropped his sword and tried to shake Gi off; then he clouted Gi on the side of the head and the olvaar sailed through the air. Poco heard the whoof of air escaping from Gi's lungs as he landed on his back some few feet away.

As the atich-ar rose unsteadily to his feet, Poco saw her knife sticking out of his back. He turned and looked at her. She rolled to a sitting position, reached out, and snatched up the sword he had dropped.

"The throat!" Retath croaked. "Aim for the throat!"

The atich-ar came at her again. Poco brought the sword around in a slashing arc.

She felt the sword strike flesh, then something wet and

warm splattered against her face as the atich-ar's weight hit her waist. She was knocked backward to the ground.

Poco had seen death before, and had witnessed more than one brutal fight on the docks of Port Bhalvar, but she had never had to kill in order to survive. Frantic to get out from under the dying atich-ar, she pushed his twitching body aside and swallowed quickly, trying to keep from being sick.

Poco turned from the gory thing that lay beside her and saw Dhal just getting off the body of the other atich-ar.

He saw her blood-smeared tunic and hurried over. "Poco, where are you hurt?"

Poco felt as if she had been pummeled by a herd of draak, but somehow she had escaped being cut by the atich-ar's blade.

Dhal used his hands to wipe the blood from her face and neck, frantically searching for the wounds he feared to find. Poco pushed his hands aside.

"It is not my blood, Dhal," she said. "It's his."

Dhal glanced at the nearby body. "Are you sure?"

She nodded and drew in a shaky breath. "What about Retath? Is he all right?"

Dhal left her and went to the old Ni. A moment later he looked up, shaking his head. "He is dead, Poco. He must have been wounded just as we came through the gate."

At the word "gate," both Dhal and Poco turned to look for Taav. He was sitting quietly right where they had left him, seemingly undisturbed by the fighting which had gone on around him.

"The gate, Dhal," Poco said quickly. "Retath said to close the gate before any more of the atich-ar could come through! Wake Taav! Hurry!"

Dhal knelt before Taav. He looked into Taav's eyes a moment, then glanced back to see that the mist which showed the passageway between the two worlds was still evident.

Dhal touched Taav's forehead with his fingertips. "Wake up, Taav. Let go of the gate!" Dhal's voice was soft but urgent.

Poco rose just as Taav collapsed into Dhal's arms. She started to go to them, then hesitated when she saw something move in the grass. A soft, whistle-click reminded her that there was one more defender unaccounted for.

She found the olvaar lying in the shadow of the tall grass.

"Dhal! Come quickly!" she said, when she saw the strange angle of the olvaar's legs and back. "It's Gi! He has been hurt!"

Gi's golden eyes were clouded with pain; he whistled mournfully as Dhal knelt beside him.

"Don't move, Gi," Dhal said softly.

"He tried to help me," Poco said. "He bit the atich-ar in the wrist and made him drop his sword. If he had not, I—"

Dhal interrupted her. "Not now, Poco! I will have to go in and see what is wrong with his back. Keep watch!"

Poco cringed at Dhal's harsh tone and backed out of the way. She watched as Dhal dropped into rapport with the olvaar. Gi's eyes closed and gradually his rapid breathing slowed.

Minutes passed. Poco kept an eye on Taav but remained where she was, ready in case Dhal needed her for anything. She had already forgiven him for snapping at her. She knew how much Gi meant to him, and she prayed that the olvaar was not beyond his help.

The sky was getting dark by the time Dhal stirred from the joining.

"Is he going to be all right?" Poco asked.

Dhal looked at her and nodded.

"What was wrong?" she asked.

"There was a slippage of one of the vertebra in his spine. I had to move it back into place. He will probably be lame for a few days, but if we keep him moving, he should be fine." Dhal's voice was heavy with fatigue. "Has Taav wakened?" he asked.

"No, not yet," she answered.

"Probably just as well."

Poco looked down at the olvaar. "Will he sleep for a while?"

"He should until morning."

"You look tired," she said, remembering how the use of his healing powers drained Dhal.

"I am," he admitted.

Poco looked at the dead bodies scattered around them. "What do we do now?"

"Let's wash this blood off, then I will take care of things here while you go and tell Screech what has happened." He touched her shoulder. "All right, Poco?"

Poco nodded, thankful that Dhal was willing to take charge. Her glance fell on the old Ni. "I wish Retath had lived. He could have answered a lot of questions for us."

"In a way, he did," Dhal said. "We know where the Tamorlee is and we know that somewhere there *is* a Jjaan-bi."

Poco looked at the bodies of the atich-ar, a worried frown marring her face. "We also know that in that other place there are Ni like those two, who plan to use the Tamorlee to invade Lach—or so Retath said." She looked at Dhal. "But how do we know if Retath was speaking the truth? Dhal, there are a few atich-ar among the Ni. Those two we killed, who were they really?"

"Retath spoke of betrayal, and of those who took the Tamorlee from Val-hrodhur."

"Yes, but who betrayed whom? If there are Ni on both sides of a fight over possession of the crystal, whose side are we on? Which side is right?"

Dhal glanced at Retath, then at the atich-ar. "I understand what you are saying, Poco, but—"

"But what?"

"The atich-ar tried to kill us. They never once tried to speak to us."

"So?"

"So I would rather believe that Retath was telling us the truth, and I think we should go on to Jjaan-bi and do as he asked us to do."

"All right, if that is what you want," Poco said. "Let's just hope that if and when we reach Jjaan-bi, we find ourselves among friends, not enemies."

Chapter 12

*P*OCO WASHED THE BLOOD FROM HER FACE, NECK, AND hands, then built a small fire and put some water on to boil. "The tea water should be ready by the time I get back," she said.

She stood and looked at Dhal. "Are you sure you do not want some help digging?"

He looked up from his work. The ground was dry, but the atich-ar blade he wielded seemed to be doing a good job of breaking up the hard-packed earth.

"No," he said. "Go and find Screech and tell him what happened. I will see to things here."

"Make it a shallow grave," she advised. "I will help you cover them when I get back."

Dhal nodded and continued to dig.

Poco found Screech sitting cross-legged on the ground, licking at his claws and furred fingers. The chest harness and sword that Dhal had purchased for him in Bannoc lay within easy reach. Behind him he had prepared a pallet of grass for sleeping; the sky was growing darker by the minute.

Poco coughed a greeting as she approached.

Screech replied in kind, then signed, *"Why here?"*

"Something has happened, Screech," she answered.

"Trouble?"

Poco shook her head. "The trouble is past, I hope."

"Sit and tell." Screech patted his grass pallet.

Poco nodded and took the proffered seat. She noticed that Screech's outer ring of eye-fur moved as he sniffed the air.

"I smell blood. Whose?"

"It is atich-ar blood you smell."

"Taav is hurt?"

"Not Taav. Another atich-ar."

The derkat eyes narrowed. *"Tell me what has happened."*

Ssaal-lr listened without interruption as Poco spoke. When she came to the part about killing the atich-ar with his own sword, Screech growled softly.

"You did well," he signed. *"I am proud you are my radg."*

Poco was not sure she should be proud of a killing; that was not as Trass had taught her.

"Was the Healer hurt? Taav? Little Fur?" Screech asked.

"Dhal and Taav are fine, but Gi was injured while trying to protect me. Dhal used his healing powers to—"

Suddenly Screech stiffened. A second later his furred hand pressed against her lips. With his other hand he signed silence.

Reading finger movement was difficult in the semi-darkness, but Poco nodded, telling Screech she understood.

"What is it?" Poco signed, as Screech took his hand away from her mouth.

"Listen!"

Poco sat quietly, her ears tuned to the sounds around

them. What did Screech hear that she did not? Her thoughts jumped from one possibillity to another. Draak? Gensvolf? Had they not closed the world gate properly and had more atich-ar come through?

The moments of silence stretched into a minute. Screech turned his head and sniffed the air.

"What do you smell?" Poco asked.

"Derkat. Close."

"One?"

"Many."

"Dhal! We must warn him!"

Poco was moving before she had finished signing, but Screech was faster. He caught her around the hips and dragged her down, smothering her cry of protest by pressing her face into his furry chest.

She struggled but a moment before realizing that each of her movements was countered by a tighter grip which was crushing the breath from her lungs. She forced herself to relax, remembering that the one who held her was Screech and not an enemy.

When Screech felt her go limp, he loosened his hold, though he did not release her completely.

Suddenly she became aware of movement in the tall grass off to her left. A soft swishing sound evoked in her mind a picture of derkat moving with practiced stealth through shoulder-high grass. She lifted her head and peered over Screech's shoulder, but the night had grown too dark to see anything but the tops of the grass swaying to movement below. A bubble of fear caught in her throat as she thought of Taav and Dhal in camp, unaware of their danger.

Frantic with the need to warn Dhal, Poco tried to push away from Screech. The arms about her tightened once more. Screech knew it was too late to help anyone; all they could do now was to stay quietly where they were and hope they were overlooked in the confusion of the attack about to take place.

A loud, ear-splitting cry made Poco jump—that sound came from no human throat. The first cry was followed by others. Derkat! A lot of them!

"Let me go, Screech! We have to warn—"

Poco's face was pushed into fur. She strained against Screech's arms and legs, shaking with muffled cries of protest until she finally lost consciousness.

Cool, fresh air rushed into Poco's lungs; at first she could not seem to get enough. Screech was lying half on top of her and she could feel his warm breath against her face. She ignored the furred fingers that stroked her upper right arm and lay still, listening.

All was quiet; the only sound she could hear was the soft intake of air through Ssaal-lr's short nose. She opened her eyes and looked up at the stars overhead.

Deep in her heart, Poco knew that Screech had probably saved her life, yet somehow she felt that he had betrayed her.

"Are they gone, Screech?" she asked softly.

The fingers on her arm stopped moving. Poco could not see the derkat's face, but she knew he could see hers.

He rose and pulled Poco to a sitting position. Softly he coughed a greeting.

Poco hesitated, then imitated the cough, telling Screech that all was well between them.

"Screech," she said, keeping her voice low. "Do you know what has happened to Dhal—or Taav?"

Screech growled.

In the dark, Poco could not tell if he was signing or not. Suddenly she felt his furred hands at either side of her face. Gently he moved her head back and forth, describing a negative response.

"Have the derkat gone?" she asked.

Screech moved her head up and down. *Yes.*

"We have to go and look for Dhal, Screech."

Screech tapped Poco's shoulder and moved her head to signal no. Then he took her hand and placed it against his chest and moved her head up and down. The message was clear: you, no; me, yes.

Poco reached out and grabbed the derkat's arms. "I am going with you, Screech! I have to know what happened to Dhal! I will not stay here alone!" Praying for you to come back, she added silently.

Screech pushed her away and stood up.

She scrambled to her feet, and her right hand brushed his fur.

"Please, Screech—together?"

For a moment the derkat did not respond, then he growled softly and took her by the wrist. He pulled her toward the path leading back to their camp, then hesitated. He stopped and left her and went back toward his pallet. When he returned, he pressed his sword into her hands.

Poco shifted the sword to her right hand as Screech offered her a hold on his tail. He knew she was night blind and did not want her stumbling in the dark.

She concentrated on moving as quietly as possible as she followed Screech down the grassy path. She strained her eyes trying to see ahead, but there was nothing but darkness; not the empty kind of darkness that frightened her because it hid the unknown, but a darkness that was composed of natural things that she could hear and feel, such as the chitter of night insects and the touch of grass brushing against her arms and face.

She tried not to think about what lay ahead, but her mind continued to paint gory scenes, and she had to fight the rising fear that threatened to choke her.

Suddenly Screech stopped.

Poco could hear him sniffing the air. She followed his example and smelled smoke, grass and—something she could not name.

The derkat moved a few paces forward, then turned and pressed her shoulders, pushing her down.

She sank to her knees and grabbed the hilt of the sword with both hands. Her heart beat heavily in her chest as she peered into the darkness. She wished she had Screech's night vision.

He growled softly in her ear, then patted her shoulder. A moment later he was gone, moving away from her so quickly that her outstretched arm encountered nothing but air.

Crouched where he had left her, Poco waited, braced for the hunting screams of derkat. Damn you, Screech, she thought, come back here!

The minutes dragged by. Finally, Screech returned. As he pulled her up, he made a sound she had never heard him use before, a low whine that sent shivers down her back.

"Screech, did you find Dhal?" she asked, pushing her greatest fear into the open.

The derkat did not respond.

Poco reached out and followed Screech's arm down to his hand. "Sign to me," she commanded him. "Did you find Dhal?"

Screech's hand closed into a fist turned downward, signing *no*.

"You are sure he is not here?"

"Yes. Sure."

"Do you think the derkat took him?"

His clenched fist turned upward. *Yes*.

"Gi and Taav? Are they gone too?"

"Yes."

"Do you think they might still be alive?"

Screech did not answer the last question. Silently he took Poco's arm and led her away from the camp.

She allowed herself to be drawn away, sick with the feeling of helplessness and numbed by the thought that Dhal was lost to her forever.

Screech made her lie down when they reached the place where he had made his night camp. He then lay down beside her and pulled her close, offering comfort in the only way he knew.

Poco buried her face in his chest fur and cried herself into a state of exhaustion. Sleep finally claimed her.

Chapter 13

POCO AND SCREECH RETURNED TO THE CAMP EARLY THE
next morning hoping to find some sign of a trail left
by the derkat raiders. They found everything gone—
bomal, packs, weapons, even the bodies of Retath and
the dead atich-ar.

Poco felt a moment of queasiness when Screech found
a large, black bloodstain on the ground.

"Whose blood, Screech?" she asked, forcing the words
past her lips.

"*Bomal. Favorite meat of the derkat,*" he answered.

Poco took a shaky breath and looked around the camp.
Waves of despair washed over her as she thought about
Dhal and wondered whether he was dead or alive.

She turned to find Screech standing nearby. His face
showed no emotion, but his silent watchfulness told her
that he was worried about her. She believed that her show
of weakness the night before had touched some respon-

sive chord within him, a protectiveness that he had never before shown openly.

Poco rubbed her eyes; they still felt swollen. She had not cried like that for a long time. Not since the night Trass died, she thought, ten—no fifteen—years ago.

She knew that Screech was waiting for her to decide what they would do next. Why doesn't he take the lead? she wondered. Why leave it up to me?

Poco was tired, body and soul; her head ached and she was hungry and thirsty, and she certainly did not feel up to making any decisions at that moment.

Screech moved closer. *"Are you ill?"* he asked.

Poco shook her head. "Just tired, Screech."

Blue eyes locked with yellow as Poco took a deep breath and released it. "Can we follow them, Screech?"

Screech's tail flicked back and forth in short, whiplash movements as he signed. *"We can follow. The trail is clear."*

"How long will it take for us to catch up with them?"

"Two days if we move quickly."

"We have no food and only the water you have in your flagon," she reminded him.

"I will find what we need," he assured her.

Poco nodded, then asked one last question. "Do you think Dhal might still be alive?"

"We will know once we are on the trail. If he lives, he will be walking and I will find his prints."

A little while later, Screech stopped and pointed to the ground. When Poco saw the print of a boot heel at the edge of an anthill, a surge of relief flowed through her.

"Dhal?" she asked, looking at Screech.

"Yes," he answered.

Poco and Screech did not catch up with the derkat raiders for three days, then they took another two days to circle ahead and find a place where they could lie in wait for the approaching derkat radg. With each day that passed, the Chen-garry Mountains loomed closer. Screech believed that the derkat radg would travel straight east to the mountains, then follow the foothills southeast into the Reaches.

One day Poco and Screech came close enough to the main radg to see a line of twenty-six derkat, divided by twos; each pair of derkat carried a litter on which rested bundles of bomal hides, a commodity tradable in the markets of the Reaches.

Each night when they stopped to rest, Screech and Poco discussed ways to approach the radg without putting themselves in too great a danger. The task seemed impossible.

Poco and Screech sat side by side while they waited for the shadows on the grass to grow longer. Earlier that day they had approached the radg close enough to see Dhal and Taav; both seemed alive and unharmed.

Poco finished sucking the last of the wild bora root that Screech had found that morning. The vegetable had satisfied her thirst, but not her hunger. Her hands were sticky with root sap and had pieces of grass adhering to them. She wiped them on her pants, wondering if she would ever feel clean again.

Keeping up with the derkat radg had taxed her to the limit. Her back and legs ached from the steady, ground-eating pace Screech had set, and though he had managed to find something for them to eat each day, it never was enough. One day they had eaten raw plains-hen, a plump, brown bird with a strange whirring call. Another day all they had had was a bitter, red root which was hard to chew.

Poco was tired and still hungry, but she forced herself to pay attention as Screech pointed out the defensive positions of the derkat at rest.

"Notice how the old and young lie at center camp," he signed. *"Around them you find the mature females, and in the outermost sleeping circle are the mature males."*

Poco glanced around the three distinct circles of sleeping enemies. They were scattered over a good size area, but as Screech pointed out, the lines of defense were plain. She could see five guards moving about, and she wondered how many more she was not seeing. She had been surprised to learn that the derkat did most of their traveling by night. Stopping by late morning, the radg would set a day camp, then all but a few would curl up and go to sleep.

Poco and Screech were situated on a slight rise overlooking the derkat camp. The flatlands had changed to rolling hills as they neared the Chen-garry Mountains, and the grass was beginning to give way to scattered clumps of bushes and trees.

Poco looked at the mountains rising steeply to the northeast. If she and Screech managed to free Dhal and the others, they would have to make a fast run to the mountain forests, for only there might they find a defensible position should the derkat give chase.

"Screech, your eyes are better than mine. Do you see Dahl?" Poco asked.

Screech pointed to the left of the second circle. *"He is near the stack of trade goods. There is one guard nearby."*

Poco strained her eyes but still could not see Dhal. "I wish we did not have to do this in daylight."

"It is the only way. When darkness comes, the radg will wake and move on again. We cannot wait any longer. Those hunters who left the radg yesterday, will return soon. We must free our friends before they arrive."

Poco hoped that Screech had not been so long away from his people that he had forgotten their ways. Screech had been only ten years old when Utura trappers had severed him from his radg in the Semco Hills and sold him to an exotic animal dealer in Port Cestar; in the fifteen years since his departure from the plains, he had lived a strange, furtive life in Port Bhalvar. Poco could not help but wonder if time and aloneness over the years might have warped Screech's images of his kin. Was everything as he remembered it, or was he discovering a world he did not know? She found no answer in those calm, yellow eyes.

"Screech, what will happen if we are caught?" she asked.

"We die, or we become saato, something to be traded,"

"Would they trade with us if we went down and talked to them?"

"What do we trade?" he asked.

Poco shook her head. Between them they had one sword, a knife, a wooden pendant, and a Ni armband. The armband might be worth one life, but never three, and in her heart Poco knew that she could not agree to a trade for Dhal and leave Gi and Taav to fend for themselves.

She looked down at the camp. The thought of going into such a gathering of derkat left her feeling sick. There has to be another way, she thought.

Screech stood and took a quick look around; then he came and sat down behind her. He reached out and pulled her back against him. *"Rest now,"* he signed, bringing his hands around in front of her. *"I will watch. When it is time, I will wake you."*

"I cannot sleep, Screech, not now."

"Try."

Poco leaned back against his soft-furred chest and closed her eyes for a few moments, but her thoughts would not let her relax.

"Screech, do you know for sure that this radg is *not* the same one from which you were taken years ago?"

"No."

"No, it isn't? Or no, you do not know?"

"I do not know," he answered.

"It is possible then?"

"Yes."

"If it was your clan, would they welcome you back?"

"Many years have passed. I am no longer the one they would recognize."

"But you would know some of them, wouldn't you?"

"*Some.*"

Poco was silent for a little while; a new thought formed in her mind, one that had to be voiced. She sat up and turned halfway around so she could see his face.

"Screech, if this radg turned out to be your home clan, would you want to stay with them? I mean—I would understand if you did want to stay. I always thought you might go home one day. It is just that we have been friends so long that—that I would miss you very much."

"*There are many radgs on the plains. Chances are few that this one is my home radg.*"

"But if it is?" Poco pressed.

"*It would not matter now. You, Little Fur, and the Healer are my radg now.*" Screech brushed the right side of her face with the back of his hand. "*Is this not so?*"

Poco looked at the derkat and felt an easing of troubled thoughts. "It is so." She smiled, and settled back against his furred chest.

Chapter 14

FINALLY THE TIME CAME TO MOVE. WITH A NOD SCREECH started down the hill, keeping low. Poco followed. She carried her sword tucked under her right arm, hand on the hilt, the point sticking up and out behind her.

Nervous, she checked the knife in her wrist sheath. Her job was to free Dhal and the others from their ropes while Screech silenced the guard keeping watch over the prisoners.

Ra-shun had slipped below the horizon and Ra-gar was casting long shadows in the grass. Screech estimated that they had approximately two hours before the derkat began to stir from their slumber. In that time Poco and Screech had to free their friends, leave the derkat camp as quickly and quietly as possible, and put as much distance between themselves and the camp as time allowed.

The derkat would, upon waking, realize that their prisoners had escaped. Screech openly admitted that the chances of the derkat going on without giving chase, were slim. Still, they had to take the risk.

Poco moved only at Screech's signal once they were off the hill. He would go a few paces ahead of her, stop, peer over the top of the grass, then wave her forward. Four times he made abrupt detours either to the left or to the right. Poco followed. She realized the reason for the detours when, through a thin veil of grass, she saw the recumbent figure of a sleeping derkat.

Moving with all the stealth at her command, Poco watched Screech stalk the derkat who stood guard over the pile of trade goods. They were by then well within the outer circle of sleeping derkat and working their way toward the second circle which, according to Screech, were all female and equally as fierce as the males when challenged.

The guard turned his back to them and moved away.

Screech looked back and signaled her forward.

"*Keep low,*" he signed, as she reached his side. "*Go straight ahead. The Healer is there.*"

"*You?*" she signed.

"*I will take the guard.*"

"*Meet you where after?*"

"*Go north toward the mountains. I will follow.*"

Poco looked into Screech's eyes and realized that if anything went wrong, she might never see him again. In the next few minutes, either of them might be killed or captured.

Poco knew that she loved this great, gray-furred being with a portion of her heart that would never belong to Dhal. The thought of losing him brought tears to her eyes. She reached out and caressed the fur over Screech's left eye.

"*Take care,*" she signed.

She did not wait for him to respond, but turned and started in the direction he had indicated. As she neared the pile of bomal hides that marked the location of the

trade packs, she saw Dhal and Taav lying against one of
the rolled hides, their eyes closed in sleep.

Carefully she pushed the grass aside and moved into
the open where the grass had all been trampled. She
stopped and looked for movement among the sleeping
derkat. There was no sign of Screech or the guard.

She hurried forward. When she reached Dhal, she carefully set her sword down and drew her knife; before she
cut Dhal's bonds, she clamped a hand over his mouth.

His eyes snapped open. Fear showed on his face but
a moment, then he recognized Poco's disheveled figure.

Poco lifted her hand from his mouth and signed slowly.
"Be still."

Dhal nodded and quickly rolled to one side, offering
her the ropes that held his arms behind his back. She
quickly freed his hands, then went to work on the draak-
hide cording that held his ankles together.

Dhal tried to revive the circulation in his hands as he
watched Poco work. Every few seconds he glanced at the
derkat sleeping nearby.

The last piece of cording broke. Poco looked up and
smiled, then she saw the pain in Dhal's face and took a
good look at his wrists, which were red and swollen where
the ropes had been too tight. But she knew that Dhal
could deal with his own pain. Swiftly she turned and began
to work on Taav's ropes.

Suddenly the scream of a derkat pierced the air. Taav
jerked away, his eyes wide in fear. Poco sawed frantically
at the ropes holding Taav's legs.

But already she was too late. The air filled with the
rumble of anger as the entire radg woke.

"Here, Dhal! Use this!" She slammed the hilt of her
knife into Dhal's hand.

Then she turned, scooped up her sword, and moved
to stand at Dhal's back. A moment later Screech bounded
around the mound of trade packs, his claws dripping blood.
Poco did not bother to ask what had happened: obviously

Screech had fought, but had failed to silence the derkat guard.

They were surrounded by derkat so quickly that there was no time to think of escape. The growls rose in timbre as more and more of the furred beings pressed closer. A young, male derkat, bolder than the others, made a move toward Screech.

Screech growled fiercely, warning the young male back.

The derkat surrounding them took exception to Screech's warning and replied with a chorus of growls that made the air vibrate with thunder.

Dhal, Poco, and Screech stood in an arc, their backs to each other. Taav lay near their feet. Both Dhal and Poco raised their weapons, ready to strike.

Suddenly Screech let loose with a scream that raised the hair on the back of Poco's neck. She desperately wanted to turn around to see what was happening behind her, but she could not take her eyes off the circle of derkat closing in.

Dhal, who stood to her left, was in a better position to see. He watched as Screech stepped forward a pace and signed to a female derkat with sagging teats.

The rumble of anger faded as Screech continued to sign.

"What is going on, Dhal?" Poco asked, keeping her voice low.

"Screech is talking to one of them, a female," Dhal answered without turning. "Keep your position."

"I will. What is he saying?"

"He is going too fast," Dhal answered. "I cannot read his signing."

Another female, gold and tawny, pushed her way through the crowd. She snarled when she saw Poco and Dhal; then she saw the tall, gray-furred derkat who stood with them, and she raised her voice in a yowl that brought instant silence.

Screech took a step backward, which allowed him a quick glance at the new arrival. She was younger than the derkat he had addressed; the intricately woven leather band around her waist told Screech that he had been talking to the wrong female.

Dhal, Screech, and Poco stood almost shoulder to shoulder, their backs to the pile of bomal hides. Taav crouched near their legs, his glance darting fearfully from one derkat to another.

Poco took a deep breath, trying to steady her nerves, then moved a half step to the side, so she could keep her eyes on the young female derkat who had just arrived. Poco knew little about derkat radgs, or their hierarchy, but it did not take much to guess that the newcomer was a being of some importance.

The other members of the radg stepped back, allowing the young female room to pace back and forth in front of Dhal, Poco, and Screech. Finally, she stopped in front of Screech. Her amber eyes narrowed, and her thin, black lips drew back in a silent snarl of distaste, as she signed to Screech.

"There is Cergar blood on your claws, Graysides. Why do you attack this radg?"

"You took from my radg!" Screech answered. *"I came to retrieve that which was taken!"*

The female's glance touched the three who were not derkat. *"Name yourself and your radg!"* she signed, speaking to Screech.

"I am called 'Ssaal-lr.' *My radg is* 'Jamba.'" Screech spoke his name and the name of his radg aloud.

"I have never heard of the radg 'amba'!" the female said, imitating the sound she had heard. *"Who is your tiyah?"*

Poco missed the last word; she had never seen that sign before. She concentrated on the interplay of hands and fingers as the female derkat spoke again. Poco forgot about the sword she held until she felt Dhal's hand on her wrist.

"Let me take it," Dhal whispered. "You read sign better than I do. Tell me what they are saying."

Poco nodded. Releasing her sword, she stepped behind Dhal and moved to stand beside Screech. The gray-furred derkat was aware of the change in positions but did not take his eyes from the female derkat.

"*Who is your tiyah?*" the female derkat repeated.

Screech started to sign but was interrupted by a male derkat pushing through the crowd. The male touched the young female on the arm to gain her attention, then he signed.

"*They are alone.*"

The female derkat turned to Screech, her eyes narrowed in suspicion.

"*You have no radg! You are renegade!*" she signed.

"*No!*" Screech responded. "*I am no renegade! My radg is small. It is what you see. Once I was of the Salgar radg. I was taken from the plains by trappers. For fifteen cool seasons I have lived in a man-place called* 'Bhalvar.' *I returned to the plains with my radg in order to find something the Green One has lost.*"

The female looked at Dhal. "*The Green Ones are no longer seen on the plains. Tell me, what has he lost here?*"

"*The truth about his people,*" Screech answered.

"*What truth?*"

"*Where they have gone.*"

The female looked at Dhal and Poco, then faced Screech again. "*I still see no tiyah. There can be no radg without a tiyah.*"

"Screech," Poco said softly. "She keeps using a sign I do not understand. What does it mean?"

Screech continued to stare at the female derkat as he answered Poco's question. He made the sign for *tiyah* slowly, so Poco could see the sound pattern. "*It means leader. The tiyah is always female.*"

"And we are not a radg because we do not have a female derkat with us?" Poco said softly.

"*We have a tiyah,*" Screech responded.

Screech drew Poco out in front of him. Startled, she

froze as Screech reached around her and signed to the female derkat.

"This is our tiyah, and in her name I call challenge, one to one."

"Screech, what are you doing?" Poco snapped, trying to keep her voice low.

Screech did not answer.

Poco looked at the derkat surrounding them. They all were watching quietly; their looks of expectation sent chills down Poco's back.

"Screech, what is this about a challenge?" Poco demanded.

Unable to keep up with the entire conversation, Dhal finally chanced a few words. "What's happening, Poco?"

He had kept his voice low, but his interruption did not set well with the derkat closest to him. Their growls of displeasure were quickly taken up by others behind them.

Distracted, the female derkat growled and again there was instant silence. She looked at Poco.

"You are no tiyah!" the female signed.

Something in the female's manner stirred Poco's ire. She was not sure what Screech was trying to do but she decided to follow the lead he had set.

She pushed Screech's arm aside and answered the female's challenge. *"I am* Pocalina-fel-Jamba, *and I am tiyah of this radg."*

The female stood quietly, her large, amber eyes unreadable as she gazed at Poco.

She is trying to stare me down, Poco thought.

Knowing how good Screech was at that game, Poco refused to play. With Screech standing behind her to back her up, she decided to take the initiative.

Relax and do this right, she thought. Make a mistake and none of us will live to regret it. She looked at the female derkat and coughed a greeting.

"I have given you my name. I ask yours in return," she signed.

The female derkat was startled; she hesitated, then returned Poco's cough as courtesy demanded.

Poco waited, presenting an appearance of calm she did not feel.

Finally the female growled softly and lifted her hands to sign.

"*I am 'Ho-law,' tiyah of the radg Cergar*."

Poco acknowledged the introduction with a nod. Now what? she wondered. In the back of her mind, she wondered if Dhal was following the conversation.

When Ho-law made no move to continue the conversation, Poco spoke again, trying to find out just where she stood.

"*Our radg is new to the plains. We did not mean to intrude upon your hunting territory. We only wanted to pass through*."

"*Your male attacked one of mine!*" Ho-law accused.

"*True*," Poco agreed. "*But only that he might free members of his own radg*."

"*There is blood between us and your male has called a challenge. Do you agree?*"

Screech nudged Poco in the back.

"*I agree*," Poco signed, hoping she had not misread Screech's silent command.

Ho-law growled softly and her upper lip lifted in a derkat expression of satisfaction.

"Screech, what have I just agreed to?" Poco asked aloud, hoping the other derkat did not understand trader.

"*A fight*," Screech answered.

"Between the two radgs?"

"*No. I called the challenge. I will fight Ho-law's champion*."

Poco was prevented from asking any further questions because Ho-law was signing to her again. "*The challenge will be answered tonight upon the return of my hunters*," the derkat told her. "*You will march with us until that time. Agreed?*"

Again came that gentle nudge in the back. "*Agreed*," Poco signed.

Ho-law nodded, then began giving orders to her followers. The barks, growls, and coughing noises which accompanied her signing made Poco think of a pack of gensvolf fighting over a bone.

As the derkat began to disperse, each to some unknown task, Dhal lowered his sword and turned to Poco. "Would someone kindly tell me what is going on now?" he said. "Where is everyone going? Are we free to leave?"

Poco glanced at the five female derkat who remained in a loose circle around them. "No, Dhal, not free. Not yet. It seems we have got to fight for our freedom."

"Fight?" he echoed.

"Screech against one of their champions."

Dhal looked at Screech and frowned. "When does this fight take place?"

"Some time tonight after their hunters return," Poco answered. "We are to march with them until that time."

"What are the terms of the fight?"

"I don't know. Screech, I think you had better explain that to both of us."

"*It is simple,*" Screech signed. "*I win, we gain our freedom. I lose, I die and you become saato again.*"

"Die?" Poco said, a chill settling in her stomach. "What do you mean, Screech?"

"*Derkat challenge is to the death. It is our way.*"

"Isn't there any other way we can get out of this mess?" Poco said.

"*Once a challenge is accepted, there is a peace pact between the radgs until the fight is over.*" Screech looked at the five derkat standing around them. "*We are Cergar guests now, but we would not be allowed to wander away from the radg. The challenge will have to be met.*"

Damn! Poco thought as she turned away. Her eyes were suddenly moist with tears. She kept her head down as she reached for the knife in Dhal's hand.

"Here, let me have that. I will cut Taav loose."

She quickly cut the ropes holding Taav. As Dhal helped the atich-ar to his feet, Poco wiped at the tears in her eyes, then stood up, resolved not to show weakness before their derkat guards.

Suddenly it dawned on Poco that they were one member shy.

"Dhal, where is Gi-arobi?" she asked.

Dhal shook his head. "I don't know, Poco. I have not seen him since that night in camp. One of the derkat picked him up and put him in a sack. The morning after the raid, when the derkat finally stopped their march, I asked about Gi, but none of the derkat seemed to understand me, or if they did, they pretended not to. And with my hands tied I could not sign to them." Dhal's voice dropped. "During the day when it was quiet, I listened for his whistle, but I have heard nothing so far."

"Is it possible he has not regained consciousness?" Poco asked.

"After five days?"

The hopeless look on Dhal's face was almost more than Poco could stand. Again she felt the pressure of tears and cursed herself for a weakling. What a crybaby you are getting to be, fel-Jamba. Snap out of it! She banished her tears by sheer willpower.

"Screech," Poco said, turning to the derkat. "Is there any way we can find out if they have Gi?"

"*We can ask*," Screech signed.

He left them and walked over to one of the guards. His hand movements were shielded by his body so Poco was not able to see what he said, nor was she able to see the guard's answer.

When Screech returned, Poco's heartbeat quickened. If anything had happened to Gi...

"*Little Fur still lives*," Screech signed. "*His kind are not common to the plains. Ho-law keeps him for her own.*"

"What will she do with him, Screech?" Poco asked.

"*Play with him. Eat him. Anything she wishes.*"

Poco felt her stomach turn.

"Is Gi all right, Screech? Can we see him?" Dhal asked.

"Little Fur sleeps much of the time and does not eat."

Dhal's frown deepened. "Screech, I have got to see him! If he is sick, he may need my help!"

"No!" The growl accompanying Screech's refusal startled both Poco and Dhal.

"What do you mean, no?" Dhal demanded angrily.

"Easy, Dhal," Poco said, putting a hand on his arm. "Let him explain. Screech, please, why can't Dhal help Gi?"

Screech made sure none of the derkat could see his hands as he tried to explain. *"If Ho-law learns that Dhal is a Healer, she will never let him go."*

"Even if you win the challenge fight?" Poco asked.

"If I won she would release us, then send her hunters out to capture us again."

"Then we would just challenge her again," Poco said.

"She would not accept."

"Are you saying that if Ho-law knew what Dhal was, she would keep him and make him use his power for her own people?"

Screech nodded. *"The derkat know of the Green Ones, and some have witnessed Healer magic. They would be willing to risk much to possess one like Dhal."*

Dhal shook his head. "That may be, Screech, but it does not alter the fact that I must see Gi!"

Screech nodded in understanding. *"I will ask again."*

When Screech returned, he still had no positive answer. *"The guard will speak to Ho-law. I told her that Little Fur was of our radg and asked that he be returned to us."*

"Do you think she will let him go, Screech?" Poco asked.

Screech looked down at her. *"The tiyah will do as she pleases. The only way Little Fur might be returned to us is if you, as our tiyah, demand that he be included in any agreements made."*

Chapter 15

THE NIGHT WAS GROWING DARKER BY THE MINUTE. POCO judged that they had been marching with the Cergar radg for a good four hours. While it was still light, she had been able to count the number of derkat in the radg; the count was thirty-two adult and seven young, including the ten hunters still away from the radg.

Screech told her that it was one of the largest radgs he had ever heard about. His own radg had numbered only seventeen.

When Poco asked Screech about the yearly migration route of the derkat, he explained that each radg had a home territory, usually somewhere in the Ha-far Mountains to the west of the High Plains. Each year at the end of the warm season, the derkat left their cave homes and followed the herds of bomal which grazed the plains during the cool passage, hunting and trading with other radgs along the way.

Since the arrival of men in that area, the derkat had

also begun to trade with them, but trust between the two peoples was still a tentative thing, and peace agreements were easily overlooked by either group if chance of gain was in the foreseeable future.

The yearly trek back and forth across the plains took the derkat radgs ten months to accomplish, their routes ranging from the Chen-garry Mountains to the northern edge of the Enzaar Sea.

Dhal asked if anyone guarded the derkat's home territory when they were gone.

Screech said no, explaining that the cave homes were used only during the birthing season, when for four months time the derkat radgs settled down.

"All radg leaders are chosen at this same time," Screech signed. *"A tiyah may reign one year or many. It depends upon how well she leads."*

"How many radgs are there?" Poco asked.

"Many small ones, some no more than our number. Only a few as large as the Cergar radg."

As they walked with their guards, Poco went over the different points Screech had said she must make during the trading session preceding the fight: freedom for them all, the return of their packs and weapons, food and water for four days, a promise that they would not be followed after leaving the Cergar radg—and a pact of nonaggression should the two radgs meet again that season.

Poco glanced past Dhal to Taav. The atich-ar walked close to Dhal and held tightly to a fold of Dhal's tunic. It was obvious that he was frightened by the number of derkat that surrounded them. The days in which Dhal and Taav had been prisoners had sent the atich-ar back into his own silent world; not once since releasing him had he tried to sign to them. Poco hoped that Taav's mental progress would not suffer because of the fright he had sustained. If irreparable damage had occurred to him, they might well have lost their entrance into the world of the atich-ar, wherever it was.

"Poco?"

She turned and looked at Dhal, but all she could see was the outline of his head against the sky.

"Poco, are you all right?" Dhal asked, a worried tone in his voice.

"Yes, Dhal. I am fine," she answered.

"You have been quiet a long time."

"Just thinking."

"About what?"

"Everything. About us, Gi, the fight coming up. About Taav and the gate. You haven't told me what happened that night after I left."

"The night Taav and I were captured?"

"Yes."

"Not much to tell. I was digging the grave and thinking about the atich-ar we had killed, then suddenly I was surrounded by derkat. They approached so silently that I never heard them. I used the sword I had been digging with, but only managed to nick a couple of them before I was taken from behind. While I was being tied up, I saw several derkat pick up Gi and Taav. I watched while they killed one of the bomal, then one of them doused the fire with water and it was too dark to see.

"I spent the rest of the night running or walking between two derkat—one of them used the points of his claws to keep me moving. In the morning when they stopped, I located Taav. Ho-law was looking him over. When she finished with him, she came and looked at me. I tried to speak to her, but she just growled and showed her teeth.

"I had no idea what they had planned for us, but whatever it was, I was glad you were not there to share it. After two days, when they failed to bring you or Screech in, I was sure that you had both escaped."

Dhal paused. "You should not have come with us, Poco. I wish the two of you had just kept going."

"Where?" Poco asked softly.

"On to Jjaan-bi."

"No, Dhal, not without you." She squeezed his arm.

"Be honest with me," she said. "If it had been Screech and I who were captured and not you, would you have gone off and left us in the hands of the derkat?"

"You always have the right answers, don't you?"

"I wish."

She started to say something else but was interrupted by a derkat scream coming from behind them. Suddenly Screech's arm blocked Poco's path.

"What is wrong?" Dhal asked, stopping beside Poco.

"I don't know," Poco answered. "All I can see are shadows."

Dhal and Poco stood quietly waiting, trusting that Screech's night vision would give them warning if danger approached.

More derkat screams echoed in the night. Two of the females who had been guarding them growled in response, then abruptly disappeared, their shadowed figures melting into the darkness beyond Poco's sight.

All was confusion during the next few minutes. Dhal, Taav, Poco, and Screech stood in a tight circle and kept watch on the shifting figures around them. The noises made by the derkat gave no indication of the cause of their unrest.

Poco found Screech's arm and followed it down to his hand.

"Screech, sign to me," she said. "Can you see what is happening?"

Screech's fist clenched into the sign for *yes*. They had played this game before. Signing by touch was an awkward way to communicate, but it worked.

"Are we under attack?" she asked.

"*No. The hunters have returned*," Screech signed.

"Screech, is there any way we could slip away in all this confusion?" Dhal asked.

Poco relayed Screech's answer. "No."

Minutes passed. The waiting made Poco nervous.

Finally a torch was lighted, pushing back the darkness. Poco looked around and saw Ho-law approach. Beside her walked a young male derkat carrying a torch. Other torches were being lighted somewhere ahead.

Ho-law stopped before them and looked at Poco as she signed. *"My hunters have returned. The challenge circle is being prepared. It is time to talk."*

Poco glanced at Screech. He nodded. The waiting was at an end. Poco turned back to Ho-law and signed, *"I am ready."*

A few minutes later Poco was seated on the ground facing Ho-law. Screech, Dhal, and Taav sat a pace behind her. As tiyah of her radg it was Poco's responsibility to make all decisions concerning the division of food, war and peace, and trade.

The ground where they were seated was level; the tall, dried grass had been trampled flat. Ho-law sat on a length of yellow cloth. Her belt of authority lay across her knees. A dozen members of her radg crouched behind her.

Poco glanced around the trade circle. The five torches that lighted the small gathering were held by strong-looking females; their chest harnesses were decorated with round pieces of metal which glinted in the firelight. In her mind's eye Poco could see herself confronting any one of the five—and coming out the loser. Poco hoped that Screech knew what he was doing.

Ho-law coughed in greeting.

Poco returned the cough and sat quietly waiting. Screech had coached her in the details of making an agreement and had cautioned her against appearing nervous or hurried.

For long moments Poco and Ho-law just stared at each other, blue and yellow eyes locked in combat.

Ho-law's fingers began to move. *"As the one challenged, I will state my demands first,"* Ho-law signed. *"Agreed?"*

"No," Poco signed.

Ho-law sat a bit straighter, startled by the refusal of her right as the one challenged.

Before the female derkat could become angry, Poco

signed again, at the same time speaking aloud, both for Dhal's benefit, and as a way of maintaining pride in her own identity.

"There is one missing from my radg," she said. "His name is Gi-arobi. He is olvaar. I ask to see him before any agreements are made."

Ho-law's eyes narrowed with indecision, as if she was unsure how to handle this strange tiyah. Perhaps what decided her was Poco's unwavering stare, or perhaps it was the belief that Poco's champion was no match for her own, and that all that belonged to Poco would soon be hers. Whatever her reasoning, Ho-law turned and signed to one of those behind her.

"Bring the olvaar."

The wait was brief. A young male derkat entered the trade circle carrying a small, grass basket. He placed the basket in front of Ho-law and stepped back to his place behind several of his elders.

Ho-law unwound the twine which held the basket closed, then she opened the lid and waved her hand in a gesture that told Poco to look.

Poco leaned forward and peered down into the basket. Gi lay there, curled into a ball. He is so still, Poco thought, as she put her hand on Gi's head.

"Gi," she said softly. "Gi-arobi, wake up."

Dhal reached out and touched Poco's shoulder. "Is he all right, Poco?"

Dhal squeezed Poco's shoulder so hard that it was painful but the pain she felt was nothing compared to the fear that had entered her heart. Poco picked up the basket, turned and pushed it into Dhal's outstretched hands.

"I do not think he is breathing, Dhal," she said.

Poco's voice was whisper-soft, but Dhal heard her. The horror mirrored on Dhal's face was like a blow to Poco's stomach. She felt the pressure of tears behind her eyes as Dhal scooped Gi out of the basket and cradled him in his arms.

Something touched Poco's arm. She turned and saw Screech signing to her; his look was grim and unyielding.

"*Ho-law waits*," Screech signed.

Sick at heart, Poco turned around, realizing that if she failed to be the leader Screech had named her, they might all end up as Gi-arobi, their coffins nothing but baskets made of grass.

She faced Ho-law and took a deep breath. As she exhaled slowly, she tried to push thoughts of Gi to the back of her mind; it was not an easy task, for she could still visualize Dhal clutching Gi in his arms, the small, furry body lost in his embrace.

Ho-law signed. "*As tiyah of the Cergar radg, I claim full possession of your radg should my champion win. Agreed?*"

Poco swallowed nervously, though Screech had warned her that in such a challenge fight the stakes were always high.

"*Agreed*," she signed.

Then it was her turn. Though she would have been within her rights to demand authority over the Cergar radg if Screech won the challenge fight, he had advised against it. All they really needed was their freedom, their weapons, and food to tide them over until they reached the mountains where they could forage for themselves.

Poco listed her demands, signing carefully so there would be no misunderstanding.

Ho-law agreed to all that Poco asked for, then added, "*The challenge circle will be ready soon. Your champion should prepare himself. You will have an escort to the circle when it is time.*"

At that, the derkat tiyah and her followers stood and moved off toward the ring of torches a short distance away.

Poco noticed that the number of guards who remained behind had doubled, a sign that Ho-law did not trust her and her companions. She dismissed the guards from her mind and turned to look at Dhal. A tight knot filled her throat as she thought about Gi, but her fear for the olvaar's life vanished when she saw the smile that lighted Dhal's face.

He lifted Gi-arobi up to her. "He is all right, Poco! He was only sleeping!"

Poco shook her head, bewildered. "I could have sworn he was not breathing."

Poco reached out and took Gi under the arms. She brought him close so she could look into his eyes.

"Gi, *are* you all right?" she asked him.

Gi whistled yes.

"You scared me half to death," Poco said. "Why didn't you move when I touched you?"

"Gi sick," the olvaar responded, reverting to trader.

"But you are all right now." she said.

Gi bobbed his head.

Poco gave Gi a hug, which Gi happily returned.

"What was wrong with him, Dhal," Poco asked, keeping her voice down. "Did you have to go in?"

Dhal cast a quick glance around, then nodded. "One of the derkat must have been rough with him that first night, hit him in the head or something. There was blood in his right inner ear. It was throwing him off balance. Each time he tried to move, it made him sick. That is why he wouldn't eat."

Dhal patted Gi's stomach. "But he is fine now, except for an empty stomach."

"Is under-stay-mint, Dhal," Gi said, tilting his head to one side. "Gi hungry enough to eat a derkat, yes!"

"Well, that is something we can fix," Poco said, and handed Gi a piece of wild root she had tucked into one pocket.

As Gi stuffed the root into his mouth, Screech leaned over and rubbed his fingers across the top of the olvaar's head, greeting Gi in his own special way.

Chapter 16

*P*OCO ESTIMATED THE CHALLENGE CIRCLE TO BE AP-
proximately fifteen meters across. All the grass within
the circle had been torn from the ground.

She shivered as the glint of torchlight reflected in the
eyes of the watching derkat. There was an aura of wild-
ness about the plains derkat, a threat of physical danger
that was enhanced by the glow of anticipation in their
eyes.

Poco realized that she had made a mistake in judging
all derkat by her friendship with Screech. Screech had
been civilized by his years of living in Port Bhalvar. She
looked at the Cergar champion and felt a knot of fear
settle in her stomach. Had she done wrong? By taming
the wild in Screech, had she sentenced them all to the
living death of slavery?

The Cergar champion's name was Rhel. He was taller
than Screech by a full head and heavier in the upper body.

His tawny fur glinted golden in the torchlight, matching his eyes, which at that moment were directed at Ho-law.

Poco could not see Ho-law's signing, but she guessed from the way Ho-law's tail was snapping back and forth that the female derkat was excited by the thought of the upcoming battle and was giving her champion last minute instructions.

Poco turned to Screech, who was calmly removing his chest harness and gold armband. Screech gave his harness to Dhal to hold; the armband went to Poco.

"What weapons are you allowed, Screech?" Poco asked.

"*No weapons*," Screech answered.

Before Poco or Dhal could voice their surprise, Screech held out his hands, palms up. Suddenly twin sets of claws appeared, clean and sharpened to points. A second later the claws disappeared, retracting back into the fur covering the back of Screech's fingers.

"*It is the derkat way*," Screech signed. "*Teeth and claws—to the death.*"

Impulsively Poco threw her arms around Screech, hugging him fiercely. The derkat's arms tightened around her, returning her embrace. Was he as scared as she was? Poco wondered.

"I love you, Screech," Poco said softly.

Screech answered her with a purring sound that emanated from somewhere in his chest. Again Poco felt tears come to her eyes.

"I think it is time, Poco," Dhal said.

Poco released Screech. "Our luck to you, Screech. Please, be careful."

She felt Dhal's hand on her arm. She stood a little straighter, and with her head up she turned to face the fight circle.

Rhel already stood in the center of the circle. Screech stepped onto the bared earth without hesitation. His gray fur glinted silver as he moved toward Rhel.

Poco squeezed Dhal's hand. "Here goes," she whispered. "Pray for him, Dhal! Pray for all of us!"

Dhal said nothing, but the return pressure on her hand told Poco that he was filled with the same fear and excitement she was.

Get him, Screech! Poco thought. Kill him! You can do it!

The two male derkat coughed in ritual greeting, then like mirror images they leaped apart, claws extended. Slowly they circled. Rhel let loose with a yowl that made Poco want to cover her ears. Screech answered with his own cry of defiance, drowning Rhel's scream.

Poco jumped as the two derkat lunged at each other. Rhel feinted to the left and swung one clawed hand at Screech's face. The stroke missed as Screech turned, dropped back a step, and bounded away, hands up, elbows out in a posture of defense.

The two derkat circled once more, each gauging the other's defensive stance and movements. Suddenly Rhel lunged forward. Screech did not back away, and the two derkat met in midair. When they fell to the ground, Screech was under the heavier Rhel.

They rolled over and over, claws raking for a hold. Their growls of rage filled the night air as they each fought for a death grip.

There were answering growls from the watching derkat, all of whom were firmly caught up in the battle.

Poco became aware of Taav's body pressing close to hers. She could feel him tremble and knew he was frightened, but there was nothing she could do at that moment.

Screech and Rhel rolled into the legs of some of the derkat who were watching. Instantly they broke apart. The two fighters quickly regained their feet and turned to face each other.

There were patches of blood marring Rhel's tawny coat, one large spot on his right hip, another spot on his left shoulder. Screech seemed to have fared a little better in the first skirmish, with only one dark blotch high on his left side.

Rhel and Screech circled again. Suddenly Ho-law loosed an ear-splitting cry that spurred Rhel into action. The two fighters met again.

A *whoof* of escaping air exploded from Screech's lungs as Rhel carried him to the ground. Rhel's teeth showed as he went in for a kill.

Somehow Screech managed to protect his throat, but in doing so he left himself open to Rhel's claws.

Time and time again Poco lost sight of Screech, unable to tell one derkat from the other as they tumbled and spun around. The two fighters clawed and bit at each other until droplets of blood spattered their audience.

The derkat surrounding the challenge circle were wild with excitement; the din of their yowling made thought impossible.

Again the two champions broke apart. Both were tiring. Blood was running down Screech's left side, and he favored that leg as he moved around the circle. Rhel was breathing hard and was well marked by Screech's teeth and claws, but of the two, he looked to be in better shape.

Rhel cut across the circle. Screech retreated before him. Suddenly Screech faltered and fell to one knee. Rhel did not hesitate; he leaped forward, claws extended, teeth aimed for Screech's unprotected neck.

Poco's silent scream was followed by a gasp for air, for just as Rhel struck, Screech dropped onto his back and slashed upward at his opponent's eyes. The blow sliced across Rhel's face, lacerating nose and eyes.

The Cergar champion screamed in pain and rage and rolled off to one side, giving Screech a moment to recover. That one moment was all Screech needed. He was on top of Rhel before the large derkat could roll away. A second later he had his teeth buried in Rhel's throat.

Rhel twisted and heaved himself around, trying to throw Screech off; his claws scored Screech's back like knives, but still Screech would not let go. Within seconds Rhel's struggles lessened, then his clawed hands stopped moving.

Screech crouched over Rhel's body and held his position until the large derkat fully relaxed.

Poco became aware of the silence of the night. All that could be heard was Screech's ragged breathing as he released his hold on Rhel's throat and sat back.

Poco looked up as Ho-law stepped into the challenge circle and made her way toward her slain champion. Fearing for the battle-weakened Screech, Poco tore from Taav's embrace. She would not let Screech stand alone before Ho-law's rage!

The derkat tiyah stopped on the other side of Rhel's body and watched as Screech pushed to his feet.

Poco came up beside Screech and caught him around the waist as he started to lose his balance. She ignored the bloody fur which wet her tunic and stood quietly facing Ho-law, her look defiant.

For long moments Ho-law and Poco just stared at each other. Ho-law's eyes were narrowed and watchful, but Poco did not see the anger she had thought to find there. Were the derkat so different from men that they could accept so casually the loss of one of their own? Poco wondered. Didn't Ho-law feel anything for her slain champion?

Poco felt a sudden emptiness as she realized that she really did not know much about derkat, not how they thought or lived, or what made them the people they were.

"The challenge has been met," Ho-law signed. *"The Cergar radg yields to* 'amba.'"

Poco nodded and watched as Ho-law signaled to several of her followers to retrieve Rhel's body.

Suddenly Poco became aware of the fact that she was holding more and more of Screech's weight.

"Graysides is a good fighter, tiyah 'Jamba,'" Ho-law signed. *"Tend him, or you will lose him."*

Poco turned to call to Dhal for help and found him

standing right behind her. Gi was riding his shoulder; Taav stood a short distance away.

Poco faced Ho-law and signed for light and water. The female derkat nodded.

"Let's take him over on the grass, Dhal, away from this place," Poco said.

By the time Poco and Dhal had Screech stretched out on a patch of untrampled grass, one of Ho-law's followers had brought a hide flagon filled with water. Poco took a lighted torch from another derkat standing nearby and moved around to Dhal's right, giving him light to work by.

Ho-law lingered a few minutes, watching as Dhal tried to staunch the worst of Screech's wounds. Poco stared at Ho-law and silently willed her to go away.

Finally Ho-law signaled the seven derkat who attended her and together they left.

"Are they gone?" Dhal asked softly, not looking up.

"Yes," Poco answered.

"All of them?"

Poco peered into the darkness. "Yes, I think so. Go ahead, go in. I'll keep watch."

Dhal put his bloody rag aside and placed his hands over Screech's head, first dulling the pain centers in the brain. He then began to work on the deepest of the derkat's wounds. The green aura of light which quickly surrounded Dhal's hands indicated that his healing energy was at work deep inside the derkat's body, mending broken blood vessels and reknitting layers of skin cell by cell.

Poco sat on the grass in the flickering light of her dying torch. Dhal and Screech lay asleep behind her. Dhal had fallen asleep shortly after finishing his work, exhausted by his efforts of healing. Before he dropped off, he told Poco that Screech would be weak for a while from the loss of blood, but that he was in no danger of dying.

She felt Taav move beside her. He and Gi-arobi had joined her in watching the derkat fire just a short distance away where Ho-law was burning Rhel's body atop a small funeral pyre made of bomal hides.

Poco listened to the subdued growling rumble of derkat voices as they moved in matched steps around the fire. The sounds conveyed feelings of loss rather than of anger.

Eventually the fire died down and the derkat moved away from the ashes of their comrade.

Gi stirred in Poco's lap. "Someone comes," he said.

Poco sat a little straighter as five shadowed figures approached. Taav edged closer to her.

She slipped her knife from its sheath and waited quietly, her heart thumping heavily in her chest.

The derkat milled around for a few moments, then they moved away.

Gi-arobi left Poco's lap.

"Where are you going, Gi?" Poco asked.

"Being back soon," Gi answered.

True to his word, Gi returned a minute later and settled down beside Poco's leg.

"What did they want, Gi?" Poco asked.

"Derkat leave packs, food, and water," Gi said.

Poco dropped a hand on top of Gi's head and stroked gently. "Are they leaving now?" she asked him.

"No," Gi answered. "Ho-law comes."

The female derkat approached alone. She stopped in front of Poco and crouched in the glow of the torchlight. "*Graysides lives?*" she signed.

"*Yes,*" Poco answered.

"*It is good. He is one worth ten.*"

Ho-law rubbed at her nose, her glance moving to Taav, then back to Poco. "*Your radg seeks the Green Ones, yes?*"

"*Yes.*" Poco wondered what Ho-law intended.

"*Go north over the mountains,*" the derkat signed. "*You will find a big freshwater lake. Go east from there. The Green Ones will be found if they wish to be.*"

"*Thank you,*" Poco signed, surprised.

Ho-law gazed quietly at Poco then rose and turned away. A moment later she was lost to the darkness.

Although she was exhausted in both mind and body, Poco knew she should stay awake and keep watch—but she had reckoned without Gi-arobi.

Gi ducked out from under her hand, turned, and pushed against her side. "Poco sleeps now. Gi keep watch," he said.

"No, Gi. I'll stay awake. It will be safer if—"

Suddenly a pair of sharp teeth caught at Poco's wrist, biting down gently but firmly. Before Poco could even think to pull away, Gi had released her.

"Poco sleeps now!" he said, his lisping speech acquiring an authoritative tone Poco had never heard him use before.

She was startled by Gi's behavior, but she was too tired to argue. Trusting him to wake her if he needed help, she lay down between Dhal and Taav and quickly drifted off to sleep.

In the morning, Poco and Gi inspected the small mound of packs left by the derkat. She was pleased to see that most of their personal packs were still intact, along with their few cooking utensils.

She sorted through several of the hide wrappers that contained food. She found dried bomal meat, dried fruit, and five packets of a hard, flat, grayish substance stacked in layers separated by large, dried, green leaves.

Curious, Poco nibbled at a corner of one of the gray cakes and gingerly chewed the grainy dough. In a few moments she began to detect a spicy flavor, and the longer she had the cake in her mouth, the softer and more chewy it became. She swallowed, satisifed that the cakes were edible, then rewrapped the packet.

She was in the process of planning who would carry what when she heard Dhal call her. She went to him, glad that he had wakened. He looked tired, as he always did after healing.

"What is happening?" he asked, as she sat down beside him.

"Nothing at the moment," she replied. "I slept most of the night while Gi kept watch. It has been quiet since I woke. Taav is still asleep."

"What about the derkat?"

"If you mean Ho-law and her radg, they are gone. After they burned Rhel's body, they brought us our packs and left. Ho-law also gave me some instructions on where we might find some of the Green Ones."

"What did she say?"

Poco repeated Ho-law's directions word for word.

"She didn't mention the Owri River?" Dhal asked.

"No."

"Great!"

"It means that we have a choice to make."

"Yes," he said. "Either we go straight north over the mountains or we go east to the Owri and follow the river north."

"I am not that fond of climbing," Poco said, "but it sounds to me as if the route straight north would be shorter."

"I agree."

"Then we go north from here?"

"Yes. I don't know that we will save any time, but it is worth a try."

Poco glanced at Screech, who was lying on his side, facing them. His eyes were still closed in sleep. He looked the worse for wear and Poco realized that it would be some time before he could regrow the fur he had lost in his fight with Rhel.

"Will we try to do any traveling today?" Poco asked.

"Screech lost a lot of blood last night. He will be weak for days. It might be best if we stay here today and give him a chance to rest. If the other derkat are gone, we should be safe enough here."

"How are *you* feeling?" Poco asked.

"Tired."

"Would you like something to eat or drink?"

"Both, thanks."

A little while later, Poco and Dhal shared their first meal together in seven days. After they ate, Dhal sat staring out across the open grasslands.

He was quiet for so long that Poco grew worried. "Something wrong, Dhal?"

"No. I was just thinking about Retath," he responded.

"What about him?"

"Do you remember what he said about Singers and Sensitives?"

Poco shook her head. "To be truthful, all I remember about that day is being scared."

"I have been thinking about him for days now." He smiled. "That is, whenever I wasn't thinking about escaping the derkat. I keep remembering him asking about the gate. Remember, he said, 'Who holds the gate for you?' and then he said that when the atich-ar first took the Tamorlee, they killed all of the Singers and Sensitives, those who could make and hold the world gate."

Poco thought back, trying to recall the old Ni's words.

Dhal continued. "When I spoke with the Ancients back in the old Val-hrodhur, they also mentioned Sensitives and the energy patterns that could create doors."

He reached out and took Poco's hand. "That song you sang, Poco—the one called 'Green Draak Dreaming'— also tells about a Singer who walks the patterned way. Put it all together, Poco! A Singer to set the pattern! A Sensitive to hold the gate! You and Taav! You two are the keys to the world gate!"

"Taav and I?"

"Yes! Think about it, Poco! It makes sense! You sing and create a gate to another reality and somehow Taav can hold that gate open. It means that we can go back to that place whenever we want to."

"Back?" Poco shook her head. "Oh, no! Not by ourselves! Promise me, Dhal, not by ourselves!"

"Easy, Poco, don't get upset. I just said that we could

go back. I promise, we will go on to Jjaan-bi and pass on Retath's warning. The Ni will help us. I know they will."

If we can find them, Poco thought, and if they believe us.

Chapter 17

THEY WALKED FOR FIVE DAYS TO REACH THE HEAVILY forested slopes of the Chen-garry Mountains. Screech walked without a pack, but he continually lagged behind, causing the small band of travelers to stop often to let him catch up. The derkat knew he was slowing them down, but each time he told them to go on without him, promising that he would catch up, they refused to leave him.

"We are in no hurry, Screech," Poco told him. "A few hours here or there, or even a few days, are not going to make any difference to us. We are lucky to have gotten this far without losing someone, and I intend to see that our luck holds—meaning we stay together, no matter what! Right, Gi?"

Gi pulled his head out of the food sack in which he had been rummaging. "Staying together, yes, Big Fur," he said. "No needing to hurry. Jjaan-bi waits for us."

Screech growled.

150

Poco shook her head. She knew his growl was directed not at Gi but himself; the derkat was not used to being weak or ill, and was impatient with his slow recovery.

Poco got up and went to see what Gi was poking his nose into.

"Find anything in there, Gi?" she asked, smiling.

"Gray cakes," Gi answered, moving back so Poco could look.

Screech had explained that the flat, gray cakes were a staple for the wandering radgs of derkat. The dried roots of the optra were ground down and cooked along with water, tree sap, and the leaves of the emlar bush. The resultant grayish mixture was then baked for five days in the sun on large flat stones. The spicy flavor came from the leaves, the chewiness from the sap.

Poco pulled out the last of the gray cakes and gave one to Screech. She broke another one in half for herself and Gi, and the last one she saved for Dhal and Táav, who were out foraging.

She glanced around the narrow hollow where they had stopped to camp. The cold passage was almost over, but the foliage looked much as it would in the warm months ahead. Some trees and bushes lost their leaves during the cold passage, but most of the green plants merely stopped growing, their leaves remaining unchanged until the warm spring rains provided the needed moisture to start a new life cycle. The giant aban trees were of the latter variety, their large, spreading branches shading the forest floor and preventing all but the most sturdy and persistent of plants to grow.

Poco had never before seen a forest where the aban trees were so dense. She was reminded of the park in Port Bhalvar, except where the park was filled with patterns of dappled shade and sunlight, the mountain wood was all half-light and mysterious shadows.

Poco heard the sound of water running off to her left. She stood and slung the three hide flagons to her shoulder.

"I am going for some water," she told Screech and Gi.

"While I am gone, why don't you two gather some sticks for a fire. If any gensvolf come skulking around after dark, we will want plenty of wood for our fire."

Screech growled to catch Poco's attention. "*Draak like water places*," he signed. "*Be careful.*"

Poco nodded. "I will, Screech."

"Want Gi to come, Poco?" Gi piped up.

"No, Gi, I won't be gone long. Stay and help Screech gather some wood, will you?"

"Will," Gi replied.

Poco left their temporary camp and climbed the steep, mossy slope to the west of the hollow. When she reached the top of the rise, she could see the small stream down on the other side of the ridge.

She filled the flagons in the stream and turned to go back the way she had come, but out of the corner of her eye she saw a large patch of sunlight through the trees. Giving in to the desire to feel the warmth of the sun after days in the chilly shadows under the giant abans, she followed the stream to a small, open field where the water dropped over a series of shallow, shale steps leading to a natural rock basin.

Poco stepped out into the sunshine and stood looking down at the water. No more than three times her height either in length or width, the small basin did not appear to be very deep. She smiled at the thought of a much needed bath and took a careful look around the glen, quickly walking the circumference of the basin to check for animal prints.

She set the water flagons down and quickly stripped. The water was cold but she discovered that on one side of the rock basin the water was shallow and sun-warmed. She stretched out on a rock shelf that was partly submerged, and closed her eyes.

Time slipped by until Poco finally decided that she had lingered long enough. She got out of the water and sat on the rim of the basin, feeling clean and refreshed. She was humming softly to herself when suddenly she heard something behind her.

"That is the first time I have heard you sing since that night on the plains."

Poco jumped at the sound of Dhal's voice. He stood on the ledge of rock above the basin.

"Are you alone?" she asked, searching for Taav. "Anything wrong?"

"No, nothing wrong." Dhal walked down the steps to the edge of the basin. "But you were gone longer than you promised and Screech was getting worried. I came back just as he was about to go looking for you. I told him I would."

Dhal squatted down beside her and put his hand into the water. "How is the water?"

"Wonderful," she answered, reaching for her clothes.

"It looks good. I would not mind a bath myself."

Poco smiled. "No one is stopping you."

As Dhal stripped and stepped into the pool, Poco asked him what, if anything, he had found for their supper.

"It is a surprise," he said, lowering himself into the water.

"I'll bet!" Poco laughed.

Dhal went under the water to wet his hair, which was getting longer every week. Soon, Poco realized, he could begin braiding it as was the Ni custom.

He returned to the surface and blew water from his mouth; then he lay back, floating as free as a leaf in the water.

Poco watched him for a little while then turned to sort out her clothing. Everything was dirty. She hated the very thought of putting her clothes back on the way they were.

"Dhal, is there any reason why we cannot stay here a few days? We could all use the rest, and it would give me a chance to do some washing. My clothes are terrible and your's could not be much better."

There was no answer to her question.

She turned to find Dhal swimming toward her, a smile on his face. "You are beautiful," he said.

Poco arched her eyebrows in question. "Just getting around to noticing that, are you?"

Dhal closed the distance between them and rested on the rock ledge below the water. "Oh, I have noticed," he said. "It's just that seeing you sitting there in the sunshine, naked, your hair wet, you just seem different. It's almost as if I'm seeing you for the first time. You *are* beautiful, Poco."

"One doesn't get a compliment like that every day."

Dhal's smile widened. "Do I get a reward?"

Poco smiled and leaned down to hit the water with her hand, splashing it into his face.

Laughing, he lunged forward just as Poco started to her hands and knees. He caught her by one ankle and pulled her into the water. Poco floundered a moment or two until he let go of her leg, then she righted herself and splashed him again.

Dhal chased Poco to the rock ledge and caught her around the waist. He laughed and demanded his reward. Poco offered only token resistance as he drew her close.

Their surroundings, and the knowledge of the dangers through which they had passed during the last few weeks, had made both Dhal and Poco realize how much they loved each other, and how easily that love could be lost.

Later, they lay together on the grass, their bodies warm against each other, and for a while they talked, forgetting that their friends might be worried about them. Finally the shadows from the trees reached them. Poco sat up and tried to comb her hair with her fingers, an impossible task.

Suddenly she sat a bit straighter and looked quickly around the glen.

"Something wrong?" Dhal asked.

"I suddenly had the feeling that we are being watched."

Dhal's glance swept the circle of trees surrounding

them. "We *are* being watched, Poco," he said softly. "Over there, at the edge of the trees. Look."

Poco looked but all she saw were shadows, then suddenly one of the shadows moved.

Dhal whistled, a sharp up and down warble that ended with a trill on the end. "It's just Gi," he explained. "I told him to come down."

Poco's heartbeat returned to normal when she saw Gi leave the shadows and amble down toward them, following the stream. When he reached the small waterfall, he stopped and peered over the edge.

Poco cast a quick glance at her clothes, then realized that it was much too late for modesty.

She stood, stepped into the water and waded over to the ledge of rock. From that position Gi was almost at eye level with her.

"Would you like to join us, Gi?" she asked. "We were just having a bath."

Gi looked down at Dhal, who was sitting near the edge of the basin, then his glance returned to Poco. Gi's thrumming laughter was a warm and happy sound.

"Gi thinks Poco making under-stay-mint, yes?"

Dhal and Poco exchanged glances, then burst out laughing.

Chapter 18

THE DAYS PASSED QUICKLY AS DHAL, POCO, AND THEIR small band climbed higher and deeper into the Chengarry Mountains. Screech regained most of his strength and again took a position in the lead, his superior eyesight and keen sense of smell helping them avoid direct confrontations with draak, which they began to sight more and more often.

The mountain draak were smaller than those commonly seen in the flatlands and marshes, but they were faster and therefore far more dangerous. The scarcity of gensvolf also made Poco nervous, for the long-legged carnivore seldom abandoned an area unless the game was gone, or unless something far more dangerous then they drove them off.

The shadowed forest floor was springy with years of fallen leaves and layers of moss. As Poco walked, she could not help but wonder how many men, if any, had ever passed that way. As far as she knew there were no man settlements north of the Reaches. Man eventually might enter the strange brooding forest, she knew, but until he tamed the land he already held, he would probably leave such places to draak—and to whatever other creatures lurked in its shadowed valleys.

Dhal came up from behind. "Everything all right?"

Poco glanced at Taav, who was walking just ahead of her. "If you mean Taav, he is doing fine. If you mean me, I'm feeling edgy—and lonely."

Dhal dropped his arm around her shoulders. "I'm here, Poco, and Screech and Gi. You certainly are not alone."

"I know. It's just this place, the trees, and the shadows. They seem to go on forever. We climb and climb and everything seems to stay the same. I am beginning to wonder if this mountain has a top."

"It does," he assured her with a smile, "and we will find it."

"And when we reach the top? What then?" she asked.

Dhal's smile faded. "We look for Jjaan-bi."

"What if we don't find it?"

Dhal looked at her; his face was a study in resolution. "We have to find it, Poco! Either we find Jjaan-bi, or we will have to try the world gate again."

Screech chose the base of a large, climbable aban tree for their night camp. Following a supper of wild root stew and hot rayil tea, Gi and Screech refilled the water flagons from the small stream they had been following for three days. Poco and Dhal sorted through the wildland foods they had gathered along the trail. They had been lucky in their daily search for food, though Poco was growing tired of nabob root and clingor-vine soup; both were too bitter for her taste.

She sat with her back against the aban tree and closed her eyes, dreaming of draak steak and boiled nida and a tall glass of wine. In the past few days she had also developed a craving for jarri, a hard, crystal candy with a soft mint center, imported from Amla-Bagor.

Poco heard Dhal speak to Screech and Gi-arobi, who

had just returned from the stream. She opened her eyes and looked at the derkat.

"Did you see anything, Screech?" she asked aloud.

He shook his head.

"Dhal, don't you think it odd that we have not been bothered by any gensvolf since we entered the mountains?" Poco asked.

Dhal looked up. "Odd, yes, but explainable, I think. Draak and gensvolf both hunt the same game. With the number of draak we have seen these past few days, I would say that the gensvolf have sought a better hunting territory, where there is less competition for food."

Poco glanced at the silent forest surrounding them; she continued to feel that they were being watched, a feeling that her companions had begun to share.

Night closed in. The forest was still but for the tiny rustling noises made by small night creatures. The snapping of a branch startled Poco. She opened her eyes and saw Screech adding branches to the fire.

"Awake, Poco?" Dhal asked.

She turned and saw him watching her from across the fire. His eyes reflected the gold of the flames. His expression betrayed his thoughts—he too was worried about the watchers.

Poco shivered in the chill of the night air. "How many do you think are out there, Dhal?"

He hesitated a moment. "More than one, less than twenty," he answered.

They had discussed the watchers earlier that day. Dhal thought that the watchers might be men from the Reaches, out hunting—but if they were men, why had they not made their presence known?

Screech returned to his place beside Poco and signed to Dhal. *"Best to keep double watch tonight."*

Dhal nodded. "Will you and Gi take fire watch, Screech?"

"Yes."

"Screech, do you think those who watch us could be derkat?" Poco asked.

"*No. I would smell them.*"

"You don't smell the watchers?"

"*Smell them, yes,*" he answered. "*Draak smell, but not draak.*"

Poco shook her head. "They smell like draak, but they are not draak; they number as many as twenty, yet they leave no tracks. What are we dealing with?"

"Whoever or whatever they are, I believe they are intelligent," Dhal said. "And they are not about to let themselves be seen until they think the time is right."

"Do you think they could be Ni?"

"Anything is possible, Poco. I just hope that if and when they decide to introduce themselves, they will do it peacefully."

He glanced at Taav, who sat with his back to the fire staring out into the darkness. Poco followed the direction of Dhal's gaze and felt a strange foreboding enter her heart as she looked at Taav.

Taav's awareness of the watchers was disquieting. Until two days before he had shown little interest in his surroundings and had followed passively wherever his companions had led. But something had changed. Twice he had left the trail without warning, striking out in a direction that would take him back toward the foothills. Poco and Dhal had not thought too much about the occurrence the first time it happened, believing Taav had simply seen a bird or something that had caught his attention; but after chasing him down a third time, they had decided that Taav's strange behavior was related somehow to the watchers, whoever or whatever they were.

"I wonder what he sees out there?" Poco said softly.

"With his eyes he can see no more than we can," Dhal replied. "But I think he is using more than his eyes at the moment."

"What do you mean?"

"Poco, I am firmly convinced that Taav is what Retath

called a Sensitive and I believe that his special talent may lie in perceiving things that are invisible to others."

"Such as world gates?" Poco suggested.

"Yes." Dhal looked at the atich-ar. "Taav may not actually be able to see those who watch us, but I would bet that he could tell us something about them if we could get him to sign to us again."

Poco shook her head. If only the derkat had not frightened him; if only she had the time to stop and work with him. She felt frustrated at her inability to reach Taav.

Gi patted her arm.

"Want something, Gi?" Poco asked, looking down.

"Poco sing?" he asked.

She smiled at him. "You never get enough, do you?"

"I think he has a good idea, Poco," Dhal said. "Sing us a song. Perhaps you can take Taav's mind off whoever is out there. Who knows, once they hear you sing they might like it so much that they will come visiting."

Poco frowned. "Either that or they will start throwing rocks at us."

"*Sing*," Screech signed. *"Make you feel better."*

Poco yielded. "What would you like to hear, Gi?"

"Sing song about Galen running, yes," he answered.

Poco nodded. "Galen on the Run" was an old seafaring song which had twelve verses and a hand-clapping chorus. She sang the first verse, then warned everyone that they were to help her with the chorus.

Screech kept the beat with his hands and hummed along as Dhal and Gi-arobi joined her in singing. By the time they had reached the seventh verse, Gi was up and dancing, his hopping so comical that Poco was having a hard time not laughing. The only one who seemed not to be enjoying himself was Taav, who still sat with his back to them. For once Poco's singing did not reach him.

Suddenly he stood up and ran off into the darkness.

Screech was the first to move. He cleared the fire in one bound and was lost to sight a moment later.

Dhal grabbed up a lighted branch with one hand, his

sword with the other. "Come on, Poco! No one stays behind!" he cried. "Gi! Stay with us!"

Following Dhal's example, Poco scooped up Screech's sword and another burning branch, then she and Gi-arobi headed into the darkness. Somewhere ahead Dhal was calling to Screech, warning him to be careful. Soon she saw the flickering light of his crude torch.

"I have lost them," Dhal said, as she came running up.

Together they listened, straining to hear any sounds that would tell them which way Screech and Taav had gone.

Poco looked down. "Gi? Gi, where are you?"

The olvaar did not answer her call.

"He was just ahead of me, Dhal," Poco said.

Dhal loosed a whistle that carried high and clear. Gi's trilling whistle answered immediately.

Dhal turned toward the sound. "This way, Poco! Follow me and stay close!"

Poco silently cursed Taav as she jogged behind Dhal's shadowy figure. We should have left him where we found him, she thought.

"Something up ahead, Poco," Dhal said. "It's Gi—and Screech. He is down!"

A knot of fear tightened in Poco's stomach as she ran after Dhal. A moment later she was kneeling beside Screech and holding a lighted branch close enough so Dhal could see what was wrong with the derkat.

Screech stirred. He rolled over and shook his head and struggled to sit up, but Dhal held him back.

"Lie still, Screech," Dhal said. "Let me see what is wrong. No! Lie still!"

Screech growled but settled back onto the ground. Dhal laid his hands on Screech's head and slowly moved one hand to the back of the dekat's neck. A minute or so passed, then Dhal withdrew his hands.

"He will be all right, Poco," Dhal said. "He just took a knock on the back of his head. No internal bleeding. Help me get him up. We will take him back to camp."

"What about Taav?" Poco asked.

"He is on his own for the moment. We have done enough running around in the darkness. Come morning we will see if we can find his trail, but I am afraid by then it will be too late."

"You think the watchers have him?"

"Taav didn't knock Screech down, Poco. Whoever did it probably has Taav now."

The thought of the gentle, passive Taav in the hands of the mysterious watchers made Poco feel guilty. "We should have watched him closer—tied him up."

"It's too late to start thinking about that now, Poco," Dhal said. "Taav is gone and the only thing we can do now is try to find his trail in the morning."

"Do you think we can?"

"I don't know. It will depend upon Screech and whether or not he feels up to it," Dhal answered.

Screech growled an affirmative.

The fire had died down by the time they returned to camp, but they could see that things were not as they had left them.

Dhal swore. "Damn them! They have taken our packs!"

Poco built up the fire while Dhal investigated.

"Food, weapons, they have taken everything," Dhal snapped. "Poco, have you still got your knife?"

"Yes."

"Well, that means we have two swords and one knife and not much else. I wish I knew who the watchers are." Dhal turned to the derkat. "Screech, did you get a look at them?"

"No. They fell on me from above."

"How many?" Dhal asked.

"Two. They ran when they heard you coming."

"Did you hear them speak? Did they make any kind of noises?"

"No."

"Gi, did you see—" Dhal looked around quickly,

realizing that they were missing someone besides Taav. "Gi?"

Remembering the last time she had seen the olvaar, Poco plucked another branch from the fire and started back the way they had come.

Dhal caught her by the arm. "No, Poco, come back to the fire."

"But Gi is still out there!"

Dhal looked at her, a worried expression on his face. "I know," he said softly. "But there is nothing we can do in the dark. We will just have to wait for him to come back. Gi is smart. He won't let himself be caught."

"What could he be doing?"

"If I know Gi, he has decided to do some investigating on his own. If he is careful, he may just discover who these watchers are," Dhal said.

Poco felt a sinking sensation in the pit of her stomach. And if he isn't careful, she thought, we will have to rescue two instead of one. Damn it, Gi! Why didn't you stay with us?

Chapter 19

*P*OCO WOKE TO A HAND ACROSS HER MOUTH.

"Wake up, Poco," Dhal whispered urgently. "Gi is back."

Poco opened her eyes and saw Dhal leaning over her.

She nodded and sat up as he drew away his hand. Her eyes quickly adjusted to the murky half-light of morning.

She saw Gi-arobi and reached out to brush a hand over the top of his head. "Are you all right, Gi?"

Gi whistled softly, reassuringly.

Dhal cautioned Poco to keep her voice low. "Gi says there are watchers all around us now."

"Did he find out who they are?" she whispered.

"He says they have the form of man or Ni and they dress in draak hide."

"Did you get close enough to hear them speak, Gi?" Poco asked.

"No," Gi answered. "If draakmen speak, Gi not hearing it."

"How many are there?" she asked.

"Many hand counts, yes."

Dahl spoke. "Gi, did you see what kind of weapons they carry?"

Gi bobbed his head. "Long knives, some. Also hitting sticks."

"Did you see Taav?" Poco asked.

Gi shook his head. "Looking but not seeing."

Screech walked around behind Dhal. The derkat had been pacing restlessly, his attention on the nearby trees and bushes.

Poco turned to Dhal. "What do we do?"

"Wait until it gets lighter; then if they don't come to us, Screech will have to try and find Taav's trail."

"If he cannot?"

"Either we go on without Taav, or we sit down and wait until the draakmen get tired of hiding and decide to make their presence known."

They chose to wait. But when the shadowed light under the trees finally showed glints of sunshine, Dhal signaled Screech that it was time to go. "No sense in waiting any longer," he said. "If there is any finding to be done, it looks like we have to do it."

Screech growled softly. His tail twitched back and forth with impatience.

Poco and Dhal trusted to the keener senses of their two furred companions to warn them of danger, but as they walked along, they kept an eye on the branches overhead, remembering that Screech had been attacked from above.

Twice Screech crouched close to the ground, sniffing for Taav's scent. The second time, he turned and signed that he had lost the atich-ar's trail.

"*Stay where you are,*" he told them. "*I will circle.*"

Gi, Dhal, and Poco drew close together and stood quietly watching as the derkat walked a wide arc ahead of them. Screech widened the pattern, extending his search until he moved out of sight around a large clump of bushes near two aban trees.

Suddenly a derkat cry of rage filled the air. Dhal, Poco, and Gi ran toward the place where they had seen Screech last.

Poco swore. "Damn it! I knew we should have stayed together!"

A few seconds later they pushed through the barrier of branches and came upon a scene neither would ever forget: Screech was rolling on the ground, claws and teeth tearing at the vine which covered him.

The six men who controlled the netting, if men they were, were having a hard time holding down the derkat. The strangers wore leggings and sleeveless tunics made of tanned draak hide; their masklike head coverings, which obscured all but their mouths and lower jaws, were also made of hide.

"They are unarmed, Poco!" Dhal cried, as he started forward. "Use your sword!"

There was no time for thought. Poco followed Dhal as he closed on the draakmen.

Poco raised her sword and came up behind one of the draakmen holding Screech, but before she could strike, something dropped in front of her, knocking her sword down. That blur of motion solidified into another of the draakmen, armed with a stout branch that he whirled in front of her face.

Ducking, Poco lashed out at the draakman's legs. He stepped to the left and blocked her sword with his staff. The thunk of metal against wood was audible even above Screech's yowling.

Fingers stinging with the shock of the counterblow, Poco jumped backward as her opponent aimed a blow at her side. She brought her sword up to a guard position, trying to ignore the hideous mask as she concentrated on the staff the draakman wielded so dexterously.

Out of the corner of her eye, Poco saw that Dhal was having a similar problem—only doubled! She danced back a few steps to give herself a moment's breathing space. Her opponent followed, his staff flipping from hand to hand and always before him, ready to block her next thrust.

Gi whistled a warning just as the draakman facing Poco lifted his voice in a high fluting call that brought more reinforcements.

A moment later Poco was grabbed from behind. Recalling some tactics she had learned from one of her friends on the docks, she stamped down on the draakman's foot. He grunted in pain but did not let go. Poco doubled over and drew the draakman off balance, then twisted out of his hold.

She turned just as the first draakman came at her from the side to hit her on the left shoulder with his staff. She cried out and fell to the ground, pain lancing through her chest and neck. She felt herself sliding into a darkened world and fought to remain conscious.

Her next awareness was of a solid weight sitting on her back. She tried to roll over, but failed to dislodge the draakman who straddled her body. One of the draakmen picked up her sword. Another went past her to help with the net holding Screech.

As she was hauled to her feet, Poco saw Dhal on the ground, also a prisoner. He looked at her and for a moment she saw anger on his face; then it was gone, replaced by an alertness that told her that he was already searching for a way out.

She turned and looked at Screech, who was being quickly and efficiently wrapped in vine netting. The draakmen secured the derkat's arms first, then cut the netting over his head and pulled it away from his eyes. The rumble of anger which issued from Screech's throat made the draakmen handle their quarry with the utmost caution. One of them placed a vine rope over Screech's head and drew the rope tight. Screech let loose with a yowl that echoed around the hills.

Another draakman was holding Gi by the scruff of his

neck. The olvaar's whistle of protest ended in a fit of coughing.

Fearing Gi might choke to death, Poco kicked the draakman on her right. The toe of her shoe found a solid target on his shin. The draakman gasped and released her.

Poco jerked free and ran up to the draakman who held Gi.

"Stop it!" she yelled. "You are hurting him! Give him to me!"

The masked draakman just looked at her. Two others closed on Poco from behind, but did not touch her as she reached for the olvaar.

She cradled Gi in her arms and gently massaged the back of his neck. "Are you all right, Gi?"

Gi whistled yes, then added, "What we do now?"

A hand closed on Poco's hair, jerking her head back.

"Keep him quiet or he will be taken from you! Understood?" The words were in trader.

Poco looked at the draakman who had spoken, and nodded. He released her hair and walked over to stand before Dhal.

"You are Ni," the draakman said. The statement sounded to Poco like an accusation.

Dhal hesitated, then nodded, knowing that he would gain nothing by denying the obvious.

"You have strange companions," the draakman said. He glanced at Screech. "Very strange and very dangerous. Who are you? Where do you come from?"

"My name is Dhalvad. My friends and I come from Annaroth and Port Bhalvar. We—"

"Sarissa!" the draakman hissed.

"No! No, we are not Sarissa! We were chased from our homes by the Sarissa!" Dhal protested.

The draakman just stared at Dhal; his silence was unnerving. Poco felt a chill down her back as she looked at the other draakmen standing around them. Their masks made it impossible to read their reactions to Dhal's statement.

Dhal spoke angrily. "Tell us who *you* are! Why do you attack us? What wrong have we done?"

The draakman's voice dropped to a threatening tone. "You are where you should not be! You were attacked because you failed to give the code for passage!"

"What code?" Dhal demanded.

"If you were a friend, you would know the code," the draakman responded.

Poco's curiosity was pricked by the slight accent with which the draakman spoke trades. Who were these people and why were they guarding this shadowy forest?

Dhal looked intently at the draakman standing before him, trying to pierce the shadows created by the man's mask.

"We did not mean to trespass," Dhal said, his tone less hostile. "We were on our way to the great freshwater lake beyond the mountains. We are not exactly sure where it lies, but we were told—"

"Why do you wish to go to this lake?" the draakman interrupted.

"We search for a legend," Dhal answered evasively.

The draakman looked at Dhal a moment, then turned and signaled to those who held Screech.

"Get the derkat on his feet and keep a close watch on him. Make sure those vines are tight. We have far to go and I do not want him to get loose."

Poco stepped forward and spoke to the one draakman who seemed to be in command. "We have come far and we mean you no harm. Please, all we ask is that you return our friend to us and let us go on our way. You have our word that we will not linger in your territory any longer than is absolutely necessary."

The draakman waved her to silence.

"I have heard you. You are not guests here, but prisoners. You will come with us and do as you are told. There will be no bargains made. Also, there will be no talking among you or you will be gagged as well as tied."

"Where are you taking us?" Dhal asked.

"Where we have taken your friend. He has not been harmed. Nor will you be, as long as you obey all of my commands."

Chapter 20 ◄

A FEW HOURS OF STEADY CLIMBING BROUGHT THE
draakmen and their prisoners to a large open meadow,
in the middle of which stood a tower of gray-green stone,
rising above the tops of the nearest aban trees. The word
watchtower entered Poco's mind as soon as she saw the
building.

She nudged Dhal in the side with her elbow. "Dhal,
what does it remind you of?"

Dhal answered without turning. "The Ni-lach tower in
Port Bhalvar, only this one is still intact."

"And occupied," Poco added, keeping her voice low.

One of the draakmen left the shelter of the trees and
walked toward the tower. Dhal turned to Poco. "Are you
thinking what I am?" he whispered.

"That the Ni-lach built the tower?"

"Yes," he answered.

"Now all we have to figure out is who these draakmen

are and why they came into possession of what was obviously once Ni territory."

The single draakman approached the tower and disappeared around a flight of steps at the base of the building. He was gone for some time.

Poco studied the tower, noting the narrow windows spaced unevenly at different levels, the three small balconies facing in different directions.

"If it is like the one in Port Bhalvar," Dhal said, "there should be a winding staircase inside that leads to the top. They could see a long distance from up there. That could be how they spotted us."

"I doubt it, Dhal. The trees are too thick for them to have seen us. The tower must have another use."

The head draakman turned and glared at them. "No more talk or you will be gagged," he warned.

Dhal and Poco exchanged glances, but neither was willing to test their captor's patience. They sat down on the ground. Screech and Gi also settled down once it became evident that they were going to have a long wait.

With nothing else to do, Poco studied the hideous masks that the draakmen wore. She wondered how the masks were formed, what kind of special pastes had been used to give them the appearance of folded layers of skin. The colors ranged from dark brown to green-blue. The eye sockets in each mask were outlined with a black pigment, which gave the draakmen the appearance of walking dead.

Why the masks? she wondered. What secret do they guard so carefully?

The single draakman returned from the tower about two hours later. Poco, Dhal, and the others were ordered to their feet and soon they were walking again, winding their way past the stone tower and upward along a tree-shaded trail that looked well used.

By midday the lead draakman ordered the prisoners blindfolded, including Gi-arobi, who now rode in a makeshift shoulder pouch that Dhal had fashioned. Though strong and healthy, Gi's short legs were no match for the pace set by the quick-striding draakmen.

By late afternoon Poco was exhausted by the effort of walking blind, and she was relieved to hear the lead draakman call for a halt. Someone pulled down on Poco's arms, indicating that she should sit.

"Feed them and give them something to drink," the lead draakman said, as he passed by. "And see that their eyes remain covered."

Poco thought to protest, but then decided that it would not do any good. She ate the food that was placed in her hands: small, chewy balls of dough that tasted of salt, ardu nuts, and honey; dried kansa, a fruit common only to marshlands; and smooth paton wine.

The rest was brief—the draakmen seemed in a hurry to press on.

The climbing became steeper as the day wore on, then suddenly leveled off. Poco was glad for the respite, for the back of her legs ached with the strain of the climb. She noticed the warmth of sun on her back and decided that they had finally left the forest behind. But shortly they were again plunged into the coolness of shadows.

The damp air that hit her neck and face told Poco that they had entered some kind of a cave. The draakmen who walked to either side of Poco held her arms tightly as the floor began to slant downward. Were they protecting her from a fall, she wondered, or was there opportunity for escape? With her eyes covered she had no way to tell.

Curiosity finally got the better of her. Lifting her bound wrists, she pretended to scratch her cheek. In the process, one of her fingers caught in a fold of the cloth covering her eyes and she tugged the blindfold down.

Her vision was blurred for a few seconds. The bouncing torchlight cast grotesque shadows on cave walls.

Suddenly one of the draakmen saw that her blindfold had slipped. He quickly pulled the cloth back into place, then squeezed her arm until Poco winced. She realized that he was warning her to behave.

Who were these draakmen? Where were they being taken? The two questions went round and round in her mind until she grew disgusted with herself.

She soon lost track of the time. She knew they had been in the cave longer than an hour, but beyond that she would have been guessing. The darkness and repetitive shuffle of feet disoriented her.

Suddenly she heard a strange buzzing in her ears, and a moment later she was falling. Hands caught her, lowering her to the floor. She was aware of someone cursing, then darkness claimed her.

Poco woke to find herself lying flat on her back. Dhal was leaning over her. He sat back when he saw that her eyes were open. He looked worried.

"Are you all right, Poco?"

"What happened?" she asked.

"I think you fainted."

"Fainted?" Her disbelief was plain.

Dhal nodded.

"But I have never fainted!" she protested.

"Well you have now," Dhal replied. "I think you surprised everyone, especially me. I didn't know you were the fainting type."

"I'm not!" she snapped, sitting up. "At least, I never was before."

"Never mind, Poco, it doesn't matter," Dhal said. "I want you to lie back down for a minute, so I can check you over."

She pushed his hands away. "No! I am fine!"

"I want to make sure," Dhal said firmly.

"No!"

Suddenly Screech stepped into view. He had been standing behind the raised pallet upon which Poco lay. He leaned over and pushed her back down on the pallet.

"*You will let the Healer see what is wrong with you*," he signed.

"There is nothing wrong with me!"

Screech would accept no argument. He signed that she was to stay where he had put her, then he touched Dhal's shoulder, signaling that the Healer should continue with his examination.

Dhal nodded to Screech, then turned back to Poco. "I wish I could make you behave that easily," he said.

Poco made a face, consciously biting back words that would be better left unsaid.

Dhal leaned over and kissed her. "If there is anything wrong with you, I will find it," he promised.

"I am just tired and hungry," she answered. "Hunger can make people faint."

"I know," Dhal agreed. "But let's make sure, all right?"

Poco knew what Dhal meant to do, but she had never experienced his healing touch and was hesitant.

"Where are we?" she asked, trying to delay the inevitable.

Dhal glanced around the small cell. The walls were dark stone, the single door was wood.

"My guess is that we are somewhere inside the mountain," he said. He leaned across her and brushed his fingertips against the wall; they came away wet. "Quite a way underground, if I'm not wrong."

"Dhal, what do you think they will do with us?" Poco asked.

"I don't know. I have thought of several possibilities, but until I know more about these draakmen, I would only be guessing."

Screech growled softly to get their attention.

"*They have the smell of Utura trappers*," he signed. "*If we do not escape soon, we may find ourselves separated and sold to the highest bidder at some slave market.*"

The word slave made Poco freeze inside. She had seen the cruelty of slavery in Port Sulta and Port Bhalvar, and

the prospect of joining the ranks of slaves who served
Sarissa masters made her close her eyes and pray for some
kinder fate.

Dhal took her hands. "Poco, look at me. I know what
you are thinking, but it has not happened yet. We may
not be free, but we are together and we do not know that
these draakmen are slavers."

Poco nodded. "Right. Don't jump overboard until the
boat is ready to sink."

"What?"

"Something Trass used to say to me," she responded,
memory of the old half-blood softening the worry lines
on her forehead.

Dhal released her hands. "Are you ready to let me
check you over now?"

"Yes, I suppose so," she answered. "Will I feel anything?"

"No, I don't think so, but I could make you sleep if
you would prefer."

She shook her head. "No, I want to stay awake."

Dhal moved his hands up and down the length of her
body, not quite touching her. She stifled a nervous urge
to giggle and took several deep breaths, trying to relax.

She looked around, trying to ignore Dhal's healing
touch. The small room was lighted by three glowing clumps
of fayyal rocks, the luminescent sea rocks that the upper-
class Sarissa used instead of oil lanterns in their homes.

Dhal quickly finished his examination and slowly raised
his head. A smile lighted his face.

"Well?" Poco said.

Dhal leaned down and whispered, "You are pregnant."

Poco's mouth dropped open in surprise. Her thoughts
flicked over the days and weeks they had spent crossing
the plains and she realized that she had lost track of time.
"Really, Dhal?"

"Really," he answered, laughing.

Disbelief, dismay, pleasure—a variety of emotions

surged through her. Her last feelings were of happiness. Sitting up, she went into Dhal's arms and held him tight.

"Happy?" he whispered in her ear.

She laughed. "Yes, though it is the last thing we need at this moment!"

"Don't worry, things will work out." He hugged her. "I love you, Poco!"

"And I you!"

Gi whistled for attention. "What wrong with Poco?" he asked, looking from one to the other.

"Nothing, Gi," Dhal answered, smiling. "Nothing at all."

"Singer is not ill?" Screech asked.

Dhal shook his head. "She is not ill, Screech. She is pregnant."

Gi let loose with a shrill whistle that was all but lost in Ssaal-lr's triumphant roar.

Suddenly the door to the cell opened. At Gi's whistled warning, Screech whirled and faced the two draakmen who entered the cell. The derkat's growl halted the two men in the shadow of the doorway and for a few seconds no one moved. Then slowly, one of the men moved into the cell; he wore no mask.

Dhal jumped to his feet, his attention riveted on the draakman's green hair.

"You are Ni!" he cried softly, hardly daring to believe.

The Ni turned and spoke to the draakman behind him. "Take your mask off, Paa-tol, and come in, please."

Poco and Dhal watched as the second draakman untied the lacing that held his hide mask in place.

Gi whistled his excitement as the mask was removed and the second man entered the cell: Paa-tol was also one of the Green Ones.

The first Ni glanced at Screech, then stepped toward Dhal. The draak-hide costume he wore was similar to that worn by the other draakmen except for the silver-colored chest harness and a red draak-hide sheath that held a sword with intricate carvings on the hilt. His waist-length green braids told Poco that he was of some importance among his people.

"My name is Chulu," he said. "I am leader of the Gerri Mountain Draak Watch. You will give me your names please."

Dhal hesitated then said, "I am called Dhalvad. I am foster son to Haradan sar Nath."

"Haradan? Is that not a Sarissa name?" the old Ni asked.

"Haradan was not Sarissa," Dhal replied. "Twice he saved me from the Sarissa, once when I was a little child, and again a few months ago while we were in the Mountains of the Lost in Val-hrodhur. He died doing it!"

Chulu's eyes narrowed. "You have been in Val-hrodhur that recently? All of you?"

"Yes, but we found it deserted. That is why we came here. We are looking for the Ni of Jjaan-bi. Do you know of them?"

Chulu glanced at Paa-tol, then turned back to Dhal. "*We* are the Ni-lach of Jjaan-bi."

"This is Jjaan-bi?" Dhal asked, confused.

Chulu nodded. "A part of it." He gestured to Dhal with his hand. "Come with me. We will talk."

Dhal straightened. "I go nowhere without my friends. We will not be separated except by force."

Screech growled, emphasizing Dhal's statement.

Both Ni looked at the derkat, then Chulu looked at Poco. "Can the woman walk?" he asked Dhal.

"Yes," Dhal answered. "If it isn't too far."

"What is wrong with her?" Paa-tol asked.

"Nothing," Dhal replied. "She was just tired."

"May I ask what you were doing to her when we entered?" Chulu asked.

Dhal glanced at the door and for the first time noticed several small holes at eye level. "How long have you been watching us?" he demanded.

"Long enough. Will you answer my question, please?"

Dhal hesitated then, deciding that the truth would serve

better than a lie, he answered. "I am a Healer, saan. I was checking to see if she—"

"Did you say *Healer*?" Chulu's surprise was evident.

"Yes, and a very good one," Poco answered. She swung her legs off the raised pallet and stood beside Dhal. "It's what got us started in this hunt for legends."

Chulu looked confused.

"The legend of the Tamorlee," Poco explained. "The Sarissa believed it was a vast treasure trove. They tried to find it by following Dhal, only he didn't know any more about it than they did. We came to—"

"Do you let the Sarissa woman do your talking for you?" Paa-tol demanded. His eyes were narrowed in anger as he looked at Dhal.

"Poco speaks when and where she will," Dhal responded softly. If the look in his eyes was not threat enough, the tone of Dhal's voice should have warned Paa-tol that he was swimming in dangerous waters.

Before Poco could do or say anything to ease the tension, Chulu intervened. "Everyone will be given a chance to speak, Paa-tol. Please, go and see to our escort."

Paa-tol accepted Chulu's subtle rebuke with a stiff nod and stepped out of the cell to speak with someone waiting beyond the doorway. His words were in Ni. A few minutes later Dhal, Poco, and their two furred companions were being herded down a stone corridor lighted with fayyal rocks.

Poco leaned close to Dhal as they walked along. "The Ni seem to have a liking for caves and tunnels," she said softly. "This is very much like Val-hrodhur."

"Such places are safe from draak and gensvolf," Dhal pointed out. "And they are easy to defend."

"True, but would you like living the rest of your life in stone tunnels?"

"No," Dhal replied. "I love the forests too much. Don't worry, Poco, you won't lose me to another way of life. I promise."

But is that a promise you can keep, my love? Poco wondered.

They followed their guides down the twisting corridors, then were ushered through a large, wooden portal into an oval meeting room lined with wood benches.

At the far end of the room was a raised platform upon which lay a beautifully woven rug in Ni colors of blue and green. Poco's gaze traced the lines of color in toward the center of the rug to the image of a large seven-pointed star, the same symbol they had found in the sun chamber in Val-hrodhur.

Chulu waved them to a seat and turned to speak to Paa-tol. Poco could not hear what was being said, but the ten guards backed off and took positions along the walls. The look Paa-tol gave her as he joined the guard was anything but friendly. For the first time since joining Dhal, Poco wondered if her being a half-blood was going to be a detriment to Dhal's reunion with his people. If the Ni did not trust her, would they trust Dhal? She could not really blame them if they didn't. After all, the war with the Sarissa had cost them many lives.

Chulu sat down on the rug opposite Dhal and glanced at Screech and Gi-arobi.

"You have some very interesting companions, Dhalvad," Chulu said, speaking trader. "The furred ones seldom choose company other than their own."

"My companions may seem strange to you, saan," Dhal answered carefully, "but there is trust and love between us. In the absence of others they have become my family."

"I see." Chulu looked at Poco, then turned back to Dhal. "Would you introduce me to your friends, please?"

Dhal looked to his left and indicated Screech. "This is Ssaal-lr."

Screech coughed a greeting that Chulu imitated, demonstrating that derkat customs were recognized by the mountain Ni.

"Beside him is Gi-arobi," Dhal continued. "Gi and I

lived in the Deep, a marshland north of Annaroth. We have been friends a long time."

Gi whistle-clicked a greeting, but this time Chulu did not respond in kind.

"I don't think he understood you, Gi," Dhal said.

Gi cocked his head to one side, then stood up and strode forward to stand close to Chulu's leg. "Gi saying avto, Chulu. Happy being here. Long time coming, yes."

Chulu looked bemused. "I don't believe I have ever heard of the fur children speaking trader," he said. "Is it a common occurrence in this Deep of yours?"

"No. I think Gi has taught a few of his friends to speak trader, but most of them just use their own language."

"Do *you* understand the olvaar whistle tongue?"

"Yes," Dhal answered.

"There are a few of us who have taken the time to learn the olvaar tongue, but not many. The olvaar are few in this territory."

Chulu's glance lifted from the olvaar and came to rest on Poco.

Dhal took Poco's hand. "This is Pocalina-fel-Jamba, my mate."

"Is she Sarissa?"

Dhal looked at Poco. "I think I will let her answer that, saan."

"I am half-blood Ni," Poco said. "My father's name was Askel. He was killed during the Sarissa war against our people."

"*Our* people? Do you consider yourself Ni then?"

"Yes, part of me," she answered.

"And your loyalty lies where?"

"With Dhal," she replied firmly.

Chulu looked at Dhal. "How long have you known her?"

"Half a year," Dhal responded.

"You believe that she is Ni, or at least part Ni?"

"Yes."

"Because she told you so?"

"Because she is." Softly, softly came that last answer. Dhal obviously did not like the direction of the questioning.

But Chulu was not about to let Dhal's anger put him off. "You must admit that she hasn't the look of the Nilach. How do you know she shares our heritage? What proof does she offer?"

"I know because I have heard her sing," Dhal said. "It is all the proof I need!"

Chulu again glanced at Poco. "Her singing is special in some way?"

"Yes!"

"How?" Chulu demanded.

Poco could see that Dhal was barely holding onto his temper. "You need not explain anything to him, Dhal," she said. "Not when he uses that tone of voice!"

"Do you know about world gates, Chulu?" Dhal asked. "Do you know about the Singers who can find and open those gates? Poco *is* such a Singer!" Dhal paused, then continued. "We have come far in search of the Tamorlee, and we have discovered some very unusual things along the way. I have learned to use a Seeker ring and have traveled to the world of the Ancients; I have learned about the Ral-jenobb and believe there is a link between them and mankind; I have heard Poco sing of other places and seen them live in her chalk pictures; and we have met an old Ni who claimed that he was once a Seeker, one of those responsible for taking the Tamorlee to safety in another world! He died while trying to escape the atichar who followed us back through the world gate!"

Poco squeezed Dhal's arm, trying to warn him that he was saying too much.

He ignored her. "We did not come this far to betray you to your enemies!" Dhal said. "We came to learn, and to warn you of danger! If what the old Ni said was true, you have more than the Sarissa to worry about! And that says nothing about the return of the Tamorlee! It isn't here is it? It's lost to you, but we know where it can be found!"

Chulu silently studied Dhal, as if gauging the truth behind his statements. Not a flicker of emotion touched his face as he looked from Dhal to Poco, then on to Screech and Gi.

Chulu turned and summoned Paa-tol.

"Go and find Tidul and Amet," Chulu said, when Paa-tol stopped before him. "Tell them—" Chulu hesitated. "—tell them it concerns the Tamorlee."

Paa-tol left and Chulu turned to Dhal. "You said that you are a Healer. Judging from what you said just moments ago, you also claim to be a Seeker." Chulu's voice had softened. "Is this true?"

Dhal nodded stiffly, not yet ready to lower his guard.

"You are extremely gifted then, almost impossibly so," Chulu said. "Those I have sent for will be better able to judge your claims than I. While we wait for them, would you allow me to see your ring?"

Dhal glanced at Poco. She nodded and he slipped the Seeker ring from his finger.

Chulu was still studying the ring when Paa-tol returned. With him were two more Ni, their braids of authority falling to their chests. Chulu apparently had called in others of equal rank to help him sort out the truth.

Chapter 21

POCO UNCROSSED HER LEGS AND STRETCHED, EASING cramped muscles. The floor, even covered with a rug, was a hard surface on which to sit for so long. She was tired and thirsty, and she was becoming impatient.

Amet held out his hand. "May I look at the pendant you found in Val-hrodhur, Pocalina?"

Poco drew the chain and pendant over her head and handed them to the thin-faced Ni at Chulu's right. She then glanced at Dhal, who looked as tired as she felt. Their story had taken him hours to tell, due to the continuing barrage of questions put to him by the three Ni.

When Tidul opened his mouth to ask another question, Poco began to wonder if he would ever be satisfied. Tidul was younger than Amet and Chulu, but Ni longevity made it difficult to guess his age. He was heavier in build than Amet and his green hair was so light that it was almost a white-gold.

"I am interested in the elder Ni you met in the atich-ar's world," Tidul said. "What did you say his name was?" The question was addressed to Dhal.

"Retath," Dhal answered.

"And tell us again, what did he say about the atich-ar planning an attack?"

"There wasn't time for long conversations. I told you, we were being chased by—"

"Chulu! Look at this!" Amet interrupted. "Read!" he said, pushing the wood pendant toward Chulu's face. "I know of only one Ni with that name symbol! Zaa-ob, the Singer of Aphicoran, the one who discovered the I-naal gate!"

Chulu took the pendant and carefully studied the glyphs on the back.

"Well," Amet pressed. "It is Zaa-ob's, isn't it?"

Chulu nodded. "It looks like it, but I cannot understand it being found at Val-hrodhur unless—"

"Unless what?" Amet demanded.

Both Ni were speaking their own language now. Poco glanced at Dhal, wondering if he was keeping up with the conversation.

Gray-crystal eyes clouded as Chulu looked at the pendant. "Unless Zaa-ob returned there sometime after we all left."

"But why go back there? Why not come through here instead? After what happened in Val-hrodhur, he must have realized that there would be no one left there to help him."

"He may have had no choice. Think what might have happened if he had opened the I-naal gate and led the atich-ar here."

Tidul broke in. "I have just thought of something. If Zaa-ob did make it back to Val-hrodhur, he could not have come alone. No Singer, even as fine a one as Zaa-ob, could make and hold a gate alone. Who came with him, I wonder, and why haven't we heard from them?"

"The answer to that last question would depend upon

how long his namepiece has been lying there," Chulu said, glancing at Poco.

Dhal interrupted before anyone else could speak. "Please, both Poco and I understand some Ni, but it would be easier for us to understand what is being said if you would speak trader. You *are* talking about the world gate and the moving of the Tamorlee, aren't you?"

The three Ni exchanged glances, then Chulu spoke in trader. "Yes, we are talking about the Tamorlee and about the Ni who had it in their care."

Poco sat a bit straighter, wondering if they were finally going to get some answers to their questions. She realized that the Ni still did not trust her, so she decided to remain quiet and let Dhal do the talking.

"What I told you about the atich-ar in that other world—you already knew about them, didn't you?" Dhal said.

Chulu nodded. "We know about the atich-ar, yes. And we know they are our enemies."

"Were we right about the Tamorlee being taken into the atich-ar's world to safeguard it from the Sarissa?"

"Yes," Chulu said.

Dhal frowned. "Tell us what happened. Why wasn't the Tamorlee brought back to Lach?" When Chulu did not respond immediately, Dhal pressed him. "You did intend to bring it back didn't you?"

"Yes, that was our intention," Chulu responded. "But before we can answer any more of your questions, there is another who must be brought into this. Amet, bring the atich-ar in, will you?"

"Do you mean Taav?" Dhal asked, as Amet stood and walked away.

"Yes, *if* that is his true name," Chulu answered.

Poco and Dhal exchanged glances, then Dhal voiced their shared thought. "What do you mean 'if'? What does his name matter? How can you—"

Poco was one step ahead of Dhal. "You see him as a danger to you. Why?"

"You are very perceptive," Chulu said, addressing Poco directly.

So I am perceptive, Poco thought. Answer my question!

"Is Poco right?" Dhal asked. "Do you see Taav as some kind of a danger?"

"He is atich-ar," Chulu answered.

"But not one of *them*!" Poco said quickly. "Dhal told you how we found him. Taav may not be his right name, but if he has another, he has never been able to tell us what it is."

"Hasn't or won't?" Chulu said softly.

"You would not ask that if you had seen him back in Port Sulta," Poco said, forgetting her intention to remain quiet. "A few weeks ago Taav's mind was little more than that of a pet nida. Since Dhal healed Taav, Taav's mental alertness has improved, but in many ways he is still a child and certainly no danger to anyone, least of all his own people."

Chulu looked at Dhal. "I am most interested in observing your healing gift, Dhalvad, but until I do, I am afraid I must reserve judgment on whether or not the atich-ar was *healed* by you, or was only playing a part."

Dhal frowned. "Are you saying that Taav might be one of the enemy atich-ar from this other world?"

"It is possible. Before the I-naal gate was closed, more than a handful of atich-ar slipped through. It was they who killed the two Sensitives who held the gate on our side and twenty-four more of our people. When the battle was over, all but three of the enemy atich-ar were killed. Those three escaped into the forest near Val-hrodhur. Only one was ever caught. We never learned what happened to the other two."

There was no way Taav could have fooled them this long, Poco felt sure. Dhal would have discovered any attempts at subterfuge long ago—or would he? Dhal's ability to link his mind with the body of another in order to heal did not necessarily mean that he could touch the

thoughts of his host. At least Dhal had never explained
it that way. Still, it would seem that if Taav had been
faking idiocy, Dhal would have sensed it.

Poco's thoughts were interrupted by Amet's return.
Taav looked small and vulnerable walking between Amet
and another Ni. As the three neared the platform, Taav
saw Dhal and immediately began to struggle to free himself. The Ni to Taav's right pulled Taav's arm around and
up in a painful hold. Taav made no noise of protest, but
by the look on his face Poco knew Taav was being hurt.
Then she noticed the gash below his left eye.

She stood up and stepped down from the platform, but
Dhal was already ahead of her. He reached Taav in six
long strides.

"There is no need for that!" Dhal snapped, stopping
before Amet. "Release him to me!"

Amet and the other Ni stiffened at Dhal's tone of voice.
Amet started to say something, then hesitated uncer-
tainly. Who was this strange Ni who claimed to be both
Healer and Seeker? Who came to them with stories of
time travel and world gates? Poco felt she could almost
read Amet's thoughts as he looked to Chulu for direction.

Poco was aware of Screech moving up behind her, his
furred hand coming to rest on her shoulder, but her attention remained on Taav. She could see that he had
sustained several other injuries. Besides the gash under
his eye, his lower lip was cut and swollen and there were
red marks on his neck as if something had been drawn
tight around his throat.

"That split lip looks new," Poco observed.

Amet answered her criticism without turning. "He was
violent yesterday. It took three to subdue him."

Poco glared at the side of Amet's head. "Taav has
never shown himself to be violent, at least not in our care.
May I ask what you were doing to him?"

Amet turned; his crystal eyes were cold with dislike
for anyone linked with the Sarissa. "We were trying to

break through his silence. We had questions we wanted answered."

"And you were not above a little physical persuasion to get those answers were you?" Poco snapped.

Amet started to reply but was interrupted by Chulu. "Enough! What has been done cannot be undone!" Chulu turned to Poco. "If we have made a mistake, we will apologize, but until we know whether or not this atichar is a friend or an enemy, he must be handled with extreme caution. The lives of our friends and the recovery of the Tamorlee are at risk!"

Chulu's words died away and suddenly everyone became aware that Dhal was talking softly to Taav, whose eyes had closed as if he were asleep. Poco knew what Dhal was going to do the moment he raised his hands to cup Taav's face and head.

Well, they wanted a demonstration of his powers, she thought. Now they were going to get one.

Chulu and Tidul moved closer as Dhal closed his eyes to better concentrate on the job before him. Amet opened his mouth to speak, but was waved to silence by Chulu. Poco realized that Chulu, at least, had at some time witnessed a Healer's trance and was willing to let Dhal perform.

Several minutes passed. No one moved or spoke. Suddenly Taav's eyes fluttered open, and a second later Dhal withdrew his hands. Poco caught one quick glimpse of Taav's face and knew that Dhal's healing touch had been successful. Anticipating his need, she moved up behind Dhal and wrapped her arms around his waist. She could feel the tremor in his legs and knew he had to sit down.

"Screech, help me put him over there," she said, indicating the platform.

Dhal gratefully sank to a seat as Chulu, Tidul, and Amet stood and stared at Taav. Taav brushed his fingertips across the cheek that had been cut and the lips that had tasted of blood. Ignoring the presence of the other

Ni, Taav came and knelt at Dhal's knees; then he took the Healer's hand and brought it to his lips.

The look of gratitude that filled Taav's face made Poco's eyes mist.

Dhal gently withdrew his hand. "You are welcome, Taav. Come, sit here beside me. Everything is going to be all right now. I promise."

Chulu was the first to voice his thoughts. "That was most impressive, Dhalvad," he said, returning Dhal's ring. "Any doubts about you have been answered."

"Agreed," said Amet, a look of grim respect on his face. "But I am afraid his display of skill has done nothing to prove that his friends are not more than they seem."

"Dhal has proved that he is what he claims, and therefore is to be trusted," Poco said. "If Taav and I could show you what we can do as Ni, would you extend that trust to us?"

Dhal dropped a hand on Poco's leg. "Do you mean to open the world gate, Poco?"

"No, not that one," she replied. She glanced up at Chulu. "Not that one until we have someone to back us up." She looked at Dhal again. "I know how determined you are to find the Tamorlee, but I also know that we will never be able to do anything about it alone. If we can convince these people that we are not their enemies, perhaps they will consent to help us—or to let us help them," she added, looking up at Amet.

"Where will you take us?" Dhal asked.

"To Port Bhalvar. Taav and I have done it once before, remember?"

Dhal nodded, then looked up at Chulu. "Well?" If she can show you another place on Lach, a place far from here, and Taav can hold that place for all to see, would you admit that they are both Ni and therefore *not* your enemies?"

Chulu looked from Dhal to Poco, then back. "We must talk a moment privately," he said, taking Amet's arm. "Please excuse us."

In but a few moments, Chulu and Amet returned to make their decision known.

"We will accept the woman's offer and give her and the atich-ar an opportunity to prove themselves," Chulu said. "If they can do as they claim, we will revise our judgment and accept them as friends to our cause."

"But if they cannot do as they claim," Amet added, his glance touching Poco, "they will be accorded permanent quarters in the lower tunnels. The cells down there are quite roomy and well-ventilated, but that is all I can say for them."

Poco ignored Amet's threat and turned to Taav. "Come on, Taav, let's show them what we can do."

She stood and stepped around in front of Dhal and came to sit on Taav's left. For a moment she wished for her chalks. Building her song pictures was much easier when reinforced by her artist's skills. But she had done without them before, she could do so again.

Shutting off awareness of those around her, she looked into Taav's eyes and began to sing of Port Bhalvar, a merchant's world of water, boats, docks, and fishermen; a world of climbing stairways and flowered gardens; a world where the Sarissa ruled and the Ni-lach were no more.

The energy patterns swirled and locked as Taav listened to the words and melody that flowed from Poco's lips. Moving shadows danced in his eyes and became reality. Poco saw her home port mirrored in Taav's eyes and was content. She let her song die to the softest of whispers and leaned back, inviting Chulu, Tidul, and Amet to look at the scene she had created. As they did, Poco wondered at the possibility of traveling to Port Bhalvar as she and Dhal had traveled to the world of the atich-ar.

Chulu stepped back to allow Amet a better view into Taav's eyes. "A lesser gate," he said, looking down at Poco. "You have created a lesser gate, yet you claim to be only a half-blood. It is difficult to believe."

Dhal's arm dropped around Poco's shoulders. "What do you mean by a lesser gate?" he asked.

"As a Seeker you should know that," Chulu responded.

"Well I don't, so tell me!"

Poco cringed inwardly at the sudden anger in Dhal's voice. She knew that he felt frustrated by his lack of training in the use of his Seeker powers; after all they had been through in the past few months, he was in no mood to be told what he should and should not know.

Chulu hesitated, then explained. "A lesser gate is what the Seekers use to teleport from one destination to another. They lock into the energy of the Tamorlee through the fire stones they carry and are able to create small corridors in space through which they can pass. We call them lesser gates because only Seekers can use them, as opposed to world gates through which anyone can pass, Seekers and non-Seekers alike."

"Is it unusual for a Singer to build one of these gates?" Dhal asked.

"No," Chulu answered. "Not if the Singer has a talent for it. One out of fifty Singers may be so gifted."

"What is unusual," Amet said, turning his attention from Taav to the conversation, "is that such a group of gifted, yet untrained people would come together and, seemingly by accident, create the energy pattern needed to build a world gate—and not just any gate, but the one leading to the atich-ar and the Tamorlee. The more I think about it, the more I begin to believe there is more than chance at work here."

"What do you mean?" Chulu asked.

Amet's gray eyes narrowed. "What if it isn't chance, but design."

"Whose design?" Dhal asked, standing.

"The Tamorlee's," Amet answered.

"The crystal?" Poco could not keep the disbelief from her voice.

"Is that possible?" Dhal asked.

Amet and Chulu exchanged glances. Chulu spoke.

"The Tamorlee is unlike any other life form the Ni have ever discovered, in this world or any of the other worlds touching ours. Though we have studied it and have come to look upon it as a deathless historian, we do not really understand its life force or how it came into being. We are not sure just how it grows, nor why it is driven to learn all within its sphere of observation, but we do know that it is capable of molding and directing energy in order to communicate and to function as a life form."

"Through the Seeker rings," Dhal finished for him.

Chulu looked down at the ring on Dhal's raised hand. "Yes, through the fire stones, like the one you carry."

"Are you saying that the Tamorlee drew us to that world gate by exerting some kind of energy through Dhal's ring?" Poco asked.

"It is possible," Chulu responded.

"It is also possible that your finding of the I-naal gate was still only an accident," Tidul said. "If you had not discovered Zaa-ob's namepiece, you might never have discovered the right energy pattern to open the gate and therefore would know nothing about the Tamorlee or its loss."

"But we did know." Poco's statement brought all eyes to her.

She realized that she had spoken out of turn, and tried to explain. "What I meant to say is that Dhal *knew* or at least suspected that the crystal was gone from Lach. That is why we came here, to find the Ni and ask about the Tamorlee."

"Ah yes, you spoke about visiting the Ancients and seeing the Tamorlee as it existed in the past," Chulu said. "That does explain your being here, but it also deepens the mystery concerning the I-naal gate."

"I don't understand," said Dhal.

Chulu looked at him. "Your journey into the past, was it reality, or was it only a dream? If a dream, did it come from within or did it originate in the fire stone? If the answer is the fire stone, then we are back to the Tamorlee."

Poco looked at Chulu, her face betraying her confusion. "Is it possible the Tamorlee's energy could reach through a closed gate?"

Chulu shook his head. "We don't really know, but if it is possible, some of our new Seekers should have picked up on it before now."

"New Seekers?" Dhal asked.

Chulu looked at Dhal and his companions. "I think before you ask any more questions, we all should sit down. We have much to discuss and we might as well be comfortable while we are about it. I would also suggest that you release the atich-ar. Sensitives tire very easily."

Chapter 22

*P*OCO, *D*HAL, *AND THEIR COMPANIONS WERE SEATED ON* the raised platform with Chulu and Tidul. The guards had been dismissed, and Amet and Paa-tol had left to make housing arrangements down in the city of Jjaan-bi. Chulu was speaking, describing the beginning of the Sarissa war against the Ni-lach; the one-sided battles as small holdings of Ni were overrun by hundreds of Sarissa mercenaries; the cruelty of the men who seemed to delight in the deaths of the Green Ones.

"We had given them no cause to hate us," he said, his eyes on Poco. "We did not covet their land or food supplies. We did not interfere with their forms of government. Some of us even lived among them and worked to help them secure their lands from draak. Never—never did we wish them ill. Yet they spoke of us as the enemy, and killed us on sight."

Poco looked down at her hands. The sadness she saw on Chulu's face, the anguish she heard in his voice, were almost more than she could bear, reminding her of her own losses and bringing to mind scenes long buried: her home in flames, Ni playmates screaming and running from the men who came at them with drawn swords, her father lying dead near the steps leading from their home to the river.

She closed her eyes and tried to block out the memories, but she could still feel her mother's arms tight around her, squeezing her so hard that she couldn't breathe. Hiding in a clump of bushes near their home, mother and daughter had witnessed the carnage taking place around them and had lived to walk away, but the hate born in Poco that day burned deep. She hated the Sarissa, hated them for what they had done to her father and her friends—and to her.

She felt the pressure of tears behind her eyes and fought to keep them from spilling over. She swallowed several times and took a deep breath, then released it slowly, trying to regain her composure. As her thoughts turned from the past, Poco realized that Chulu had stopped speaking and that Tidul had taken over.

"The Sarissa were afraid of things they could not understand or possess," Tidul said.

Dhal nodded. "That is what Haradan told me, that men were afraid of the powers we used. It's why he made me hide my healing talents. He was afraid of what would happen should the authorities hear about it—and he was right."

"Haradan was your foster father," Tidul said.

"Yes."

"He must have loved you to hide you for so long a time," Chulu said.

"He did," Dhal said.

Poco looked at Dhal, her own pain forgotten for the moment as she remembered how Haradan had died trying to defend Dhal.

Dhal changed the subject. "Tell us about the Tamorlee. How and why was it taken from Lach?"

"The Tamorlee was taken into another world in order to keep it from Sarissa hands," Chulu explained. "We had to use a world gate because there simply was no other way to get it out of Val-hrodhur. The crystal was too large to move through any of the tunnelways."

"How many world gates are there?" Dhal asked.

"We know of five at the present. Three lead to very inhospitable lands, where the temperatures are either too hot or too cold for any of our kind to survive very long. The other two gates lead to worlds much like our own. One is called Trothgar, a world inhabited by a race of intelligent, heavily furred beings who are three times our size and who look upon any entry into their world as an invasion. We lost three Seekers to the Trothgar giants before we learned our lesson."

"And the other world?" Dhal pressed.

"The last world gate discovered was located in the same year the Sarissa declared war on our people. It is called the I-naal gate and it leads to a world called Ari-al."

Five or six questions popped into Poco's mind, but she pushed them aside to concentrate on Chulu's words.

"Though the knowledge of the world gates has been with us a long time, we had no real need to use them and were satisfied to let our Seekers do all our exploring for us. But then came the war and the safety of the crystal was threatened. A decision was made to move the Tamorlee through one of the world gates, but which one? Before a final decision was reached, Zaa-ob, one of our finest Singers, discovered a new world gate."

Chulu looked at Poco. "Like yourself, Zaa-ob could create energy patterns with his songs. Some patterns were dream images which lived only while he sang—and some patterns were real. Up until the day he discovered the I-naal gate, all of his real patterns existed on Lach. If not for a Seeker named Lar-nol, who witnessed Zaa-ob's find and knew it for what it was, Zaa-ob's discovery might have gone unnoticed."

"You mean he found a gate but didn't know what it was?" Dhal asked.

"Yes. He thought it was just another dream image until Lar-nol proved to him that it wasn't. Lar-nol, Zaa-ob, and another Seeker named Resset then did some exploring. What they discovered created such ripples of excitement among the Ni-lach that even the war with the Sarissa was forgotten for a while."

Poco's thoughts leaped ahead. "They found the atich-ar!"

"Yes," Chulu answered.

"Blood kin to the Ni-lach!" Poco cried softly.

Chulu's eyebrows raised in surprise. "Yes, Pocalina, so we believe. You know then the legends of the first Ni-lach?"

"Yes," she answered. "They were told to me by an old friend. The legends of Ni origin center around a lake named Mar-lion, where the Ni were said to have first walked on land. The scaled ones, which we now refer to as atich-ar, left the security of their water homes to seek a new way of life on land."

"So it is told," Chulu said.

Dhal interrupted. "Wait! Are you both saying that the atich-ar from this other world, and the Ni-lach are some-how linked?"

Chulu turned to Dhal. "The scaled ones whom Lar-nol, Zaa-ob, and Resset discovered, spoke a form of Ni that they could understand. What do you think the chances are of two different peoples from two different worlds speaking the same language, Dhalvad? My guess would be almost nil—unless, of course, they shared a common ancestry."

"How could such a thing happen?" Dhal asked.

"A world gate, a natural one perhaps, one that needs no opening or closing," Chulu offered. "Did the Ni-lach come from the seas and rivers of this world, as some believe, or did they unknowingly discover a subterranean world gate and use it for passage to a new world that they quickly adopted as their own? No one knows for sure what the atich-ar sought when they left the waters of Lake Mar-lion, but whatever it was, they must have found it, because they never went back to their own world. Perhaps they were outcasts among their own people. Perhaps they were wanderers or explorers, or perhaps they were only curious. The truth is buried in the past and there it shall remain until our Seekers have time to look into the matter."

Dhal frowned. "Is it possible for such natural gates to exist?"

"You, a Seeker, can ask me that?" Chulu said, smiling. "Do you forget your own power to move from one place to another by simply envisioning your destination? The lesser gates which you use as a Seeker are natural, the energy patterns within your mind forming a bridge from one reality to another. It helps, of course, to have a fire stone in your possession, which boosts your power to draw on the energy around you."

Chulu looked at Dhal a moment before speaking again. "I do not mean to embarrass you or belittle your power as a Seeker, Dhalvad, but I must say that you seem to know very little about being a Seeker."

"I don't, but I am ready to learn," Dhal replied honestly.

Chulu nodded.

"Before you two get off on another subject," Poco said. "Chulu, would you please tell us more about these atich-ar in this other world. What did they think of this kinship? Did they accept it?"

"The evidence was too strong to refute, Pocalina," Chulu replied. "We shared a common language, our eyes and hair coloring are the same, and we could even show them a few of our own atich-ar, Ni like your friend Taav, who are born with scales. Once they accepted the possibility of some of their ancestors accidentally populating another world, they greeted us as kin and offered to help us safeguard the Tamorlee. Would that we had realized their motives at that time."

"What happened?" Poco asked.

"The war with the Sarissa had already started when Zaa-ob discovered the I-naal gate. Most of our people were on their way out of the lands surrounding the Enzaar Sea by the time we made our first contacts with the atich-ar of Ari-al. Even Val-hrodhur was being evacuated of all but the Seekers, Singers, and Sensitives who were to take the Tamorlee through the gate. At that time we still had not decided which gate we would use."

"Then you found Ari-al," Dhal prompted.

"Yes, and after just a few weeks of meetings with the atich-ar, we confided in one of their leaders and told them about the crystal and our need to keep it safe. Their leader's name was Chemii. He was the ruler of a territory they call the Errlog Waterways. According to Chemii, it is one of the greater domains inhabited by the atich-ar. This, of course, we had no time to verify. In truth, there was much we didn't know about the atich-ar, but time was against us and we decided there would be opportunity for learning at a later date.

"Once we decided to trust the atich-ar, plans went ahead quickly. It was our intention to make two gates using the I-naal pattern. What we hoped to do was to take the crystal from Val-hrodhur to Ari-al, then from Ari-al to Jjaan-bi without actually having to move the crystal more than a few hundred meters."

"You were only going to use Ari-al as a transfer point, then," Dhal said.

"Yes," Chulu replied.

"Then any of the gates would have done as well wouldn't they?"

"No, because there was an element of time to consider. It requires a great amount of energy to hold a world gate open. The Sensitives who do that work were—and still are—few. We believed it would take us at least three hours to move the Tamorlee through the I-naal gate one way. Even dividing the energy load among the eight Sensitives we had at that time, we knew it was going to be

a close thing. There was no way we could reopen the gate
back to Jjaan-bi until after the Sensitives had rested."

"How long a rest?" Dhal asked.

"A day at the least," Chulu answered, "during which
time our people were open to betrayal."

"Why didn't you use one of the lesser gates and go
straight from Val-hrodhur to Jjaan-bi?" Poco asked.

"It was tried. The Seekers were too few and the crystal
too heavy a mass to move in that manner. I am not sure
it could have been accomplished had we had five times
our number of Seekers."

"You spoke of betrayal," Dhal said, bringing the conversation back to the enemy atich-ar.

"Yes," Chulu replied. "I believe it began when Chemii,
leader of the atich-ar, visited Val-hrodhur during those
first weeks after the gate was discovered. On one of his
visits he was taken to see the Tamorlee. It is my guess
that once he saw the crystal and recognized it as the
source of power enhancing the natural talents of the Ni,
he decided to have it for his own. All that followed was
a fulfillment of that desire."

"What happened?" Dhal asked, crystal eyes intent upon
the older Ni.

"Zaa-ob and the Singers he had trained opened the I-
naal gate and we took the crystal through. It required one
hundred of our people to move the Tamorlee, and at least
that many of the atich-ar. Once we had the crystal through
the gate, some of us went back for the Sensitives who
were still entranced and holding the gate open. After we
carried them through, the gate was to be released and we
would be closed off from Lach until our Singers created
another gate leading to Jjaan-bi."

Chulu paused, his eyes focusing on a scene from the
past. "Amet and I were the last to go through the gate.
It was our responsibility to see that no one was left behind.
Val-hrodhur was to be completely abandoned—for how
long we dared not even guess."

Chulu's voice softened. "Val-hrodhur was my home.

I had never thought to leave there. I realize now that we would have been better off to have stayed and fought the Sarissa. We might have won, and we still would have Valhrodhur *and* the Tamorlee. It is so easy to look back and see one's mistakes."

"Please go on," Dhal said. "What happened at the gate?"

"A youngling by the name of Ree was the last Sensitive on our side of the gate. Amet and I started to pick him up, then we heard someone screaming. We looked up just as a group of our people came running back through the gate. For a moment there was such confusion that Amet and I did not realize what was going on. Then suddenly there were atich-ar among us, wielding swords and killing indiscriminately. More and more of our people appeared and right behind them ran more of the atich-ar. Amet and I fought side by side trying to defend Ree, who was still entranced."

Chulu shook his head. "It seemed that the battle went on for a long time, but it could not have been more than a few minutes. When it was over there were dead all around us. Ree was among them—and the I-naal gate was closed."

Chulu took a deep breath, then continued. "It did not take long to realize that of all those who had made it back through the gate, not one was a Singer. Amet later told of seeing Zaa-ob on the other side of the gate just before it closed. He said the Singer was being restrained by several of the enemy atich-ar.

"Of the one hundred-odd Ni who crossed into Ari-al, thirty-six made it back to Lach, and of those thirty-six, only fifteen survived the battle with the atich-ar who crossed to our side of the gate.

"Our greatest loss, except for the crystal itself, was the loss of l'Tamorlee, our Speaker, he who is in direct contact with the crystal. He was young and adventurous, and he chose to travel with the crystal rather than use his Seeker powers to teleport safely to Jjaan-bi."

"Was he one of those who died at the gate?" Dhal asked.

"No. His body was not among those we buried in Valhrodhur. He may be alive; he may be dead. We have no way of knowing."

"What happened after the gate closed?" Dhal asked.

"With the gate closed and no Singer on our side to open it again, all we could do was wait to see what would happen. There was some talk of a possible invasion of Lach by the atich-ar, but it never came to pass. There are some who ascribe to the theory that once the atich-ar have time to study the crystal and the captured Ni, they will use the gate to launch an attack."

"After so many years do you think it likely?" Poco asked.

"More than twenty years have passed since we lost the Tamorlee. Many believe that if the atich-ar planned an invasion, they would have made their move by now. Others disagree and believe that the atich-ar are using this time to build forces, so that when they invade, they will have the numbers to destroy us. After witnessing the ferocity of their attack years ago, I find myself leaning toward the second theory. When the atich-ar are ready, they will attack."

Though Chulu's fear closely paralleled Retath's warning, Poco found herself wondering. "I don't understand why they would want to make war on the Ni," she said. "Knowing they share a common ancestry with the Nilach, why wouldn't they seek to link with you in friendship?"

"I don't know," Chulu answered. "But I would guess that like the Sarissa, the atich-ar feared something they did not understand. Perhaps they even thought that by taking the Tamorlee from us, it would weaken our powers, and we would no longer be a threat to them."

"Do you think the atich-ar will some day try to invade Lach?" Dhal asked.

Chulu nodded. "Yes, I do. And think on this! If you

were Chemii and you wanted to keep what you had stolen, wouldn't you try to safeguard it from being retaken? And if your enemies had the power to create doors into your world, doors for which you had no locks, what would you do?"

Dhal thought a moment. "If I could not control the doors, I would try to control the ones who could make them."

"Correct. There is a possibility that Chemii has coerced the Ni he captured into helping him. If he has, he could already be sending his spies among us. That is why we were so careful with all of you. As it is, I doubt Amet trusts you yet."

"Do you?" Dhal asked bluntly.

Chulu looked around the circle, his glance touching each of them briefly. "Do not ask me why but, yes, I think I do trust you, all of you."

"A moment ago you spoke about Chemii sending spies to Lach," Poco said, "Have you sent anyone to Ari-al recently?"

"In the last few years, yes, a few."

"Have you learned anything from them?"

"I am sorry, Pocalina, that I cannot tell you. All I can say is that for years we have been working and planning toward the retaking of the Tamorlee. What has held us up so long has been finding and training enough Sensitives and Singers to hold the I-naal pattern for as long as it need be held. We now have twelve Singers who are familiar with the energy pattern of the gate, and there are nine Sensitives now working with us."

"Ten if you count Taav," Dhal said softly.

Chulu glanced at the atich-ar, then looked back at Dhal. "By that can I assume that you and your friends are interested in helping us retrieve the Tamorlee?"

Dhal nodded.

Chulu looked at Poco. "And you, Singer, can we enlist your help in opening the I-naal gate?"

"The atich-ar will be watching for us," Poco warned.

"As we have been watching for them," Chulu responded.

Poco hesitated, but only for a moment. "If you trust me enough to ask for my help, I guess I have no reason to refuse."

Chapter 23 ✒

*P*OCO, *DHAL*, *SCREECH*, *GI*, *AND TAAV FOUND LIFE IN* the Ni-lach city of Jjaan-bi unlike anything they had ever experienced before. Each day they toured a different section of the mountain city, walking down tree-shaded lanes which wound among giant aban trees, and up and down stone stairways which hugged the contours of the mountainside.

On their third day in the city, their guide, a Ni named Caaras, took them to Lake Hadrach, which bordered the city to the north. The lake was so large that they could not see the farthest shore.

They arrived early enough in the morning to watch some fishing boats move out into the green mist which overhung the water.

"Do the Ni still use draak to help them with their catches?" Dhal asked.

"Yes," Caaras replied. "While most of the Ni work on setting the nets, several of our finest Draak Singers go out to call the water draak to service, then they guide the draak in toward the place where the nets are set."

Dhal stood on the docks looking back at the city. "How many people live in Jjaan-bi?"

"We used to number around five hundred. We are closer to two thousand now," Caaras answered.

"Is the increase due to your preparation for a war with the atich-ar?"

"Yes, partly. The Ni were widely scattered before the war with the Sarissa and the loss of the Tamorlee. Our way was to live in small groups. But we learned that if we wanted to survive as a people, against both the Sarissa and the atich-ar, we had to unite and make plans for our defense."

A few days later, Poco and Dhal visited the Jjaan-bi Learning Arc, a large, wood building erected on a well-protected plateau, treetop high above the lake. There they saw young Ni being taught to read and write and sing—and to understand the history of the Ni and the importance of the giant crystalline life form called the Tamorlee.

From there they toured some of the lower tunnelways that honeycombed the mountainside. The tunnels were used both for living room and storage. Because of the large growth in the population, many Ni chose to live in these underground rooms in order to be close to the center of the city. Those who had been longer in residence usually had tree homes. Long vine and wood walkways linked tree home to tree home in an unending labyrinth.

The tree home that Dhal, Poco, Screech, Gi, and Taav shared belonged to Caaras, and was on one of the higher slopes above the storage caves. From there it was a ten-minute walk to the main Trade Gardens, a large, walled-in square where all types of goods were displayed for sale or trade. According to Caaras, the Trade Gardens were open to all, even to the small contingent of men who in the past had made their way up the Owri River from the Reaches.

On the morning of their ninth day in Jjaan-bi, Poco

stood at a window overlooking Lake Hadrach. Her back
was to Dhal, who was just rising from a late afternoon
nap, a luxury they had shared together.

She gazed downvalley. Jjaan-bi is beautiful, she thought.
Here all is order and privacy. The planning which had
gone into the forest city was striking in contrast to the
hodge-podge of stone stairways, sprawling buildings, and
webbed streets of Port Bhalvar.

She stretched her arms and turned to find Dhal watching her from the thick grass mat which served them as a
bed.

She smiled as she walked across the floor. "Think you
have had enough sleep?" she asked him.

"For a while," he replied. He reached up and took her
hand.

Poco gave in to the gentle tug on her arm and lay down
beside him. She let him kiss her, but pushed him away
when his hands started to stroke her back, hips, and buttocks.

"No, Dhal!" She laughed. "Enough of that! We cannot
lie here all afternoon making love."

Dhal pushed himself up onto his elbows and grinned.
"Why not? We have nowhere special to go."

"What if Caaras should come up?"

"He would not barge in without giving a holler. Anyway, we are to eat at his parent's home tonight. He won't
bother us unless we fail to show up on time."

"Caaras has become a good friend, hasn't he?" she
asked.

"Yes, I like him," Dhal admitted.

"You have made a lot of friends here."

Dhal sobered. "I think part of it is being accepted for
what I am, Poco. Here I can walk among people without
hiding my hair or eyes; and here no one calls me devil-
spawned when I use my power to heal. I haven't felt this
free since the days before I learned who I really was."

"I am glad for you, Dhal. I really am."

Poco leaned forward and brushed his cheek with her

lips. I only hope that some day they will accept me as easily, she thought.

She lay quietly in Dhal's arms, her ear pressed against his chest listening to his heart beat. She felt strange, frightened, as if suddenly she was on the brink of losing something, a part of herself that she could not name. Damn, she thought, but I am getting moody lately. Must be the pregnancy.

She tightened her arms around Dhal. Here is reality, she thought. Dhal, Jjaan-bi, the Ni-lach. There is nothing to be afraid of. Just relax and stop creating problems where they don't exist.

"Poco, is something wrong?" Dhal said softly.

Poco released Dhal and rolled to a sitting position. She avoided his eyes as she combed her hair with her fingers, shaking it out behind her.

"I think it's time we were up and moving," she said.

"Poco, tell me what is wrong," Dhal said.

She turned to face him. "Nothing is wrong. I was—I was just thinking about Taav," she lied. "I was wondering who he really is, and where he comes from. Do you think there is any chance of his being one of the enemy atichar?"

Dhal sat up. He studied her, then shrugged, accepting her lie. "He could be, Poco, but it is something we cannot worry about now. In his present state I don't think he presents much of a risk one way or the other."

Poco stood and went back toward the window. "I wonder where Screech, Taav, and Gi are. They have been gone all afternoon."

"Where do we usually find them?" he said, as he padded across to the window to join her.

Screech and Gi shared one common trait, curiosity. Whenever they were long absent, they could usually be found wandering about the open stalls in the Trade Gardens, poking fingers and noses into anything that captured their interest. Gi was especially fond of lingering near the food stalls, while Screech spent most of his time looking over Ni jewelry; his fascination for Ni art was becoming an obsession.

Poco looked at Dhal as he stood in the windowlight. His green hair fell free to his shoulders; his pale skin had taken on a blue shadow that accented bone and muscle. In that moment Poco saw him not as her lover and mate, but rather as a Ni Healer, one of the mysterious Green Ones, the illusive forest folk whom man had yet to tame to his way of life.

She watched Dhal out of the corner of her eye and again felt that flicker of uneasiness. I am going to lose him, she thought. If not to this war with the atich-ar, then to his own people.

The words came unbidden to her mind and though she flinched from them, she also recognized a truth. She had witnessed the changes taking place in Dhal ever since their discovery of Val-hrodhur, and week by week, as they made their way out of Port Sulta and across the plains, she had seen him grow and mature.

And he was not the only one who had changed, she acknowledged. Where was that chalk artist who wandered the streets of Port Bhalvar looking for that something in life that would have it all make sense? What had happened to Pocalina-fel-Jamba, the woman who thought she knew everything there was to know about men and their desires; who took pity on a Ni being hunted by the Port Guard and who found herself unable to let him walk out of her life?

Dhal turned to look at her, then stepped close and pulled her into a hug. "What is wrong, Poco?" he asked softly. "Please, tell me how I can help."

Poco returned his embrace, hiding her face in his hair. "There is no help for me," she answered. "I am just dreaming up problems that will never see daylight. It's a favorite pastime these days."

"Are you sure that's all?"

"Yes. I'll tell you about them sometime. You'll laugh."

"Tell me now."

"No, not now. Later."

Dhal knew when not to press. "All right, later. Why don't we go down to the lake for a swim. Then we'll come back and get ready for supper. Maybe by that time Gi, Taav, and Screech will show up. If not, we can go look for them."

"Sounds good," she said.

Dhal and Poco swam for a while, then sat on the rocks near the diving pools and watched young Ni plummet from the cliffs, their graceful dives into the deep water below making Poco think of blue-feathered rimsang birds which fished the shores, their brightly colored bodies blurs of motion as they dove into the sea to fish. She was delighted by the fluid grace and perfection of the divers and would gladly have sat there the rest of the afternoon, but Dhal reminded her of their promise to Caaras and together they returned to the tree home that they shared with their friends.

Poco was sitting on the grass mat combing Dhal's hair when she heard Gi's whistle.

"About time," she said.

Dhal laughed. "I told you they would be back before suppertime. Gi never misses a meal."

Poco patted Dhal's shoulder. "All finished. Soon your hair will be long enough for braids if you want to wear it that way."

"Maybe," he said. "Find us both a fresh tunic, Poco. Caaras left some in that kist over there."

Poco was pleasantly surprised at the quality of the tunics she found. She was sure she had never owned any that were woven with so rich or soft a fabric. She chose a blue ankle-length tunic for herself, and for Dhal she found a dark green hip-length tunic which would go nicely with the buff pants he had put on fresh that morning. Within the kist she also discovered several gold sashes. She decided that the sandals given them earlier that week would serve for footwear.

Poco hated to admit it, but she was excited by the

prospect of having supper with Caaras's parents. She understood that there would be other guests present, which meant a party of sorts, a rare event among the working class of Port Bhalvar. As she draped the clothes over the cushioned bench by their eating table, she could not help but wonder what price would be exacted for the gifts that Caaras had given them. She had learned early in life that few things ever came free.

She returned to the other room to find Gi sitting on the grass pallet talking to Dhal. Gi was excited about some new find in the Trade Gardens and his whistle-clicks came so fast that Poco did not even try to make sense of the conversation. Dhal would give her a translation later.

She walked over to the window where Taav and Screech were standing. Poco and Screech exchanged the derkat form of greeting, then Taav startled them both by imitating Poco's coughing sound.

Poco smiled. "You are learning, Taav."

She took Taav's arm and led him toward Dhal and Gi. "Come on, let's hear what Gi is telling Dhal. From the sounds of it, you must have had quite a day."

Screech sat quietly through Gi's rambling account of their travels that day. Poco was not alone in noticing his silence.

"You haven't once corrected Gi, Screech," Dhal said, looking at the derkat. "Has he been that truthful?"

"*Little Fur sees many things*," Screech signed. "*But not everything.*"

"You mean there *is* something he missed," Dhal said, his glance catching Gi as he smiled.

The olvaar turned to Screech. "What Gi miss?" he demanded.

"*We were followed all day*," the derkat answered.

"Followed?" Poco echoed. "By whom?"

"*No names. Each day different Ni.*"

"Screech, are you telling us that you have been followed before?" Dhal asked.

"*All of us*," Screech answered.

Poco thought back, trying to remember if she had seen anyone in the past few days who had looked suspicious. After a moment of reflection, she decided not. Like Dhal, she had been so caught up in sightseeing that if they had been followed, she had not been aware of it.

"Why didn't you tell us before, Screech?" Poco asked.

"One or two days, I thought the Ni were just curious. But still they watch us. Why?"

Why indeed? Poco wondered. "It sounds as if they still don't trust us," she said. "What do you think, Dhal?"

Dhal was looking at the derkat. "Screech, are you sure about this? You know how much interest you and Gi stir up when you wander around."

"I am sure. Those who follow us never come close to speak. They just watch."

"I don't like the sound of it, Dhal," Poco said.

"No more than I. But what do we do about it?"

"Confront them?"

"When?"

"Why not tonight?" she said. "Caaras might be able to give us some answers. If not him, perhaps Chulu will. He is supposed to be there too."

Dhal nodded. "All right, tonight. You go ahead and get dressed. I'll help Taav. And you," he said, looking down at Gi. "You need a bath before you go anywhere. What is that sticky stuff on your belly?"

Gi looked down at the incriminating stain on his fur. He touched a finger to the sticky dribble and brought his finger to his mouth.

"Is lidil jam, Dhal," he said, his golden eyes wide and innocent. "Is very good."

"I'll bet. How much did you eat?"

"Not keeping count. Just tasting samples."

"Are you too full to eat supper?" Dhal asked.

Screech made a humming noise through his nose, the derkat's form of laugher. *"Take a sea draak to fill Little Fur."*

Gi clicked his indignation and made a show of chasing

the derkat from the room. But a few minutes later, as
Poco passed through the small kitchen on her way to get
dressed, she saw Screech gently helping Gi wash off his
fur.

Chapter 24

LONG AFTER THE SUPPER HOUR, POCO STOOD IN THE large, railing-enclosed porch overlooking Lake Hadrach. Most of Caaras's guests had departed. Even Gi and Screech had left, taking a sleepy Taav with them back to the tree house.

Dhal and Poco both had enjoyed meeting Caaras's friends, most of whom were young adult Ni somewhere near their own ages. They also had enjoyed the fine selection of foods at the table, as well as the entertainment provided by a trio of musicians who played a variety of stringed instruments.

She joined Dhal on the other end of the porch, where he was sitting with Chulu and his mate, Naalan. As Poco approached she heard Chulu ask Dhal if they were learning their way about the city.

"Yes," Dhal replied. "Caaras has been an excellent guide."

"You are enjoying yourself then?"

"Yes, but we would enjoy ourselves more if we were not being followed wherever we go," Dhal said.

Everyone looked up as Poco approached. "Good evening," she said. "May I join you?"

Naalan stood. "Here, take my seat. I have something I want to say to Beirna. I'll be back in a few minutes, Chulu."

Poco took the proffered seat beside Chulu. The light from the glass-enclosed candles set in the windows barely reached the far corners of the porch; Chulu's face was deep in shadow.

"Your mate is very beautiful, Dhalvad," Chulu said.

"I agree," Dhal replied.

"I think you have both made some good friends tonight."

"We hope so," Dhal said.

Poco glanced at Dhal. "Speaking of friends, perhaps you would answer Dhal's question now?"

"Question?" Chulu said.

"Why are we being followed, saan? Ssaal-lr has seen your people every day. There is no point in denying it," Poco said.

Poco was startled by a soft growl. She leaned out and saw Screech sitting on the floor deep in the shadow of Dhal's chair. She had not realized that he had returned to the party.

Chulu tried to explain about the guards sent to watch over them. While he was speaking, Caaras approached quietly and stood listening.

Poco interrupted. "Are you saying that the Ni who follow us are for our own protection?"

"Your protection and our own," Chulu responded quickly. "Amet convinced the Elder's Council that we would be foolish to let strangers wander too freely—not when we are so close to our objective."

"Are you ready to move against the atich-ar?" Dhal asked.

"Yes," Chulu responded.

"When?"

Chulu shook his head. "I am sorry, I cannot tell you. All I can say is that it will be soon."

"Being the strangers you speak about," Poco said, "are we so suspect that you no longer wish our aid in helping with the world gate? If so, there is nothing for us to do here and we might just as well leave."

Caught off guard, Chulu quickly softened his tone. "No, you must not leave! We have already added your strength to our numbers."

He paused, as if searching for a way to explain without offending. "It is not that we don't trust you, Pocalina. It is just that we cannot take a chance of making a mistake, not now, not after planning so long."

But the truth is that you don't trust us, Poco thought.

"Call off your spies, Chulu," she said. "Trust us and we will stay. Don't—and we leave. It is that simple."

Poco looked at Dhal, wondering if he would back her up. But then Caaras spoke up.

"Nothing is that simple," he said. "As things stand now, Amet would not let you leave. As Chulu said, we are too close to declaring war on the atich-ar."

Dhal stood up. "You were in on this, Caaras?"

"Yes," the young Ni answered. "I am sorry, Dhalvad. I was only doing what I was ordered to do."

"So where do we stand?" Dhal snapped. "Are we your prisoners?"

"No!" Caaras replied instantly. "Never that! I know you feel I have betrayed your trust, Dhalvad, but I haven't, and I hope that you will call me friend again one day. Personally I believe you are to be trusted, and so I have told Amet, but he has not withdrawn his people. Please do not be angry. What was done was done to protect us all, and to make sure that our attempt to regain the Tamorlee is successful."

Poco walked down the narrow lane leading away from the Learning Arc. She saw Dhal and Gi waiting for her near the entrance to the herb garden on the terraced slopes below.

The late afternoon air was fresh with the first of the spring rains. The path was still wet though Ra-gar had shone brightly for several hours.

Poco jumped a puddle and waved to Dhal. He saw her and returned her wave. A week had passed since their confrontation with Chulu, and Poco still was finding it hard to reconcile herself to the fact that somehow Caaras had convinced Dhal to forgive Amet his suspicions and keep his promise to help them retrieve the Tamorlee. Dhal, in his own way, had convinced her to give the Ni-lach another chance, but she did not like being watched and she would not stop grumbling about it.

Gi ran to meet Poco, his whistle-clicks of greeting attracting the curious glances of several garden workers. Poco swung the olvaar up into her arms and gave him a hug, then passed him over to Dhal.

"Been waiting long?" she asked.

"A while, but it's pleasant here," Dhal answered, as he set Gi on his shoulder.

"Is Taav with Screech?"

Dhal nodded and took Poco's arm, steering her toward the steps leading down to the lake. "Taav was sleeping when we left, so Screech said he would stay with him. Taav has been wandering a lot these past few days and Screech has been kept busy just keeping up with him."

"I believe Taav is more alert since coming here, Dhal. Do you think it might have something to do with seeing other Ni?"

"Could be," Dhal said. "He certainly doesn't act as if he is afraid any longer."

"Except when he sees Amet," Poco said.

Dhal nodded. "Where Amet is concerned, Taav has cause to fear. If Amet had his way, Taav would still be locked away somewhere."

"Dhal, do you think there is any possibility that Taav

is one of the two escaped atich-ar Chulu says they lost near Val-hrodhur?"

"No, I don't. Why? Do you?"

"No. But there are moments when I do wonder what happened to him and how he came by the head wound that knocked him witless."

"Well, personally, I don't see that it matters one way or the other," Dhal said. "If Taav isn't one of the enemy atich-ar, we have nothing to worry about, and if he is, what harm can he do if he is on our side of the world gate? There is no way for him to get back through to warn his people, not alone. He may be able to hold a gate, but he cannot create one."

"You're right. I guess I am just letting Amet and his people make me nervous."

They descended two flights of steps then turned eastward onto the well-trodden path leading to their tree home.

Dhal paused to set Gi down on his feet. As they started off again, Poco asked the question that had been in her mind since seeing him.

"Well, has the Council made a decision yet?"

"I don't know," Dhal replied. "All they will tell me is 'soon.' Amet doesn't trust Taav and the council doesn't trust us."

"Well, they had better start trusting or they can do without us!" Poco snapped, angry at the disappointment she heard in Dhal's voice.

Gi patted Poco's leg. Realizing that they were setting too fast a pace for the olvaar, she slowed down. "Want something, Gi?"

"Poco like singing with Niifan?" he piped up.

Aware that the olvaar disliked any show of anger and was trying to steer her thoughts away from the Council, Poco shook her head. Gi-arobi would never cease to amaze her; his perception and wisdom were so often obscured by his childlike innocence and good nature that one almost forgot how truly intelligent he was.

You win, Gi, she thought. Getting angry is not going to help.

"Yes, Gi," she said. "I do like singing with Niifan." Niifan was the only other female among the Singers who would open the I-naal gate.

Poco recalled the practice session that afternoon and felt good inside. She had been working with the Ni Singers for the better part of five days and that day, under the direction of Lurral, the oldest and most accomplished Singer in Jjaan-bi, they had sung the first sequence of music that would open the I-naal gate; the notes varied only slightly from the sound pattern Poco had discovered when holding Zaa-ob's pendant.

Earlier Poco had told Lurral about the pendant and the mysterious Singer who had taken over her voice. After examining the pendant, Lurral had explained about the vibrations that become entrapped in objects once handled.

"Picking up these vibrations is a matter of concentration," Lurral said. "It does not surprise me to learn that the pendant you carry somehow absorbed Zaa-ob's song, for the pattern of the I-naal gate was one of his greatest accomplishments, even if its finding lost us the Tamor-lee."

Dhal interrupted Poco's thoughts. "How much longer before Lurral thinks you will be ready?"

"He says that there are two more sequences to practice, so I would say three or four more days until we put it all together. If the gate did not have to be so large, fewer of us could sing and it would be easier to match our voices. But Lurral says that Chulu wants a gate large enough for twenty-five Ni walking abreast. That means using every Singer in Jjaan-bi."

Gi led the way up the large tree limb that served them as a stairway to the outside porch on the first level of their two-level tree home.

When they reached the porch Poco turned to face Dhal.

"There are still some things that bother me about the world gates," she said.

"What things?" he asked.

"Like, why doesn't it matter where we are when we set the pattern? When we used the gate before, we were somewhere on the plains and the door we passed through took us to that hill overlooking the Ni temple. According to Lurral, when we open the I-naal gate for you in a few days time, we will arrive at another place not too far from that same hill. Tell me, how can that be when Jjaan-bi is so far away from the plains? Shouldn't we enter Ari-al in another place equally distant from our original entry point? The more I think about it the more confused I get."

"Sit down," Dhal said, as he lowered himself to the edge of the porch. "I will try to explain." He smiled. "If I can.

"Poco, you are thinking of the two worlds as if they both exist in the same space and time. They don't. Time *may* be the same for the atich-ar as it is for us, but the space is different. Caaras refers to it as a different dimension or reality. As for where we start out and where we arrive when passing through a world gate, it is much like the energy patterns the Seekers use when they travel from one place to another. The image one holds in his mind directs his destination."

"Are you saying that the energy patterns we create as Singers are not bound by natural laws of movement, that if I wanted a world gate to another place on Ari-al, all I would have to do is envision it in my mind, then create a song pattern to match it?"

"Yes, something like that, but according to Resset, who is the oldest Seeker among us, the creation of a new world gate is ninety-five percent luck and only five percent design."

"Dhal, has anyone thought about the two atich-ar who followed us through the gate that day? After losing two of their people, won't the atich-ar be looking for another breakthrough into their world?"

Dhal nodded. "That is why Chulu wants so large a gate. He hopes that sending a large number of us through at the same time will improve our chances of securing the hills south of the temple. Once we have the hills, we will march on their temple, or whatever it is they have built there. He hopes to find the Tamorlee there, and the Ni who were captured years ago."

"Do you think we have the numbers to retake the crystal?"

"I don't know. The main thing against us is time. The Sensitives cannot hold the gate open forever. There is a good possibility that we will have to carry them through with us, close the gate, and then reopen it when we are ready to bring the Tamorlee back to Lach."

"That means the Singers will have to go through too."

"Yes."

Poco nodded. In the back of her mind she had really guessed as much. "What happens if the crystal has been moved?"

"The Council has discussed that possibility and has prepared contingency plans that include setting up a permanent base camp and sending out search parties headed by Seekers. The fire stones we carry should help us locate the crystal no matter where the atich-ar have it hidden. And there is a chance that they haven't moved it at all. They may believe themselves strong enough to defeat any invasion. Amet says that..."

Poco saw movement out of the corner of her eye. Turning her head slightly, she saw Taav standing in the doorway to the main living area of the tree home, watching Dhal.

"... but many on the Council do not agree," Dhal was saying. "They believe the atich-ar are too loosely organized to put up much of a battle. I guess we will know soon enough."

"I guess," Poco said. She turned suddenly and caught Taav's glance. The startled look on his face lasted but a moment, but in that moment Poco had the distinct feeling that a stranger stood in the doorway. How long had he been standing there listening? she wondered.

"Taav awake now," Gi observed, sliding off Dhal's lap and padding over to the open door.

"About time," Dhal said, turning. "Come join us, Taav." Dhal signed as he spoke.

Taav looked at Dhal, then his glance returned to Poco. He shook his head, turned, then disappeared back into the house.

"That's odd," Dhal said, startled by Taav's abrupt departure.

Yes, Poco thought, odd for the Taav we know, but what about the stranger I saw just a minute ago?

Dhal asked Gi-arobi to go and see if Taav was feeling all right. Poco watched Gi leave the porch, then turned back around and found Dhal staring at her.

"Poco, you have the strangest look on your face. Are *you* feeling all right?"

"I'm fine. I was just thinking about Taav."

"Don't worry. He has probably eaten something that didn't agree with him. I'll go in in a minute and check on him."

"No—it's not that," she said.

"Not what?" he asked, frowning.

Poco hesitated. "Taav was listening to us talk about the world gate."

"Just now?"

"Yes."

"So? We have spoken about it in front of him before."

"Yes," Poco agreed. "But this time he was listening to what we said. Really listening."

"What are you saying?"

Poco shook her head. "I don't know. I just feel that somehow Taav has changed, and suddenly I don't know that I trust him."

"Because he is atich-ar?"

"No. Because of the look I saw on his face when I caught him eavesdropping."

Chapter 25 🐟

*D*HAL WOKE IN THE EARLY HOURS OF MORNING. *HE SAT* up and muttered softly to himself.

Poco heard him and woke.

He threw back the blanket that covered him, got up, and went to the window overlooking the lake. Outlined by the faint glimmer of daylight, he paced back and forth, his naked footsteps almost soundless.

"Dhal?" Poco said softly, not wanting to wake the others.

He stopped pacing and turned to look back into the dark room. "You awake, Poco?"

"Yes. What is it?" She rose and pulled the top blanket around her.

He waited for her by the window, silent and somehow frightening. She could just make out his face in the early morning light. "What's wrong?"

"It's the Tamorlee," he said softly. "I dreamed about it."

"So?"

"It needs me—now!"

"Needs you? I don't understand."

"Neither do I. I just know that it needs me—and quickly!"

He reached out and took her arms. "Poco, I have never had a dream like this before. It was so real it scared me!"

"But it *was* just a dream, Dhal. Come back to bed and—"

"No! No, I cannot just put it out of my mind. You don't know what it was like!"

"What do you want to do? Do you want to go and find Caaras and tell him that—"

"No! Yes. I don't know. Let me think!"

Poco stood patiently, shivering in the chill morning air. A few minutes later she broke into Dhal's silence.

"Do you have any idea of how much longer it will be before the Ni-lach are ready to move?"

"No," he answered. "Every time I ask, they just keep saying soon."

Another shadow moved in the semidarkness. Screech coughed as he approached.

Poco coughed in greeting. "Dhal was wakened by a dream," she explained. "Nothing is wrong. Go back to sleep, Screech."

"No," Dhal said. "Don't go back to sleep. Screech, wake Taav and Gi and bring them here."

"Dhal, what are you going to do?" Poco asked.

"Come on. I will explain as we get dressed," he answered, and pushed her back toward their sleeping pallet. "We are leaving here."

"Leaving? For where?" she asked, dropping the blanket and searching for a light.

"We are going to Ari-al to find the Tamorlee."

"Dhal, you aren't serious!"

"Yes. I am."

"You promised me that we would never return to Ari-al by ourselves!"

"We won't be alone. Screech, Gi, and Taav will come with us. I know what I told you, Poco, and if I thought I could get Caaras, Chulu, and the Council to speed up their timetable, I would wait; but there isn't time to waste! We must move now!"

"Dhal, this is crazy! What can we accomplish by ourselves? What if this dream is just that—a dream? Why don't we sit down and talk about it. Maybe if you—"

"No, Poco! We have got to move now! We can do it! You know the pattern and Taav can hold the gate for us. Please, don't argue with me, not now. Just trust me!"

Hearing the desperation in Dhal's voice, Poco held her tongue and dressed quickly. Minutes later she was packing some food into a pouch while Screech and Dhal collected their weapons and whatever else they might need for a few days away.

When Gi and Taav showed up, Poco handed the two food pouches to Taav, who looked mystified by such early morning preparations.

"Big Fur say we leaving now," Gi piped up. "Going where, Poco?"

"Dhal has had a dream, Gi, and he tells me we have to go and find the Tamorlee, right now."

Poco shook her head. She knew how foolish this venture was; but she also knew that Dhal was deadly serious and would not be turned away from his goal.

"War happens today?" Gi asked.

Poco leaned down and picked up the olvaar. "I hope not, Gi. I sincerely hope not."

They walked for an hour to reach a small open place by the lake where Poco's singing would not wake anyone.

"I still think we should have told Caaras or someone what we are going to do," Poco said.

"They would only stop us," Dhal replied.

He led Taav to a dry place on the sand and told him to sit down; then he turned to Poco.

"I know this must all seem crazy, Poco, and I cannot explain how I know that something is threatening the

Tamorlee. I just know that it is, and that I have to try to do something about it!" Dhal was talking so fast that he was tripping over his own words.

"All right," she said, trying to calm him. "What do you want us to do?"

"I want you to sing the pattern for the I-naal gate. When the gate opens, I will go through, check around to make sure it is safe for the rest of you to follow. If it is, we will carry Taav through and close the gate behind us."

"And then?"

"And then we look for the Tamorlee. My fire stone should help me locate it."

Poco shivered. Dhal's plan was full of holes and the possibility of real danger. "Dhal, I am scared. Too many things could go wrong."

"I know, but I cannot stop myself. I have to find the Tamorlee!" Dhal took Poco in his arms. "After we close the gate, I want you, Gi, and Taav to stay close together. If anything goes wrong, if I cannot get back to you, you must use the gate again and return here."

Poco did not like the sound of that. She made herself a silent promise: We go to Ari-al together, we come back together!

Dhal was looking at her expectantly, his face just barely visible in the half-light of morning. "I love you, Poco," he said softly. "If there was another way, I would not ask this of you, not now in your condition, but—"

"But there isn't," she finished for him. She leaned close and kissed him, holding him tight.

A few moments later, she sat facing Taav. She looked at the atich-ar, remembering the startled look on his face when she had caught him eavesdropping the day before. Who was he really? Did he understand what was about to happen?

She reached out and took Taav's hands. "I am going to sing, Taav, and you must listen very closely. Do you understand?"

He nodded. He appeared statuesque in the morning light, his face devoid of expression.

"Dhal, Screech, Gi, and I are going to travel to a very special place and this time you must come along. You must not be frightened. We will be there with you."

Again Taav nodded.

Poco drew a deep breath and released it slowly. She glanced once at Dhal, then turned back to Taav. Keeping hold of his hands, she began to sing. She had been practicing the I-naal gate pattern with the other Singers of Jjaan-bi and no longer needed Zaa-ob's pendant for direction; but as she sang, that other presence filled her mind, joining and reinforcing the I-naal pattern, and for a moment, Zaa-ob lived again, the song he had created years ago drawing upon nature's forces to build a doorway from one world to another.

The words to the pattern were in Ni and as they were sung, Poco saw them take hold of Taav. His eyes became unfocused, his hands went slack, and he became the statue he had appeared to be only minutes before; and as he fixed the pattern in his mind, a green hazy mist began to grow between them.

Dhal moved to stand right behind Poco. He signed for Screech and Gi to stay where they were.

Poco continued to sing, unaware of Dhal's movements. Her attention was locked on Taav and the proper sequence of the song.

Finally the song neared its end, and Poco felt a change in the air around her; it was cool and held the hint of rain. Then the song was finished and she sat quietly, aware of the fog that surrounded her.

She felt something brush by her and looked up as Dhal disappeared into the darkness beyond the gate. "Dhal?" she cried softly.

His disembodied voice floated back to her. "Stay where you are, all of you. I'll be back soon. It is still night here and it is raining."

Minutes passed. Poco grew worried.

Screech and Gi moved up to stand within the green mist at Poco's shoulders. Taav sat quietly outside the misty gate, oblivious to their concern.

Suddenly Dhal reappeared, almost bumping into Screech who had edged farther and farther into the fog. Dhal was soaked, water running down his face.

"Come," he said. "But quietly. I find no atich-ar around but that doesn't mean they aren't here. Screech, I'll help you with Taav. Be careful not to wake him."

Poco stood and took Gi's hand, and together they stepped through the gate. She felt only momentary disorientation.

The rain that struck her face was cold, and the sky was so dark that only the green haze from the world gate gave her anything to see by. Gi tugged on the leg of her pants pulling her away from the gate as Dhal and Screech carried Taav through and set him down on the ground.

Dhal glanced once at the gate, then leaned over Taav and touched his forehead, waking him from his trance. As Taav slumped in Dhal's arms, the gate faded, leaving the five of them in wet darkness.

"We cannot stay here," Dhal whispered. "We'll have to find a safer place for Taav. Screech, you will have to be our guide. I'll carry Taav."

Screech helped lift the slumbering Taav to Dhal's shoulder, then he fastened his tail around Dhal's belt. Poco held onto a corner of Dhal's tunic.

Gi ran ahead of Screech and acted as a scout.

Poco lost track of the time. The rain, darkness, and wooded terrain all combined to make minutes seem like hours. Finally they stopped going downhill, and as the ground leveled off, the density of trees and bushes gave way to an open area that Screech described as a field of grass.

Finally Screech stopped. Dhal grunted with relief as he let Taav slip from his shoulder. The atich-ar moaned once, then was quiet again.

"Where are we?" Dhal asked.

"Near water," Gi piped up.

"Are we anywhere near the temple? We came off the hill to the left. If the waterway is in front of us, the temple should be to our right."

"Want Gi to go look?" Gi asked.

"Yes, Gi, and hurry, but be careful. The atich-ar are not friendly."

"Gi be careful."

After Gi left them, Screech moved away, returning a few minutes later. He went to Poco and took her hand.

"Trees ahead. Shelter. Come."

"Screech says there is shelter somewhere, Dhal. He wants us to follow him."

Screech lifted Taav, and led Dhal and Poco to a wooded place near the water. Using some small branches he found on the ground, and laying them across two upper branches of a nearby tree, Screech quickly erected a shelter. Some rain dripped through, but it was better than standing in the open.

The wait seemed to last forever, but finally Gi returned to tell Dhal that the atich-ar temple stood to their right at the edge of the waterway.

Dhal touched Poco's arm. "It's time for us to leave, then. Poco, you and Gi stay here with Taav. Screech and I will go and see if we can find a way inside the temple."

"There is way," Gi said. "Steps leading from waterway to gate. Gate closed. Gi crawl under. No see guards. Screech can climb gate, yes. Let Dhal in."

"No guards? Are you sure, Gi?" Dhal asked.

"Hiding from rain maybe."

"Atich-ar? I doubt that. From all Chulu told me, they like water. Rain would not bother them. Gi, did you see anything of the Tamorlee?"

"Looking but not seeing," Gi replied.

"They probably have it hidden somewhere, Dhal," Poco said.

"It's too big to hide. Retath said it was here. We will just have to find it."

"Dhal—I want to go with you," Poco said.

"No."

"If you run into guards, you may need every pair of hands you can get."

"No, Poco, I will not have you—"

"Taav will be out for hours, so he won't go anywhere, and if things look too dangerous, you can always send me back!"

"Poco, have you thought about our baby and what will happen if you are caught or stranded here?"

"Right now I am thinking more about its father, and I want to go with you! Please, Dhal, don't say no."

Dhal reached for her in the darkness. "What am I going to do with you, Pocalina-fel-Jamba?"

She hugged him. "Love me, and let me come with you."

Dhal was silent for long moments, then he pushed her away. "All right, but if I tell you to get back here, you promise you will obey?"

"I promise."

Gi led the way back to the gates facing the waterway. Dhal kept a hold on Screech's tail and Poco held onto Dhal. Their progress was slow and cautious.

The rain let up slightly as they reached the wooden gate. As Gi slipped under the gate, Screech climbed up and over.

Several minutes passed. Dhal and Poco stood near the gate listening and waiting for Screech to open it. Another minute passed and nothing happened.

"What's keeping him?" Dhal whispered.

A few moments later, a soft whistle came from down near their feet. "Screech finding guards. He comes soon," Gi said.

Suddenly Poco heard something against the gate. She reached out just as the large door began to move inward. She poked Dhal and felt him slip up beside her.

Screech took Dhal by an arm and latched onto Poco's

wrist with his tail, leading them through the doorway and into a large courtyard beyond.

"What do you see, Screech?" Poco asked softly.

The derkat did not reply, but led them to another wall and another doorway where the gate was ajar.

Through the doorway Poco and Dhal saw torchlight, and someone moving. They turned their attention to Screech as he began to sign, his hands held to the light coming from the yard beyond.

"I killed the guards at the gate. There are two more inside. They keep to a shelter. There are cages nearby. Little Fur has gone to see what is in the cages. We wait here."

Poco looked at Dhal, checking to see if he understood everything Screech had said. He nodded, then moved up cautiously behind the door and peered into the enclosure beyond.

Time seemed to stand still. Poco grew restless waiting. She was worried about Taav and the possibility of his waking alone in the darkness.

She looked back at the gate through which they had passed, and was surprised by a perceptible lightening of the sky to the east. She also noticed that the rain had stopped.

She turned to warn Dhal of the passage of time and saw him lean down and pick up Gi. She moved closer and heard the olvaar softly lisping.

"Guards talking. Not see Gi. Green Ones asleep in cages. Many hand counts."

"Are they Ni or atich-ar?" Dhal asked.

"Ni."

"Are you sure, Gi?"

"Sure," Gi replied, bobbing his head.

"The prisoners from Val-hrodhur?" Poco asked softly.

"Has to be them," Dhal answered.

"Can we do anything to help them?"

"We can try. One of them may be able to help us find the Tamorlee."

"What do we do?" she asked.

"You stay here," he told her firmly. "Screech and I will silence the guards. If anything goes wrong, you and Gi get back to Taav, wake him up and sing your way back to Lach. Agreed?"

"Agreed," she said.

Dhal leaned forward and kissed her, then he and Screech slipped through the partially opened doorway.

Poco and Gi peered around the door and watched as Screech and Dhal stalked the two guards on the other side of the courtyard.

The atich-ar guards were so engrossed in conversation that they were unaware of their danger until the very last minute. Only one cried out, and he was silenced so abruptly that only a few of the Ni prisoners began to stir.

Dhal left his victim, put his knife away, and went straight to the cages. More of the prisoners were beginning to move. Some spoke, only to be quickly hushed.

Poco watched as Dhal spoke to several of the Ni; he then left the cages and, with Screech, searched the guards. They found the key to open the cages and one by one the prisoners were freed.

The Ni began to straggle across the small courtyard. Several were limping and one or two were being carried by others.

Dhal, Screech, and several of the more active Ni reached Poco first.

"Poco, this is Favlon," Dhal said, indicating the Ni to his right. "He says he knows where the Tamorlee is! Screech and I are going with him. You and Gi lead the others back to the river to Taav, and wait for us there. If we don't come by daylight, you know what to do."

"What are you going to do when you find the crystal?" she asked.

"I don't know. Nothing maybe. I just know that I have to see it! To make sure it's all right."

Favlon turned as Ni began to pass through the doorway. "You, Llura, Dar, and Tana, come with me. There may be trouble. This Ni claims he is a Seeker and must reach the Tamorlee. The rest of you go with the female. He says she is a Singer. They have a Sensitive waiting for them outside the gates. We have no choice but to trust them!"

Poco watched Dhal and the others start across the large courtyard toward an open archway in the western wall. The series of stone towers that rose beyond the wall were still darkly shadowed, but the coming daylight worried her.

She ran ahead and caught up with the Ni who, following Favlon's orders, were heading toward the outer gate. They looked at her as she passed, but no one said anything. She almost tripped over the body of one of the guards Screech had killed.

When she reached the gate, she paused to make sure nothing was moving outside. She then motioned to the Ni to follow.

Gi-arobi appeared and Poco told him to take the lead. His soft whistle-clicks were audible for a moment or two, then they faded away as he disappeared into the shadows of the outer temple wall.

Poco counted the Ni as they passed through the gateway. Retath had said there were thirty-seven still alive, but as the last Ni shuffled past, her count had only reached twenty-five. Including Favlon and his three friends, that made twenty-nine.

She waited a moment or two longer, then poked her head back inside to check for stragglers, but the courtyard was empty. When she turned again she saw the backs of the last Ni in line and realized that if she didn't hurry, she would be left behind.

Which is exactly what you want to happen, she thought. Recognizing the duplicity in her calm acceptance of Dhal's orders, Poco went back through the gate. She stepped over the fallen guard and started across the courtyard, knowing that Dhal would be furious with her, but unable to stop herself.

When she reached the open archway leading toward the main temple and towers beyond, she hesitated, checking for any signs of guards, or Dhal's trail. Finding neither, she followed the path of least resistance, a narrow walk leading down the right side of the temple. She passed under another archway, smaller than the last and entered a garden where shoulder-high bushes lined both sides of the walk. Openings in the wall of bushes to her left appeared to lead out into a meeting place of some sort. She could just make out a series of stone benches placed in circular formations around an open walkway.

Afraid she had gone the wrong way, Poco decided to retrace her steps, but suddenly she saw a glimmer of light through the bushes to her right. She went on, moving faster and looking for a way past the bushes.

She finally reached another archway and almost stumbled over the body of an atich-ar guard lying in a pool of his own blood. One look told her that Screech was responsible for that death.

She stepped past the fallen guard and moved several paces forward until she reached an even smaller archway. Cautiously she poked her head around the corner.

A glow of green light suffused the stone enclosure beyond. The light came from a huge, round object that sat in the center of the yard.

Though she had never seen it before, Poco knew she was looking upon the famous Tamorlee. She moved slowly forward, mesmerized by the light and awed by the size of the Tamorlee. Never had she dreamed that a crystal could be so beautiful.

Poco reached Favlon and another of the Ni, who stood looking reverently upon the Tamorlee.

"Where are the others?" she whispered.

Both Ni started at the sound of her voice. "Dar and Llura and the Furred One look for more guards," Favlon answered.

"Where's Dhal?"

"The Seeker tries to communicate with the Tamorlee."

"What?" she asked, startled. "Where is he?"

"There," Favlon pointed. "At the base of the crystal to the right."

Dhal was standing in the glow of the crystal, his hands outspread and touching the green luminescent surface.

"I thought only the Speaker could touch and communicate with the crystal directly."

"Our Speaker is dead. He died many years ago," Favlon responded.

"But Dhal said it was dangerous for anyone to touch the crystal without proper safeguards!"

Poco started toward Dhal but Favlon caught her arm. "Do not interfere," he cautioned her. "That would be even more dangerous. Come, take a few steps closer and you will understand what I mean."

As they neared the crystal, Poco began to feel a strange prickling sensation; her skin itched and her hair seemed to come alive as small sparks of energy snapped and crackled around her.

Favlon pulled her back. "The Tamorlee's energy force is strong, even stronger than it was moments ago. We must move back!"

"What about Dhal?" Poco cried.

"He is a Seeker. He knows what he is doing." Favlon kept a hold on Poco's arm. "The fire stone he wears will channel the energy so he will not be harmed. But what he hopes to accomplish by this is . . ."

Favlon's words trailed off as the soft green light that was the Tamorlee's natural color began to change, fading. A pulsating white light began to move around and around inside the crystal, its trajectory changing with each passage.

Favlon pulled Poco back farther as the light intensified. By the look on his face, she knew that something was wrong.

The glaring light became too bright to watch. Poco tried to shield her eyes. She turned and saw Screech bound out and around the crystal. The two other Ni were right behind him.

"The light will bring atich-ar!" Screech signed as he stopped before her. *"We must leave!"*

"No! Not without Dhal!" Poco cried. "Let go!"

"You cannot interfere!" Favlon said.

Poco pulled from Favlon's hold, but before she could reach Dhal, the white light began to fade.

Suddenly Dhal wrenched away from the crystal. He turned and took several steps before collapsing to the ground. Screech and Poco started forward, but stopped when they heard a strange noise like hard rain cutting down through dense foliage.

Suddenly the Tamorlee seemed to fold in upon itself; within seconds it had disintegrated in a shower of crystalline shards that tinkled like glass as they fell.

Favlon and the other Ni groaned in despair. The Tamorlee was no more.

Poco and Screech ran to Dhal. He lay unmoving only steps away from the pile of crystal shards. Though the light from the crystal was gone, Poco could see Dhal plainly. She glanced up at the sky which was growing lighter by the minute. They had to get out of there and fast! "Pick him up, Screech! Hurry!"

Screech gently lifted Dhal to his shoulder and stood up. Poco turned and led the way back toward the walk, herding Favlon and the other Ni ahead of her. "There is nothing you can do here now," she told them. "Hurry! We have to get out of here before the atich-ar discover us!"

Poco remembered little of their run through the temple gardens except jumping the bodies of the dead guards. The Ni, once moving, took the lead and were the first out the temple gate. Screech and Dhal came next, with Poco acting as rear guard.

After they passed the last of the temple walls, the Ni hesitated, not knowing which direction to take. Screech and Poco caught up and led the way. In the shelter of the trees near the waterway, the other Ni were anxiously awaiting them.

As Screech let Dhal down from his shoulder, Poco glanced around, searching the shadows for Gi and Taav. She saw neither.

Some of the Ni were lying on the ground, others were huddled together for warmth. Favlon began to talk to several of those who were more alert.

Poco knelt beside Dhal and tried to rouse him, but he was still unconscious.

The voices of the Ni began to rise. The word Tamorlee was repeated over and over. The Ni obviously were upset over the destruction of the crystal.

Poco stood. "Please listen! All of you!" she cried softly, trying to keep her voice as low as possible. "The olvaar and Taav—where are they? We cannot go back without them!"

"No one was here," one of the Ni said. "The olvaar left as soon as we got here."

"We have to find them! I cannot make a gate without Taav!"

Favlon turned and looked at her, the despair on his face more eloquent than words. "It doesn't matter now. The Tamorlee is dead. All that we lived for is dead." He glanced at Dhal and his tone changed suddenly. "I don't know what happened, but I think he is responsible! He said he was a Seeker, but no Seeker would ever destroy the Tamorlee!"

Poco did not like the look in Favlon's eyes. "Don't blame him for what happened!" she snapped. "He was only trying to help the Tamorlee! It called him here!"

Favlon glared at Poco, then at Screech, who stood at her shoulder. Screech growled in the back of his throat and Favlon took several steps backward.

Poco looked at the Ni huddled behind Favlon. There was no way to explain to them what had happened. Only Dhal could do that and there was no telling how long before he would regain consciousness. There was but one thing to do: find Gi and Taav and reopen the gate before the atich-ar discovered them.

Poco kept her eyes on Favlon as she spoke. "Screech, stay here with Dhal and see that nothing happens to him. I'll go look for Gi and Taav. They could not have gone far."

Screech's furred hand dropped onto her shoulder; his claws bit into her skin as he growled softly.

Poco patted his hand. "No, Screech. I will go. I want you to watch over Dhal. I don't trust them."

Screech's claws retracted and he coughed softly.

Poco looked at Favlon. "I will be back as soon as I can. I don't care what you think about us right now, just remember, harm any one of us and you will never see Lach again!"

She turned and left the shelter of the trees. She had no idea which way Taav and Gi had gone and began her search by walking a wide circle around the clump of trees that sheltered the Ni. Softly she called Gi's name.

She repeated her call as she neared the waterway. Suddenly a piping whistle came from her left. She turned and followed the sound pushing weeds and bushes out of her way. She stopped and called again.

"Here, Poco!"

Poco saw Gi running along the edge of the waterway. She stepped out onto the pebbled beach and caught him up as he threw himself into her arms.

"Poco come! Taav in water! Not come out!" Gi said.

She put him down quickly. "Show me where!"

Gi raced back up the beach and around a small bend where a felled tree lay in the water. Poco ran to the tree and started to climb over but stopped when she saw Taav wading out into deeper water. He looked unsteady on his feet.

"Taav!" she called in Ni. "Wait! Please wait!"

Taav stopped and turned, almost losing his balance.

Poco remembered that Taav was always groggy after

waking from a song-induced trance. Slowly she climbed over the tree trunk and stepped down into the water.

"Taav, where are you going?" she asked, trying to keep her voice calm. She began to wade slowly out into the water.

Taav watched her approach. His hands lifted and for the first time since leaving the plains, he signed to her. "*I go home.*"

Poco stopped; the water was up to her thighs. "Home, Taav? What do you mean? Here? Ari-al?"

He splashed the water with his hand. "*Here is home! I stay here!*"

So Amet was right all along, Poco thought, and we were wrong. Taav is not Ni.

The atich-ar reached down and cupped water into his face, as if trying to clear his mind.

Poco's thoughts raced as she tried to think what to do. If she lunged for him and tried to wrestle him back to shore, there was a good chance she would lose him. Was there another way? Could she talk him back in?

"Taav, we need you! Dhal is lying back there unconscious. Something is wrong with him and he needs a Healer. We have to get him back to Lach. We need you to do that."

"*I stay here,*" he signed again.

"He saved your life, Taav. He healed you and protected you. He needs *your* help now."

Taav glanced at Gi who was moving out along the dead tree trunk. The olvaar whistled softly, his unspoken plea filled with sadness.

"Please help us, Taav," Poco pleaded. "I promise, I will see that you are sent back to Ari-al. I promise!"

Taav stood quietly watching her.

Suddenly the sound of a large bell echoed across the water and put fear into Poco's heart. "Please, Taav, that bell—your people know we are here! If they find Dhal they will kill him! You know what he is! Only you can save him now!"

Taav hesitated, then started toward her. Poco grabbed his hand and together they climbed over the tree trunk and hurried back along the beach.

When they reached the clump of trees, they found the Ni all on their feet, their attention on the temple.

Favlon turned as Poco led Taav under the trees. "The atich-ar have probably found the crystal and us gone! They will be here in minutes! If you can open a gate, do it! Hurry!"

Poco glanced at Dhal; he still lay unconscious on the ground. Screech crouched next to him.

Poco sat down a short distance away and pulled Taav to a seat before her. She looked into his eyes. "You have my promise, Taav. I will see that you are returned to Ari-al if I have to open the gate myself!"

She took his hands. "Ready?"

Taav glanced at Dhal, then nodded.

Poco tried to calm her thoughts as she began to sing. Her first few words trembled, then her voice steadied. She was halfway through the first sequence before there was any signs of trouble.

"Atich-ar!" someone cried softly. "They are coming this way!"

Poco closed her mind to the danger surrounding them and concentrated. The song could not be hurried or short-ened. The pattern had to be complete.

The last words were sung and the gate finally opened. Favlon began to hurry his people through. Screech bent and picked up Dhal and growled for the Ni to hurry.

Poco stood and saw a handful of atich-ar guards ap-proaching the trees cautiously, as if unsure of the resis-tance they might meet. She turned and saw that she, Gi, and Taav were the last ones on their side of the gate.

Suddenly Screech reappeared. He grabbed her by the arm and pushed her through the gate. Gi dashed past just as Screech bent to pick Taav up.

"Leave him, Screech!" Poco cried from the gate. She held a rock in her hands. "We can wake him from here!"

Screech hesitated, then bounded through the gate. Poco stepped back and threw the rock at Taav, hitting him hard in the chest. A moment passed, then the world gate wavered and disappeared, leaving Poco staring out across Lake Hadrach.

Dhal regained consciousness a day later and asked to speak to Chulu, Amet, and Caaras. The news of the Tamorlee's death had struck hard at the Ni; their faces reflected their sense of loss.

Poco ushered the three Ni to seats and then sat on the edge of Dhal's raised pallet. Gi sat at Dhal's feet, Screech on the floor nearby.

"We are all here," Poco said, as she took Dhal's hand. "What did you want to tell us?"

Dhal looked at Chulu. "It is time you know what happened to the Tamorlee."

"We know what happened!" Amet growled. "Favlon told us!"

A strange smile touched Dhal's face. "Did he?"

"We all saw it, Dhal," Poco said. "The crystal just fell apart."

Chulu leaned forward. "Dhalvad, did you have a chance to speak to the Tamorlee before it—before it died?"

"Yes, I did."

"What did it tell you? Did it give you any indication that—"

"It told me that it was dying, Chulu," Dhal interrupted. "It knew it would not live much longer so it set a plan in motion, a plan that depended upon a certain untaught Seeker who managed to stumble into the past searching for others like himself, and for the truth behind the legend of the Tamorlee."

Dhal's voice softened. "The Tamorlee knew I would reach Val-hrodhur because my arrival there was recorded in its memory, and it knew I would have a Singer with me because the fire stone I carried into the past had recorded Poco's presence. All that was needed was for Poco and I to locate a Sensitive and the pattern for the I-naal gate.

"The Tamorlee knew Poco and I were headed for Jjaan-bi in search of the Ni-lach and it knew that there we would find a Sensitive. To insure the I-naal gate pattern not be lost during the passage of years, it impressed the gate's pattern on Zaa-ob's pendant, and with Zaa-ob's help it placed the pendant in the jewelry chests that it knew we would find in Val-hrodhur."

"Did Zaa-ob return to Val-hrodhur then?" Chulu asked.

"No. There were no Sensitives left alive on Ari-al to hold the gate for him. What he did was create the gate pattern and for the few seconds it was open, he threw the pendant through."

"You said that the Tamorlee had a plan," Amet interrupted. "What plan?"

"The Tamorlee did not know the Ni of Jjaan-bi were planning a rescue. It sent Poco and I to act as a catalyst, hoping to spur the Ni to reenter Ari-al and reclaim what had once belonged to them. All that happened, happened because the Tamorlee did not want to terminate. Like all living things, it wanted to continue and it did its best to ensure that happening—and it succeeded."

"Succeeded?" Amet snapped. "What do you mean?"

Dhal smiled. "The crystal that contained the life force you know as the Tamorlee has ceased to function, but before it fell apart, the life force of the Tamorlee was transferred into this."

Dhal raised his right hand. The fire stone that lay nestled within the birdwing setting glowed with a familiar green light.

Chulu knelt and took Dhal's hand. "Dhalvad, are you saying that—that the Tamorlee now resides in your fire stone?"

"Yes. That is precisely what I am saying."

"It doesn't seem possible," Chulu said softly. "Surely so small a sphere could not hold the entire history of the Ni."

"The Tamorlee is whole, Chulu," Dhal assured him. "Like its parent crystal, this fire stone will be the Tamorlee's new home."

Dhal slipped the ring from his finger and held it out. "Here, Chulu, take the Tamorlee and keep it safely with you. In time a Speaker will be chosen and it will be his to wear. Until then you will have to be its guardian."

A little while later, after Chulu, Caaras, and Amet had left, Poco returned to sit with Dhal.

"Tell me something, Dhal," she said. "The Tamorlee knew what was going to happen because of your travels into the past. Is that right?"

He nodded.

"Well, if it knew, why did it let itself be taken to Arial? Why didn't it warn the Ni-lach about the atich-ar?"

"The Tamorlee is not omniscient, Poco. All it knew from my journey into the past was that it had been taken from Val-hrodhur for safety's sake. Since I knew nothing of the atich-ar and their betrayal of the Ni, I could not pass that information on. For all the Tamorlee knew, there was nothing in the future to fear. Only upon reaching the future—our present—could it look back and know the truth."

Poco shook her head. "I don't think I will ever understand. Past, present, future—is it all one and the same to the Tamorlee?"

"If you could live forever, Poco, might it not seem that way to you?"

Poco sighed. "I guess." She was silent for a moment. "There is one more thing."

"What?"

"Who is to be the next Speaker? Will it be you?"

Dhal chuckled. "No, I think not."

"Are you sure?"

Dhal grew serious. "Is that what you want, Poco? For me to be chosen Speaker?"

She looked down at him and shook her head. "No, that is not what I want."

He took her hand. "You would not mind living the rest of your life with a simple Healer?"

Poco leaned forward and gave Dhal a long, lingering kiss.

Screech softly growled his approval, while Gi-arobi thrummed and said, "Poco making under-stay-mint. Yes!"

About the Author

Marcia Joanne Bennett was born on June 9, 1945. Raised in a rural community, she has spent all but a few of her working years in central New York State.

After graduating from Albany Business College in 1965, she spent the next seven years in banking.

Several years ago, she established a small craft shop in her hometown. While running the shop she began writing, a hobby that quickly became an addiction. Her other interests range from reading, painting, and basketry to astrology and parapsychology.